Praise for

SISTERS & HUSBANDS

"Thought provoking." —*Sacramento Book Review*

"Easy and breezy . . . and it has a feel-good sensation that will appeal to many." —*Philadelphia Inquirer*

"This book is filled with the problems many families face in marriage today. Trying to mix two families into one due to second, even third, marriages . . . losing one's vitality . . . it's all within the pages of this work. It is good, light reading. It might even make you feel better about problems you are experiencing in your own marriage." —*Midwest Book Review*

"The main character's cold feet will resonate with a lot of women who have seen marriages around them crumble . . . but it does drive home the point that no two marriages are the same."
—*Mainstream Book Reviews*

"A hot, romantic novel . . . Keeping company with SISTERS & HUSBANDS by Connie Briscoe is the next best thing to hanging out with a group of friends. But be careful. Drama is contagious."
—Karlamass.com

"Delightful, easy-to-read . . . a wonderful novel about love, family, fidelity, and marriage. Readers will be able to identify with the characters and root for them. They will also realize how the actions of others impact everyone around them. This is a perfect book for the sultry days of summer." —ApoooBooks.com

"Lots of drama and romance." —SuperFastReader.com

"A refreshing summer read . . . Briscoe's writing is light and airy with a sprinkle of spice and a whole lot of drama."

—TheRawReviewers.com

"Heartfelt . . . intense . . . Briscoe tackles one of the most popular questions and she delivers this as wonderfully as she had with *Sisters & Lovers* fifteen years ago . . . Briscoe shows us that life isn't really perfect and that we have to be strong in order to cope with everything that happens around us." —EzineArticles.com

"What I appreciated most about the book was the practicality of the issues at hand. Briscoe considers real-life situations, like blended families, midlife crisis, and the pre-wedding jitters that many people experience prior to their first marriage . . . The page-turning drama and the situations in the novel make this an easy, fun read." —AALBC.com

SISTERS & HUSBANDS

CONNIE BRISCOE

GRAND CENTRAL PUBLISHING

NEW YORK BOSTON

This book is a work of fiction. Names, characters, places, and incidents are the product of the author's imagination or are used fictitiously. Any resemblance to actual events, locales, or persons, living or dead, is coincidental.

Copyright © 2009 by Connie Briscoe
Reading Group Guide Copyright © 2011 by Hachette Book Group
Excerpt from *Money Can't Buy Love* Copyright © 2011 by Connie Briscoe
All rights reserved. Except as permitted under the U.S. Copyright Act of 1976, no part of this publication may be reproduced, distributed, or transmitted in any form or by any means, or stored in a database or retrieval system, without the prior written permission of the publisher.

Grand Central Publishing
Hachette Book Group
237 Park Avenue
New York, NY 10017

www.HachetteBookGroup.com

Printed in the United States of America

Originally published in hardcover by Grand Central Publishing.

First Trade Edition: February 2011
10 9 8 7 6 5 4 3 2 1

Grand Central Publishing is a division of Hachette Book Group, Inc.
The Grand Central Publishing name and logo is a trademark of Hachette Book Group, Inc.

The publisher is not responsible for websites (or their content) that are not owned by the publisher.

The Library of Congress has cataloged the hardcover edition as follows:
Briscoe, Connie.
Sisters & husbands / Connie Briscoe. — 1st ed.
p. cm.
Sequel to: Sisters & Lovers.
"In this sequel to Sisters & Lovers, we follow Beverly through her struggle for love, happiness, and the ability to truly commit"—Provided by publisher.
ISBN 978-0-446-53489-5
1. Sisters—Fiction. 2. African American women—Fiction. I. Title.
PS3552.R4894S569 2009
813'.54—dc22

2008038111

ISBN 978-0-446-53488-8 (pbk.)

Book design by Charles Sutherland

SISTERS & HUSBANDS

Prologue

"I can't do this." Beverly slipped out of Julian's tight embrace and backed away from the queen-size hotel bed. With those simple words she had abruptly altered the course of her life. She had put an end to "I do." To bridal showers and wedding bells and honeymoons.

Julian sat up, and the muscles in his bare bronze chest rippled softly as he reached for a pair of dark-rimmed eyeglasses on the nightstand. "Did I do something wrong?" he asked as he put the glasses on. "Is it my breath? My underarms?" He lifted an arm and sniffed playfully. That was Julian, always joking around and making her laugh. It wasn't going to work this time.

She pulled her sleeveless black dress over her auburn shoulder-length hair, walked to the picture window of the Baltimore Hyatt, and stared at the lights shimmering on the harbor. "I'm serious, Julian. This isn't the time to be funny."

She gripped the gold brocade drapes on the window, and her voice grew faint as she forced the words from her lips. "I can't go through with the wedding tomorrow. I can't get married." The corners of her eyes stung, and she closed and opened them to fight back the tears. Somehow the lights on the harbor seemed to have grown dimmer across the night sky.

He was out of bed and standing behind her in a flash. He

touched her bare shoulders gently, spoke softly. "You're nervous, Beverly. It's normal to get cold feet the night before you get married, you know? Especially with all the problems your sisters are having with their husbands lately."

She nodded. "I admit that's getting to me. Both of their marriages are suddenly falling apart, and it's scaring me silly. Instead of hearing wedding bells ringing in my head, I've got alarms going off like crazy. I tried to shake it and I—"

"You've done this before, Bev," he interrupted anxiously. "Before me, you broke off two engagements."

"Yes, but—"

"But nothing." He squeezed her shoulders firmly. "I'm not like either one of the brothers you were with before. I'm not your sisters' husbands. Things are different with us. We talked about this."

Beverly bit her bottom lip silently. Yes, she had broken off engagements twice before. And she had been right to do it both times. She couldn't go through with marriage unless she felt sure it would work out.

"I know. I thought it was different this time too," she said. "And it is in a way. At least that's what I tell myself."

"Is there someone else?"

"What? No, no. It's nothing like that."

"You sure? You'd say so if there was?"

"Yes, I'm sure. There's no one else."

"Then what is it? I don't get it." He paused. "Is it marriage or is it me that's the problem?"

Beverly shook her head. Julian had been nothing but sweet to her ever since they met at a party a year earlier, and she was crazy about him. He was loyal, trustworthy, dependable. Best of all, he cherished her. And he had the kind of good looks and charisma that crept up slowly and reeled you in before you knew what had taken hold of you. All that made for a solid, loving relationship, and they had settled into a soothing rhythm together.

Still, her sisters had no doubt felt the same way when they got hitched and look at them now. Both of their marriages were crumbling. Beverly didn't want to go through the nuptials only to end up in divorce court. She knew the grim statistics, especially for African Americans. She had read that two-thirds of marriages among black couples ended in divorce, and she had every reason to believe it was true. She could see it all around her now with her sisters and friends. One divorce right after the other, whether they'd been married for two years or twenty. If those were the odds, why take a chance?

She turned to face Julian to make her point. She wanted him to understand where she was coming from. "I still love you, Julian. I still want to be with you. I'm just saying that we don't have to get married. If we're so happy now, why change things?"

Julian took her arms and tightened his grip as he looked down at her. "Bev, listen to me." His brows wrinkled with anxiety as he peered into her face. "You're panicking and you're not making any sense. Almost a hundred people are coming tomorrow to see us get married. My family, your family, our friends. Thousands of dollars have been spent."

She lowered her head. "I know."

"I love you and I want to get married tomorrow. Don't do this now. Don't mess us up like this."

His voice was so sad, it crushed her heart. But she knew she was right about this. And with time, Julian would come around to seeing things her way. Or maybe he wouldn't. Still, she couldn't get married just because she was afraid she might lose him. It was the wrong thing to do.

She removed the diamond ring from her third finger, left hand, and reached for his palm. He stepped back, holding his hands up and refusing to accept it. So she placed it on the wooden table in front of the picture window.

"I'm so sorry, Julian," she whispered. "But I can't go through with it." She reached out to soothe him, but he turned his back to her and signaled for her to let it go.

She shoved her teddy into her overnight bag, slipped into her sandals, and ran out of the room and down the long corridor. It felt like she had just dived into the blackness of the Baltimore Harbor.

Chapter 1

One Month Earlier

Exactly four more weeks before her wedding day and Beverly couldn't believe how calm she felt. She stepped onto the carpeted platform at Vanessa's Bridal Boutique on a balmy Saturday afternoon in early June and was startled at what she saw staring back from the three-way mirror—a svelte but healthy-looking woman, thanks to recent workouts at the gym, appearing fabulous in a strapless beaded ivory-colored satin gown.

The dress was feminine but not frilly—she couldn't stand frilliness—and youthful but not too young—she was, after all, going to be a thirty-nine-year-old bride. It was a staggering transformation from her usual self, dressed casually in blue jeans or shorts, or a simple skirt and top for the office at the newspaper where she worked. At this moment, she was the picture of elegant serenity.

The same couldn't be said for her mother, standing just below, arms folded rigidly across her gray linen suit jacket, eyes narrowed tightly as she scrutinized every movement of the seamstress. Mama looked perturbed enough for all three of them, and she could be quite intimidating when she got in that state. It was a wonder the seamstress hadn't swallowed the pins dangling from her lips.

"Shouldn't it be a little higher off the ground?" Mama asked testily.

The seamstress, a petite Latina named Isabella who looked to be in her late twenties, paused, stood up, and removed the straight pins from her mouth. It was a small fitting room at the rear of the Baltimore bridal boutique, with just enough space for the platform and three-way mirror, a couch, a coffee table piled high with back issues of *Brides* magazine, and a rack of coral-colored bridesmaid gowns. The air was filled with lint from fabrics of all kinds—silk, satin, brocade, lace—and aligned along one wall were a half-dozen pairs of well-worn white heels in various sizes and heights.

"A lot of brides prefer their gowns just touching the ground," Isabella said with a slight accent and studied patience. "For a more graceful look." She shrugged. "But I can make it long or short, whatever you wish."

"I like it like this," Beverly said firmly. "It's perfect."

Mama touched her chin thoughtfully. "Are you sure? I worry that the hemline will get dirty."

"It's not like I'll be running down the street in the dress, Ma."

"Hmm. Go ahead, then, if that's what you want."

Isabella stuck the pins in her mouth and got back down to business.

"I still can't believe you're standing here for your first fitting only a month before your wedding day," Mama said for the third time that afternoon. "When your sisters got married they had—"

"Ma, please. We're not having a gigantic over-the-top affair like they did. It's just family and close friends. Now why don't you sit down and relax?" She and Julian had agreed that they didn't want one of those three-hundred-guest gazillion-dollar extravaganzas that left everyone in debt for years to come.

Instead, they would go for something more intimate, with around a hundred people.

"I'm fine." Mama smacked her lips, glanced at her watch, peeked behind the curtain toward the entrance to the bridal shop, and whipped her cell phone out of her purse practically all at once, which told Beverly she was not fine. Not even close.

"Who are you calling, Ma?"

"Your sisters," Mama said, dialing anxiously. "They're already fifteen minutes late. I want to make sure everyone gets here for their fitting before I leave to go see the florist about the flowers for decorating the reception area."

As if on cue, Beverly heard the front door of the boutique squeak open, and a few seconds later, her oldest sister rushed into the fitting room looking slim and chic in a buttery yellow pantsuit and a pair of cute black patent-leather sandals. Beverly always found it hard to believe that Evelyn was forty-seven years old. People often thought that Evelyn was younger than their middle sister, Charmaine, who had just turned forty-five. Of course, being asked if she was the oldest always thoroughly pissed Charmaine off.

Beverly suspected that Evelyn's youthful looks had to do with the way she always managed to seem so calm and collected, so sure of herself. Beverly liked to joke that a tornado could strike, tossing and turning everything and everyone in its path, and when it was over, Evelyn would be standing with her neat pixie haircut and little designer suit perfectly in place. Even now, as Evelyn darted into the fitting room, she looked totally put together, as if she were about to take a front-row seat near the runway at a fashion show in New York or Paris.

"Sorry to be so late," Evelyn said. "Traffic was backed up coming into Baltimore like you wouldn't believe." Evelyn eyed Beverly, placed her hands on her hips, and smiled broadly. "You look absolutely stunning in that dress, girl. It's gorgeous."

Beverly smiled. “Thanks.”

“Designer?”

“Uh, no name that you would recognize, Evelyn.”

Evelyn cocked her head to the side. “Isn’t it a little too long?”

Beverly threw her hands in the air.

“That’s what I told her,” Mama said as she paced the floor and dialed another number on her cell phone.

The seamstress paused again, looking bewildered.

“Just ignore them and continue, please,” Beverly said to Isabella. “The length is *fine,*” she said with pointed finality to everyone else.

“If you say so,” Evelyn said, looking doubtful. “Don’t mind me, then. Who are you calling, Ma?”

“Charmaine,” Mama said as she put the phone to her ear.

“Oh, I meant to tell you,” Evelyn said as she placed her Fendi handbag on the coffee table. “Charmaine called just before I left the house. She’s running late because Valerie called crying and carrying on.”

“Uh-oh,” Mama said. She snapped her cell phone shut.

“What happened?” Beverly asked.

“Valerie and Otis had a big blowup last night, and now Valerie’s too upset to come here today. She wants to be fitted another time.”

Mama sighed loudly.

“That sounds serious,” Beverly said, frowning. “Wonder why she didn’t call me.” Valerie was Beverly’s somewhat kooky, motor-mouth, astrology-loving best friend, and they told each other just about everything.

“She probably didn’t want to upset you by talking about having a big fight with her fiancé on the day you’re being fitted for your wedding dress,” Mama said. “She’s trying to be a good friend to you.”

And she might also be embarrassed, Beverly thought. Valerie was forty-one years old and had been itching to get married again ever since her first marriage right after high school fizzled within two years. She and Valerie had both recently gotten engaged at about the same time and had originally planned a double wedding. Then about a week ago, Valerie changed her mind about them getting married together, saying she thought the whole idea was too corny for a couple of mature brides.

Beverly had suspected that Valerie was actually worried that Beverly would call off her wedding at the last minute. Valerie's decision not to have a double wedding had disappointed Beverly at first, but she got over it. How could she argue? She *had* broken off no less than two previous engagements—one about five years ago, the other a year before she met Julian. So Beverly and Valerie decided that Beverly would get married at the end of June, and Valerie would walk down the aisle a few weeks later. Now it looked as if Valerie's wedding might be the one called off, and Valerie was too ashamed to tell her.

"I agree with Ma," Evelyn said. "She's trying to be considerate of you."

Beverly nodded with understanding. "She's probably crushed. I'll have to call her as soon as we're done here."

"Girls, my heart goes out to Valerie," Mama said. "But I don't think this is the time or the place to dwell on that. This is Beverly's moment. We should think happy, positive thoughts. And you need to get into your dress, Evelyn. It's up there on the rack."

The seamstress paused and stood to help Evelyn pick her gown out from among the three coral satin bridesmaid gowns hanging on a rack.

"Ma is so jittery," Beverly said to Evelyn. "I think she's afraid I'll chicken out."

"Can you blame her?" Evelyn asked, folding her dress over her arm. "You have commitment issues."

Beverly's hands flew to her waist indignantly. "I don't need you to tell me that."

"Anyone who's thirty-nine years old and never been married has commitment issues," Evelyn said. "You're as bad as Julia Roberts in *Runaway Bride*."

"Did you hear me?" Beverly asked. "I'm agreeing with you. At least I'm doing something about it. I'm committing for real this time. And I need to remind you, I never waited until days or hours before the wedding to call it off."

"No, only two weeks," Evelyn said sarcastically, just before ducking behind the curtain leading into the dressing room.

"The last one was eleven days before," Mama added.

Beverly smiled guiltily. "That's better than going through with it if I'm not sure."

Mama nodded. "I agree. It's still nerve-racking. Not to mention expensive. Be glad you have such a loving father."

Now *that* made Beverly feel bad. Both times she had backed out before, her parents lost a couple of thousand nonrefundable dollars that they had put down on the reception hall. Beverly had offered to reimburse them, but her father refused to take her money, saying he'd rather lose a few bucks than have his daughter marry the wrong man. Still, her folks were in their mid-seventies and living on retirement plans. They didn't need a confused daughter wasting their money. "Sorry about that, Ma, but you don't have to worry this time. Julian's a keeper."

"It's not Julian I'm worried about," Mama said, giving Beverly a pointed look. "I can see how much he loves you."

"I'm definitely not going to change my mind this time. I think I finally got it right. No, I *know* I did."

"I sure hope so," Mama said.

Isabella stepped back. "All done. What do you think? Everything okay?"

Beverly twirled around slowly as her mother looked on proudly.

"It's beautiful," Mama said.

"I'm definitely feeling this," Beverly said as she admired the dress. "You do outstanding work, Isabella."

"So how many more fittings today?" Isabella asked as Beverly stepped down from the podium.

"We have her two sisters for the bridesmaid dresses," Mama explained. "Evelyn just went into the dressing room, and Charmaine is on her way. Unfortunately the matron of honor won't be coming. We'll have to reschedule her."

Evelyn exited the dressing room in her bridesmaid gown and stepped up onto the podium as Beverly went in to change. Beverly walked out a few minutes later in jeans and a blue-and-white-striped top just as Charmaine parted the curtains and blew into the fitting room wearing a black form-hugging skirt slit up to the thigh.

Beverly always thought of Charmaine as a force of nature. One didn't just see Charmaine or hear her talk. You felt her, breathed her, experienced her. Beverly suspected that today would be no exception as Charmaine placed her hands on her hips and struck a pose in the entryway, à la Dorothy Dandridge or Marilyn Monroe.

"I'm here, ladies!"

Chapter 2

Beverly pointed at her watch in mock indignation. "And late as usual, I might add."

"Sorry about that."

"At least you're here," Mama said. "Now I can get going. Will my girls be all right?"

"Go on to the florist, Mama," Beverly said as she handed her gown to Isabella. "We promise to behave."

"*You* promise to behave," Charmaine said, smiling slyly, her brown eyes twinkling beneath her short curly hairdo. "Just kidding, Ma."

Beverly and Evelyn laughed as Mama picked up her shoulder bag from the coffee table and headed for the doorway. "Don't forget, after you all leave here, you need to go the hotel to finalize the menu with the chef." Mama shook her head and pinched Beverly's cheek playfully. "All this last-minute stuff. I swear, you better not change your mind again, girl."

Beverly smiled, a little embarrassed, as Mama blew kisses to Charmaine and Evelyn and waved good-bye.

"Don't you dare say a word," Beverly said, narrowing her eyes and pointing to both of her sisters as soon as Mama left the shop. She knew what was coming from them, especially Charmaine—relentless teasing about breaking off two previous engagements—and she was having none of it if she could help it.

Charmaine smiled thinly. "I guess I can behave myself for one afternoon, since this is a special day for you. But you have to let me see your dress."

Beverly took Charmaine to the rack and showed her the gown that Isabella had just hung up.

"Nice! Put it on so I can see it on you," Charmaine said.

Beverly shook her head. "It's a lot of trouble getting in and out of that thing. You should have been here on time if you wanted to see it on me."

"It's not my fault I'm late," Charmaine protested. "Blame that silly-ass girlfriend of yours."

"What happened with Valerie and Otis?" Beverly asked as she and Charmaine sat on the couch and watched Isabella pin Evelyn's gown at the waist.

Charmaine sat next to Beverly and kicked off her black stilettos. "She called just as I was going out the door and said they argued last night. He shoved her and walked out."

"You mean he put his hands on her?" Beverly asked.

Charmaine nodded. "She said she fell back and hit the wall hard enough to bruise her arm."

Beverly gasped.

Evelyn frowned.

Even Isabella got in on it, shaking her head with stern disapproval.

Beverly knew that Otis had a hot temper, but Valerie had always said it came out only in yelling fits. "That's just wrong. He's never touched her like that before."

"Don't be so sure," Evelyn said. "All you know is what she tells you."

"I think she would have told me if he had hurt her," Beverly said.

Evelyn looked doubtful. "You never really know what goes on in a relationship behind closed doors. Trust me."

Beverly figured that Evelyn was speaking from her experience as a psychologist, and she supposed she couldn't argue with that. "You're probably right," Beverly said. "She could be too ashamed to tell me if he's been smacking her around."

"It could be shame," Evelyn said. "Or it could be something else entirely. There's all sorts of reasons someone might not tell you about something like that."

"I told her, be glad that sucker is gone," Charmaine said. "Hope he stays gone."

"They should try therapy," Evelyn suggested.

"You *would* think that," Charmaine said, waving her hand in Evelyn's direction. "But some relationships aren't worth trying to fix. He's a lost cause, if you ask me. Once they put their hands on you in anger, that's it."

"I agree," Beverly said.

"Still, I think she's going to go back to him," Charmaine said.

"I should hope not," Beverly said. "Why do you say that?"

"I couldn't get out of the house 'cause she was crying so hard on the phone," Charmaine said. "Talking about how she was over forty and not married. And how she wants the hubby and the picket fence, just like me and you, Evelyn." Charmaine made quotation marks in the air with her fingers. "I reminded her that I'm definitely no role model when it comes to wedded bliss. I'm on my fourth marriage mainly 'cause I don't take a lot of crap off these crazy brothers out here. I might put up with it for a while, but if you keep screwing up, I'm going to kick your ass to the curb." Charmaine snapped her fingers to make her point.

"Kevin and I are not perfect, either," Evelyn said. "We have our share of problems."

"Most of us would kill to have your problems, Evelyn," Charmaine said. "Your husband is a lawyer. You live in that big fat house. You lead a charmed life, sister."

Evelyn shrugged. “Honestly, we’re just like everyone else. We have our ups and downs and we have to work hard to keep things together.”

“Still, you and Kevin have a great relationship,” Beverly said. “Of course you have ups and downs, but you manage to work things out. That’s why you’ve been married for more than twenty years. You two are my role models for marriage.”

Evelyn smiled.

“By the way, is this your Fendi here?” Charmaine lifted the designer bag sitting on the table.

Evelyn nodded, and Charmaine carefully placed the bag back down. “Uh-huh. I am so damn jealous. How much that set you back?”

Evelyn seemed to squirm on the podium, and Beverly knew what was coming. Evelyn hated it when Charmaine got to comparing their lifestyles. In any comparison that involved money, their oldest sister would always come out on top. Charmaine would get pissed, and Evelyn would feel defensive.

“Enough,” Evelyn said.

“What’s enough?” Charmaine persisted. “Five hundred?”

“Charm,” Beverly said, nudging her middle sister in an attempt to warm the chill building rapidly in the air. If what she knew about Fendi was true, the bag had probably cost twice that, and Beverly didn’t want her sisters squabbling on the day of her bridal fitting. “It looks like Evelyn is about done. Why don’t you get into your dress?”

All was quiet as Charmaine gave the designer bag one last lingering glance and left for the dressing room. Beverly gave herself an imaginary pat on the back for handling that so well. Their mother would have been proud.

She wished she could smooth things over for her friend. No doubt Valerie was miserable now. But if Otis was smacking her around, it was good that he had left. Hopefully he would stay gone. Beverly was so thankful that Julian didn't have a bad temper. Compared to Julian, *she* was the one with the temper.

She remembered the time about ten years back when she had come within an inch of slashing her then-boyfriend Vernon's convertible top because she caught him cheating on her. The only thing that stopped her as she crept up to Vernon's car in the middle of the night was that she had accidentally locked her shoulder bag—the one with the knife needed to do the dirty deed—inside her car.

She had done a lot of growing up in the years since that awful night, and it was downright embarrassing to think that she had ever let a man mess with her head like that. She liked excitement in a relationship as much as the next woman, but some of the stunts men pulled were absolute deal breakers, and cheating and hitting were at the top of the list.

It had taken her a while to get it right, to put it all together, and watching the relationship between Evelyn and Kevin had probably helped more than anything. They had been married so long, they must be doing something right. They had a kind of give-and-take that Beverly had come to admire. When one was down, the other one lifted. When one came up short, the other filled in. They completed each other the way the right pair of shoes completed a great outfit. With Julian, Beverly knew she had finally found someone she could have that kind of relationship with.

Chapter 3

Charmaine removed the pot roast from the double oven, and the kitchen filled with the aroma of cloves as she carefully placed the pan on the stovetop. As soon as she had come in from the fitting and meeting with the chef, she kicked off her heels and got busy in the kitchen. For the past year, she had been in a Martha Stewart or B. Smith mode. She had always enjoyed doing things around the house when she had the time, and when she and Tyrone got hitched a year ago she had turned into a regular homebody, as Tyrone often teased her.

Maybe it was because she had finally found herself a decent man, or perhaps it was that her sons, Kenny and Russell, now ages fourteen and nine, were growing up and didn't need as much of her time. Whatever the reason, Charmaine had bid a permanent farewell to Betty Crocker, her constant companion of the past several years, and all the tuna casserole mixes. Instead, she was popping roasts and pies made from scratch in and out of the oven faster than her little family could sit at the table. And loving every minute of it. The only bad thing about the incessant fussing around the kitchen, as far as Charmaine could see, was that all the delicious food was starting to build up around her hips.

She had just added potatoes and carrots to the roast and popped it back into the oven when Tyrone, Kenny, and Russell came in from shooting hoops on a nearby basketball court. They headed straight for the Gatorade she had chilling in the freezer, then perched themselves on stools at the kitchen bar, sweaty bodies, dingy caps, and all. There was a time when she would have made a real stink about a bunch of funky males hanging out in her kitchen and shooed them off to shower and change. But this was the new Charmaine—sweet, patient, and tolerant with her guys.

"Smells real good, honey," Tyrone said. "What's cooking?"

"Your favorite, baby. Pot roast."

Kenny lowered the bottle of Gatorade from his lips. "Can we get that sweet potato dish with apples and marshmallows that you made last week to go with it?"

"It's already got white potatoes in it," Charmaine said.

Kenny pouted and Russell joined in. Even though Kenny was growing faster than she could clothe him and at six feet he was a couple of inches taller than Tyrone, Kenny was still only fourteen, and at times like this he looked even younger despite his height. Russell adored his older half brother and was at a stage where he always followed along with him.

"The sweet potatoes *are* good," Tyrone said. "You should whip up a bunch."

"They are off the chain!" Kenny said. "My new favorite dish."

"Mine too," Russell added.

Charmaine realized what was going on and was ashamed that Tyrone had picked up on it first. Although Tyrone and Kenny got along, she sometimes sensed a bit of jealousy on Kenny's part. After all, for the first several years of his life Kenny had had his mama all to himself. Then he became a big brother to Russell, and for a while was kind of the man of the house.

Now there was a real man in the house, and on top of that, Kenny also had a new older stepsister—Tiffany, Tyrone's fourteen-year-old daughter, who lived in Oakland, California, and visited for two weeks over the summer and a week at Christmas. Tiffany was only a few months older, but suddenly Kenny had all these other older people in his life and he wanted to assert some authority. If Charmaine was making Tyrone's favorite for dinner, Kenny would insist on his favorite too.

Shame on her for not sensing what was happening before Tyrone did, Charmaine thought. But Tyrone's compassion was one of a million things that had attracted her to this handsome butterscotch-complexioned babe.

She reached across the bar and squeezed Kenny's and Russell's cheeks playfully. "One off-the-chain sweet-potato dish coming up, then." She removed her red KitchenAid mixer from a base cabinet, then went to the bin in the refrigerator for the sweet potatoes. Kenny and Russell drained their Gatorade and left to go take showers.

"How did the fitting go?" Tyrone asked. "Or whatever it was you went to."

"The fitting and a meeting with the chef. Beverly looks real happy, but her friend Valerie had a big fight with her fiancé last night and she was fit to be tied. She called me just before I left and bawled almost nonstop for a half hour."

"Makes you glad we went to the justice of the peace, huh?"

Charmaine smiled and nodded. "And Evelyn was showing off a hot new Fendi bag. Those things start at, like, five hundred, I think."

Tyrone raised his eyebrows. "Five hundred what?"

"Dollars."

"Damn. Well, Kevin is a lawyer, she's a psychologist. That's how them rich folks do."

"Lucky for them," Charmaine said with sarcasm.

"You jealous? You're a secretary, I'm just an electrician."

"What do you mean, *just* an electrician. I'm proud of you. And proud to be married to you. I don't need no Fendi bags."

"Yeah, right."

"Okay, so I'm lying about that part. I mean, I really am happier since meeting you. That much is true. But I would still kill for a fucking Fendi."

He laughed.

"What time does Tiffany's flight get in from Oakland tomorrow evening?" Charmaine asked.

"About four."

"What you got planned for her stay?" Charmaine leaned over the sink and ran water into a large pot. "Anything special?" She knew that the days would be a marathon of nonstop activity, with Tyrone trying to fit fifty-two weeks into his daughter's two-week visit. Last summer, their first together, was full of shopping sprees and amusement parks, the beach and bowling. For fourteen days straight they barely stopped, and Tyrone must have spent a few thousand dollars, most of it on clothes, shoes, and bags for Tiffany.

The problem wasn't the nonstop pace or all the dollars he spent when Tiffany visited. Tyrone made decent enough money and was certainly entitled to spend some of it on his daughter. And Charmaine believed firmly that girls needed their fathers in their lives. She admired Tyrone for not shirking his responsibility the way too many fathers did.

The real problem was that Tyrone treated Tiffany as if she were visiting royalty, catering to her every wish and whim. Like a lot of absentee fathers, he missed his child. He was also filled with guilt about not being with her year-round. Instead of treating her like a daughter, with all the love and discipline that should mean, he treated her like a little princess. The result was a child who thought she was entitled to special treatment. And who could blame her? Any kid would lap that up.

Charmaine remembered how she had come home late from work one day last summer drop-dead tired as usual, and Tiffany indignantly asked her why she hadn't done the laundry. The girl had been visiting only a few days, but apparently she needed a special pair of jeans that she had worn on the flight. Never mind that Tiffany brought at least six pairs of jeans with her. She needed that particular pair, she explained, and she needed them first thing in the morning.

Charmaine had almost choked on her tongue. She gathered all of the girl's dirty clothes from a pile on the floor in her bedroom, dumped them in her skinny arms, and showed her to the laundry room in the basement. She calmly but firmly asked Tiffany whether she needed help working the washer and dryer. Instead of responding, Tiffany had thrown her clothes on the floor and run crying to her daddy.

Charmaine was sure Tyrone would straighten Tiffany out and make her do her own laundry or tell her to wait patiently until Charmaine was ready to do it. Instead, her new husband came riding to his daughter's rescue like some knight in shining armor and did the laundry himself. At that very moment.

That was when Charmaine realized that the honeymoon had officially ended. Over the next few hours, you could have sliced the chill in the air with a kitchen knife.

The one saving grace was that Charmaine didn't have to deal with this nonsense year-round. When she did have to put up with it, she tried to keep her nerves steady. She picked her battles carefully and let the rest slide. She knew that her life would get back to normal after Tiffany's visit and that Tyrone would go back to being his usual sweet self.

"I think we'll take it a little easier this time," Tyrone said. "And not be on the go around the clock. We can spend some days just kicking around the house relaxing, watching videos or something."

Charmaine smiled thinly. He'd said that before Tiffany's last visit at Christmas, and they still ended up going and spending nonstop for an entire week. Tiffany would bat her big hazel eyes at her daddy and get him to do and buy whatever she wanted. And what she wanted was the latest of everything, from clothes to gadgets. Still, Tyrone was a good man, and they had a great relationship as husband and wife for forty-nine weeks out of the year. Charmaine wasn't going to let a few weeks ruin that.

"Sounds good," she said as she gathered the other ingredients while the sweet potatoes boiled. "I'll get some grocery shopping done when you go to the airport to pick her up. I can rent a couple of videos then. Anything in particular you think she'll want to see?"

Taking the last swig from his Gatorade bottle, he stood up and stretched his lean and muscular self. Whenever he did that, he looked good enough to eat. If she weren't cooking, she would have devoured him then and there.

"Whatever you get should be fine with her," he said, dumping the bottle in the recycling bin.

"When does she go home, exactly?" Charmaine asked.

"August seventeenth."

Charmaine paused, spice bottle in one hand, box of brown sugar in the other. "You mean *June* seventeenth. Right?"

"No. It's August. She's staying all summer this time, remember? I told you that."

Charmaine felt little beads of sweat popping out under her newly colored honey-blond hairdo. She shifted her weight from one bare foot to the other. "No, I don't think you did."

"I definitely told you, baby. Just before I made the flight reservations last week." He blinked. "At least I thought I did."

Charmaine sighed loudly as she placed the bottle on the countertop. "No, I'm certain, you did *not*, honey."

"Okay, so she goes back August seventeenth. Her school starts on the twentieth. Sorry if I didn't tell you before."

He walked up behind her and kissed her on the neck. It was

a good thing he was behind her. If he had seen the expression on her face, Charmaine suspected he would have wanted to call an ambulance.

"I'm going on up to shower," Tyrone said.

She turned to see his heels disappear through the doorway, then slammed the sugar box on the countertop.

"Ah, *hell,* no," she muttered between clenched teeth. That didn't just happen, did it? He didn't just pull a fast one on her, did he?

The potatoes boiled over at that moment and shook Charmaine out of her stupor. She ran to the stove and quickly switched the pot to a cool burner, turned the stove off, and paused to catch her breath.

"Ma," Kenny said, entering the kitchen and opening the refrigerator.

"What?"

"You look like you just burned your fingers or something."

Damn if it didn't feel like it too, she thought.

Chapter 4

Evelyn pulled her black Mercedes sedan into the two-car garage just before dusk and leaned her head back on the soft leather cushion. She needed a few minutes to gather her thoughts before going inside. Her family had lived in this house for twenty happy, loving, fulfilling years. Yet whenever she came home lately, it felt like she was entering the house of a stranger.

Her husband was still around, of course, at least in body. His mind and spirit had vacated the premises months ago, soon after their youngest child left for college. In her work as a psychologist, Evelyn had heard many gloomy tales of men changing drastically at around age fifty. She never thought it would happen to Kevin.

She had realized that she and Kevin were growing apart, that the spark that had burned so brightly between them for so long was slowly dying out. But she had been focused on raising the children, doing her work, and earning her Ph.D. She and Kevin had spent nearly twenty-five years together, most of them very good years. She thought the foundation under their marriage was solid enough to hold things together until they both had time to work on the relationship.

As Andre and then Rebecca approached their college years and she wrapped up work on her Ph.D., Evelyn began to anticipate with eagerness the days when she and Kevin would have long stretches of time alone together. Visions of romantic dinners, cozy walks in the park, and lazy Sunday afternoons lounging in bed began to dance in her head.

Yet when the moment finally arrived shortly after Rebecca went off to Spelman College last fall, Kevin suddenly began to change at breakneck speed. He sold the law practice that he had spent nearly ten years building up. He took a job as a clerk at Blockbuster. He replaced his once beloved Mercedes SUV with an ancient BMW.

She hadn't shared any of this with a soul, not even her parents and sisters. Everyone thought they were still the perfect happily married couple. She didn't have the heart—or maybe the guts—to tell them the truth.

She exited the car and let herself into the L-shaped kitchen. The room was being remodeled and was in a shambles, with the old cabinets, countertops, and appliances ripped out and new top-of-the-line appliances waiting to be installed. To Evelyn, the whole space was a reminder of her troubled marriage. A few months ago, she had finally persuaded Kevin that it was time to have the twenty-year-old kitchen upgraded, and contractors had begun the work last week.

Yet she and Kevin had bickered about everything, large and small, all along the way. He wanted a natural material like granite for the countertops. She wanted Corian or something easier to maintain. He wanted bold paint colors. She wanted earth tones.

"I'm not living with a kitchen that reminds me of a fucking field full of dirt," he had yelled as they debated in the middle of the kitchen floor.

"Well, I don't want a kitchen that knocks me back every time I enter it," she had countered.

On and on it went. They were either yelling at each other or dishing out the silent treatment. As a psychologist, Evelyn knew that the problem was far deeper than a simple disagreement over paint colors. Kevin was in the throes of a midlife crisis or a severe case of male menopause. But as a wife, she was clueless as to how to get them through this confusing period.

She could remember when Kevin first decided to leave his job as a partner at one of Washington's top law firms to start his own firm about ten years ago. She had initially been dead set against the idea, thinking it too risky, too life altering. Yet she also saw that it was very important to Kevin, and she let him talk her into going along with it. In the end, as his firm began to take shape and do very well, she became his strongest supporter. In return, Kevin had enthusiastically backed her when she wanted to return to graduate school to pursue her Ph.D.

That kind of give-and-take, which had sustained them for so long, would never happen now. Kevin had become too self-absorbed, too stubborn, too selfish. He had erected a wall around himself, and she just couldn't seem to get through to him anymore. Yet she hadn't given up on him completely. A part of her still hoped that she would one day come home and find the man she had married waiting there for her.

She strode across the kitchen and into the foyer. She kicked off her heels, picked up the mail from the center table, and tried to clear her head of all her worries. After meeting the chef with her sisters, she had stopped by Andre's apartment in Baltimore and fixed dinner for him. It had been a long day, and her feet were aching. Kevin was probably on the computer in the den, and she wanted to relax, maybe read a good book and catch some news on CNN. She picked up her shoes and the mail and headed up the staircase.

She heard a commotion coming from the master bedroom as she reached the top landing. A couple of thumps, footsteps shuffling across the hardwood floor, drawers being slammed shut. Was Kevin cleaning or something? These days she never knew what to expect from the man.

She entered the bedroom just as Kevin closed the door to his walk-in closet. She was about to ask what all the noise was about, but instead she stopped in her tracks and stared at him—her heels dangling from one hand, Fendi bag and mail in the other. Kevin had shaved his head; not a single strand of hair was left. All thoughts of the commotion she'd just heard vanished from her mind.

"My God, Kevin. What did you do?"

"What's it look like?" he responded curtly.

It wasn't his tone that bothered Evelyn the most these days. It was the indifference in his expression. He walked toward the bed, and that's when she noticed about a dozen of his suits lying across it, including a couple of his prized Brionis.

"What are you doing with those?" she asked as he scooped them into his arms.

"Giving them to Goodwill. I won't be needing them anymore."

"You're not serious?"

"Oh, yeah," he said. "I'm very serious."

"But why? You spent thousands of dollars on those suits."

"Exactly. I told you, I'm sick and tired of this materialistic lifestyle. Hell, you're probably wearing two or three designer labels right this very minute, between the suit, the bag, and the shoes. It makes no sense."

Evelyn rolled her eyes to the ceiling. Not this again, she thought. She was about to tell him not to do something he would later regret. But given all the changes he had made in his life lately, getting rid of his designer suits was nearly nothing. "What is going on with you, Kevin? You left your law firm, a firm you spent a decade building from the ground up. You're working at Blockbuster now, for God's sake. You sold your Mercedes and bought an old beat-up BMW. When is this craziness going to stop?"

He scoffed. "I'm just getting started, and it's about time you figured that out." He brushed past her and headed toward the doorway.

"Kevin," she protested. "We need to talk about this. You're always running off." He didn't stop at the sound of her voice. He didn't even look in her direction.

She stamped her foot and stared at the empty doorway. She could no longer deny it or even rationalize it. The old Kevin—the loving, generous, ambitious family man she had married—was gone. And it was going to be hard to get him back. Maybe impossible.

Chapter 5

The second Beverly spotted Julian in the hotel restaurant—standing tall and bronze and smiling warmly in her direction—her heart did a little shuffle. They had been dating for a year, and he still had the power to melt her with a single glance.

He removed his eyeglasses and kissed her tenderly on the lips, and the masculine scent of his cologne made her heart flutter. She smiled as they slid next to each other in a quiet, secluded booth at the back of the restaurant. They had developed the naughty little practice of spending one night a month in a different local hotel. They would meet in the restaurant or bar for drinks and dinner and then head up to their reserved room. Sometimes it was a fancy hotel at the Baltimore Harbor or in Georgetown in D.C. Other times it was a simple roadside motel. Today they had chosen a chic little spot on East Lombard Street in downtown Baltimore.

The regular rendezvous were Julian's idea, and it was typical of the way he often blended the familiar with something exotic. When she was anxious about work or frustrated with the wedding preparations, she could think about the night of passion they had planned for that month. It never failed to put a smile on her face.

He ordered an apple martini for her and a regular one for himself, and she told him all about the fitting and meeting with the chef that afternoon. Julian was as manly as they come and he loved all manner of sports, with the Baltimore Ravens being his favorite ball team. His determination to get out on the golf course on weekend mornings bordered on fanatical. And yet he could sit and listen contentedly to Beverly go on about things like dresses and wedding cakes and her sisters.

When Beverly first met Julian at a party at Valerie's apartment a year earlier, it was instant attraction for the both of them. Beverly was licking French onion dip off her fingers when she turned away from the buffet table and collided with a tall, bronze-complexioned stranger wearing dark-rimmed eyeglasses. He was holding a drink that nearly spilled on her. Fortunately he pulled away just as Beverly jumped back, and some of the beverage ended up hitting the floor instead of her off-white summer dress.

They both apologized repeatedly to each other as he stooped down to blot the floor with his napkin. When he stood back up and looked at Beverly, it slowly dawned on her that this was no ordinary guy. On the surface, he looked a bit nerdish with his semi-round barrister-style eyeglasses and a crisp white shirt tucked in neatly at the waist. But he was tall—about six foot two—and well-built, with broad shoulders and a slender waist.

"You sure you're all right?" he asked her again.

She put on her best smile. "I'm fine, really."

"I didn't get any vodka and Coke on that pretty white dress, did I?"

"Nope. Not a drop."

He wiped his brow with mock relief. "Whew! Close call."

"Yes, it was a little close."

He extended his free hand a little awkwardly, as he balanced his glass and a small plate holding cheese and crackers in his other hand. "By the way, I'm Julian. And you are . . . ?"

"Beverly."

"Beverly," he repeated. "I always wanted to meet a Beverly."

"Yeah, right." She laughed. "I bet you say that to every woman you meet."

"No, not at all," he said, looking very serious. Then he cracked a devilish smile. "Only to the pretty ones."

She laughed again. For some odd reason, she found this geeky guy and his weak jokes heart-stoppingly alluring. He was nothing like the cool Casanovas she normally went for, and that was refreshing.

"So, are you a friend of Valerie's?" Julian asked.

Beverly nodded. "I've known her for years, ever since college. And she's standing right behind you."

Beverly pointed and Julian turned as Valerie, wearing an ankle-length denim skirt and a white cotton blouse with the collar turned up beneath her shoulder-length black hair, approached the two of them. "I see that you guys have bumped into each other," Valerie said as she picked up a carrot from the buffet table and dipped it into the veggie dip.

"Literally," Beverly said. She and Julian laughed.

"Oh?" Valerie looked from one to the other, not quite getting the joke.

"We came within inches of colliding," Beverly explained.

"Almost spilled my drink on her," Julian added.

"Ah," Valerie said, nodding with understanding.

"How do you two know each other?" Beverly asked. She was curious but also wanted to be sure that Julian wasn't someone Valerie was interested in before she explored him any further. Beverly and Valerie had met at Hampton University in Virginia when Beverly discovered that her then boyfriend was cheating on her with another woman. That other woman turned out to be Valerie.

Beverly had lived on campus. Valerie lived in Newport News,

a neighboring town, with her parents and a baby daughter whose father she had divorced. Beverly and Valerie met in English class, became friends, and soon realized that they were dating the same man and that each was in the dark about the other. By the end of the first semester, they had both ditched the guy. They had been friends ever since, and fighting over men was a no-no. Not that anything would necessarily develop between her and Julian, Beverly thought. But just in case, she wanted to be sure she wasn't barging in on her best friend.

"Julian works with me," Valerie said. "He's the best computer animator this side of the Atlantic."

"I wouldn't go that far," he said modestly.

"It's true," Valerie said.

"What exactly is an animator?" Beverly asked.

"I'm the one who transforms Valerie's creative ideas from hand-drawn artwork into pixels on the computer monitor."

"Fascinating." Beverly nodded and smiled. So he worked at the graphic design firm where Valerie was employed, and he really *was* a geek. The three of them chatted for a few minutes until Valerie asked Beverly to help her out in the kitchen and the girls walked off.

"My co-worker likes you," Valerie blurted out as soon as they were out of earshot. Valerie walked to the refrigerator and removed two trays filled with carrots, celery sticks, and broccoli and placed them on the countertop.

Beverly began to remove the plastic wrap covering one of the trays. "Get out. I just met the dude."

"So?" Valerie said. "I've worked side by side with Julian for a few months now, long enough to get to know him. He likes you."

"How can you tell?"

"The way he looks at you. Or rather the way he can't *stop* looking at you."

"I do think he's cute. A little geeky maybe, but cute."

"I agree," Valerie said, laughing. "He's a total geek, but anyone who thinks geeks can't be cute and sexy is dead wrong."

"I know. They're the ones who rule the world, I always say. They get the best jobs, make the most money."

"And they're less likely to cheat on you than the playas."

Beverly nodded. "I'm surprised you never mentioned him, since you two work so closely and you're always trying to fix me up with someone when you're not interested in them."

Valerie shrugged as she removed the plastic wrap from the veggies. "Guess I didn't think he was your type."

"What's my type?" Beverly asked, wondering how Valerie had pegged her.

"You know, suave, drop-dead gorgeous."

"You mean, playa."

"Unfortunately, we've both been suckers for all the suckers out there. We met in college 'cause our boyfriend was two-timing us with each other. Remember?"

"How could I forget?" Beverly said. "Sometimes I think that's why we're both still single. Given the rotten luck I've had with men all these years, maybe I need to change my type." She looked at Valerie. "You're not into him, are you? Because if you are, I'll—"

Valerie shook her head. "Nah, I got my eyes on someone else tonight."

"Cool." That was good news to Beverly's ears. It meant she could explore this budding thing with Julian. "I saw you talking to that guy with the shaved head. That him?"

Valerie nodded. "Yeah, Otis. What do you think?"

"He's hot. Kind of reminds me of a slightly older Taye Diggs. Where'd you meet him?"

"He works at my office too. He's a programmer. Just started about two weeks ago."

"Sounds like another good-looking geek," Beverly said.

Valerie laughed.

"Seriously, maybe I need to change jobs. I mean, I love working at the *Baltimore Sun*, but you got all these smart, hot brothers working with you."

Several minutes later, Beverly and Valerie walked back into the party, each carrying a tray of veggies and dip. Julian quickly sought out Beverly, and they spent much of the rest of the evening getting to know each other. Then they met for lunch midweek, followed by dinner and a movie on Saturday for two consecutive weekends. The second movie and dinner date turned into an overnighter at Julian's apartment, and he and Beverly were pretty much inseparable from that point on.

When Beverly telephoned Valerie to tell her how things were going with Julian, Valerie was shocked to learn how quickly they had become a couple.

"I wouldn't have put you two together in a million years," Valerie said. "Just goes to show you what I know."

Beverly could hardly believe it herself. She had spent years looking for someone who not only made her feel good between the sheets but also treated her good, only to become convinced that men like that showed up just in movies. Initially, she had a hard time believing her relationship with Julian could be the real deal.

That was why when he proposed to her within six weeks of their first date, she immediately turned him down. She was definitely falling for him. What was not to love? He was good-looking, owned his own house, had an exciting career as a computer animator, and was a tiger in bed. True, he was a bit geeky with the glasses and a penchant for pixels, but she had come to appreciate that. Her new motto was that nothing was better than a man with the three Ss—single, sweet, and successful.

But she had been burned so often, from Vernon to Vance. Sometimes it was obvious, as when she had walked in on the guy screwing another woman. Other times it was subtle, like the way he looked at other women—or men. Something *always* went wrong sooner or later. Julian treated her like a jewel now, but she figured that he was just more clever at hiding his vices. So she decided to enjoy the moment while she could and guard against letting herself get too attached too fast.

Then he took her to Cincinnati, Ohio, to meet his family. They stayed for a week, and by the time they left, Beverly had totally flipped her thoughts about marrying Julian. One hundred eighty degrees. This dude was the real stuff. His parents had been together for fifty years and still held hands. And not only were his folks husband and wife, they were also the best of friends. Julian had two older brothers in their forties. Both had been married longer than ten years and appeared to be very happy. The only way the signs could have gotten any better would have been if Julian had had a halo perched on top of his head.

When he proposed again a month after the visit to Cincinnati, Beverly accepted eagerly.

At the hotel restaurant in Baltimore, she placed her half-empty martini glass on the table and took Julian's hands. "I hope Valerie finds someone like you one day," she said. "Every woman should have a Julian."

He lifted her hands and kissed them both. "Every man should have a Beverly."

She sighed. He always said the right thing. She smiled and leaned forward so that he could get a good peek beneath her strapless top as she lightly licked the tips of his fingers with her tongue.

His free hand shot up and signaled the waiter for the check.

❧ ❧ ❧

As Beverly slipped into bed wearing a short black negligee, she could feel Julian's eyes following her every move with ardent appreciation. He had turned the covers down to the foot of the bed, as he insisted on doing whenever they made love. He wanted to be able to see everything.

He reached out across the queen-size bed and gently pulled her in closer. She ran her fingers slowly over his bulging biceps as his hand slid down her hips and beneath her gown. He quickly found her moist inner thighs, and she could hear him panting heavily as his lips traveled from her neck to the crevice of her breasts. In one smooth motion he pulled the negligee over her head and hoisted her on top of him. Julian seemed like a hero out of a romance novel at times, but there was nothing at all fanciful about his lovemaking.

He lifted Beverly by the hips, and she spread her legs eagerly. She grabbed the top of the headboard for support and moved with him, slowly at first, tossing her head back as each thrust filled her with more urgency. His eyes glued to her, he took obvious joy in her pleasure as he slipped his middle and ring fingers into her mouth. She sucked and then bit down in frenzied delirium, her teeth sinking further into his flesh than either had expected. He yelped softly, yanked his finger from between her lips, and laughed softly.

"Sorry," she whispered hoarsely.

She leaned down to his ear and nibbled playfully. He tossed her on the bed and landed on top of her. They faced one way, then the other, legs twisting and turning, as they moved faster and faster. The headboard bumped against the wall until Beverly suddenly heard a loud snap, and a corner of the mattress thumped heavily to the floor. The fall only served to heighten their passion, and they rolled and landed on the carpet, never missing a beat.

The muscles in his face and arms tightened as he whispered dirty thoughts into her ear. Beverly could feel his desire mounting, and the tingly sensation of his hot breath excited her as much as his words. She shuddered and moaned loudly, straining to keep from screaming until she could hold it no longer.

He rolled off her onto the floor, and they lay holding hands breathlessly while their bodies slowly came down from the peaks. Beverly closed her eyes and savored the moment.

Julian leaned up on one elbow, glanced at the bed and back down at her. He smiled. "This is why I said we should never visit the same hotel twice."

She opened her eyes and looked at him. They both burst out laughing.

Chapter 6

Charmaine danced across the kitchen floor in her bare feet and peeked into the oven at her meatloaf. She walked to the stove and checked the collard greens simmering with smoked turkey, then dropped a stick of butter and a half cup of heavy cream into the pot of steaming white potatoes. She added a chopped garlic clove to the potatoes and blended it all with her handheld electric mixer.

She had been up since early that Sunday morning to knead the dough for her homemade rolls, and when the family returned home from church she changed into denim knee-length cutoffs and a hot-pink tank top and picked up where she left off. She was fixing some of Tiffany's favorite dishes. And since Tiffany claimed that the KitchenAid mixer made potatoes too mushy and that mixing them with a spoon left them too lumpy, Charmaine was using her handheld mixer. Tiffany also didn't like tomato sauce in or on her meatloaf. In fact, she didn't want anything to do with tomatoes and other popular foods like baked chicken and pasta. Who the hell didn't like pasta?

Obviously, Tiffany was a fussy eater. Maybe that was how she stayed so slim. Girl couldn't weigh more than a hundred pounds. Charmaine didn't plan to even try to appease her all summer long, but this would be her first day visiting. Not only that, today was Russell's last day before he left for his month-long summer visitation with his father in D.C. Charmaine wanted to try and get them all together and off to a good start.

She was cleaning off the beaters when the phone rang. She could see that it was Tyrone on the caller ID, so she picked up and held the receiver between her ear and shoulder as she moved about the kitchen.

"Just got her and we're waiting for the luggage," Tyrone said, his words barely discernible above the din at the airport. "Knowing my daughter, she packed enough stuff to dress a small village, so we might be here a while." He chuckled.

"Glad everything went well," Charmaine said, smiling into the phone. He sounded happy, and it was good to hear him that way. "So the flight was on time?"

"For once, yeah."

"I should have dinner ready before you guys get here. I also rented a couple of videos for us to watch afterward. See you around five, I guess?"

"Um, dinner and the movie will have to wait a bit. She wants to stop at the mall after we leave here. There's some wedge sandals she's dying to get."

Charmaine frowned into the phone, thinking she hadn't heard right. Tyrone knew she had busted her ass going all out with this dinner to welcome Tiffany. She had even baked a chocolate cake from scratch. It was sitting right on the countertop, waiting for the cream cheese icing. "Did I hear you right? You're going shopping straight from the airport?"

"She wants to have these shoes for the summer, so I thought we would swing by Columbia Mall."

Charmaine cleared her throat. "Can't the shoes wait until tomorrow? I've been cooking all day—since last night, actually. I went through a lot of trouble to fix her favorite things. I've got meatloaf and potatoes, homemade rolls, and chocolate cake for dessert." Just in case he had forgotten how long and hard she had been slaving in a hot kitchen.

"I know. I told her that, but she really wants these shoes and some Purla handbag."

"Furla," Charmaine said, correcting him with a frown. Now it was shoes *and* a handbag, a five-hundred-dollar handbag for a teenage girl that Charmaine couldn't even afford for herself. "Do you have any idea how much those bags cost?" she asked.

"She said she knows where to get one on sale for half price."

"A Furla for half price at the mall?" Charmaine said doubtfully.

"No, some boutique in Columbia that she found online."

Charmaine found that difficult to believe. Columbia was a small city, not some large metropolis with shopping all over the place. She shut her eyes tightly, crossed herself, and said a silent prayer to muster some patience.

"We shouldn't be more than an hour longer," Tyrone said. "Probably be there by six."

Charmaine's eyes popped open. No way was he going to get in and out of a mall and then go gallivanting about Columbia in search of a nonexistent discount Furla bag with Tiffany and get here by six. It would likely be eight or nine before they got home. Still, she tried to remain calm. Tiffany had landed only moments earlier, and Charmaine did not want to lose it just yet. She would try reasoning with Tyrone.

"You know Kenny still has school for another week and he shouldn't be up late," she said. "And don't forget, today is Russell's last day before he goes to stay with Clarence. If y'all don't come soon, we won't get to watch the movie together before he leaves."

Tyrone sighed and said something to Tiffany, then came back on the line. "She's really looking forward to getting the shoes and bag tonight. I promise we won't be long. I just told her that we had to be home by about six or six-thirty. We should be able to eat and watch the video together tonight before Kenny has to turn in."

Charmaine glanced at her watch. "Tyrone, I have a hard time seeing that happen. You do realize—"

"Look, the luggage is coming," he said, interrupting her. "We'll work it out. Don't worry."

"But what—"

"I'll see you in a bit."

"Tyrone." Charmaine quickly realized that she was talking to no one. He had hung up. She slammed the phone down with all her might. "Dammit!" The prayer for patience obviously hadn't worked.

She looked around the kitchen despairingly. At that moment she was tempted to dump all the food into the garbage can. After all the trouble she had gone through to fix a special meal, Tyrone couldn't even tell his daughter to come home and eat it. All he had to do was say that the shopping spree would have to wait until tomorrow. What was the harm in that? He and Tiffany could have had a nice dinner, and watched the video with Kenny and Russell, and then shopped at the mall to their hearts' content tomorrow or the next day or the day after that. Tiffany would be visiting all summer.

But Tyrone couldn't tell his fourteen-year-old daughter no to save his life, even when it inconvenienced others. This whole relationship that he had with Tiffany was the strangest thing Charmaine had ever seen. She had noticed it when Tiffany visited last summer and again at Christmas. But she hadn't worried about it much then, thinking that Tiffany visited only a few weeks out of the year. Now she was staying much longer. If this was an example of what was to come over the next several weeks, it was going to be a long, hard summer.

❖ ❖ ❖

Something was bothering Evelyn, and it wasn't the fact that she was hunched over yanking weeds out of the vegetable garden in her backyard. Given the recent dry spell, there weren't many weeds to pull out. She stood up straight in her Capri jeans, stretched her back, and wiped the sweat from her brow as she waited for a warm breeze to hit her face. She had held off doing the yardwork until late evening, since it was so hot in the afternoon and she had been in church that morning.

She walked back toward the house and turned on the sprinkler system set up near the garden. As to what had been nagging her, she just couldn't figure it out. All she knew was that it had something to do with Kevin. They had barely spoken since their argument yesterday, even when they were both hanging around the house. But there was nothing unusual about that. In fact, that was pretty much how things were between them now. He hung around in the den; she gardened outdoors. He watched television in the rec room; she read in the bedroom. When they crossed paths it was as if neither saw the other, for all the words exchanged between them.

She walked to the shed and placed her gardening tools in a basket on the floor. Then she shut the door and locked it. At that moment her mind flashed back to the day before when she had first returned home from the bridal fitting and visiting Andre in Baltimore. She could remember hearing thumping and running noises coming from the bedroom as she climbed the stairs, and when she entered Kevin was closing the door to his walk-in closet. Then she saw Kevin's shaved head and freaked out, and the strange sounds were forgotten. But now she remembered them vividly.

The only things amiss in the bedroom were Kevin's suits on the bed, and they wouldn't explain the weird noises she'd heard. She decided to do some sleuthing. It might have been something as innocent as Kevin straightening out his closet. She certainly hoped so. But she needed to shake this nagging thought.

She entered the house from the side door, walked through the disarranged kitchen, and headed up the stairs to the bedroom. Kevin was likely in the recreation room, watching a movie. She moved quickly to his closet and opened the door.

Her eyes scanned the large closet and finally focused on two black suitcases and a black leather duffel bag in a corner. Kevin normally stored his luggage on the shelves at the top of the closet; they looked out of place there on the floor. She stepped inside, lifted one of the bags, and was surprised to realize that it was not empty. She lifted the other two. Same thing. All three bags were packed.

She stooped down and opened the duffel bag to find Kevin's socks, underwear, and toiletries. She placed one of the suitcases flat on the floor and flipped it open. It was packed with Kevin's clothes—slacks, shirts, sweaters. She was about to open the third bag when she heard a sound behind her. She turned to see Kevin standing in the doorway to his closet, a scowl on his face.

"What the hell are you doing?" he asked gruffly.

"You mean, what the hell are *you* doing?" she countered. "What is all this?" She gestured toward the bags.

"What the fuck does it look like?" he snapped.

She frowned. "Are you going on a trip?"

"You could say that. A permanent one."

She was dumbfounded. Did he mean what she thought he meant? She was too afraid to ask, too afraid of the response she might get.

"I'm leaving and I won't be back," he said pointedly, as if he sensed her reluctance to go there and wanted to get it all out.

Evelyn stumbled from the closet and back into the bedroom. She didn't need to hear this, not now. Not ever. Yes, they were going through a rough patch. But leaving? How had it come to this? She faced him as he exited the closet. "You can't be serious."

"I'm very serious. I've had it with all this, Evelyn." He jerked an arm through the air, indicating the spacious master bedroom and bath, with the matching designer bed linen and drapes, the soaking tub and the Kohler bath fixtures. "The kitchen remodeling—that's the last straw. I can't deal with this crap anymore. Or I won't."

Evelyn stared at him. She couldn't believe what she was hearing. This antimaterialistic fad he was going through—quitting his job, giving away all this clothes, shaving his head—was one thing. Now he was about to walk out on her? On two and a half decades of sharing their lives, with absolutely no warning whatsoever?

"You wanted all of this as much as I did until recently, Kevin," she protested, struggling to keep her voice calm. "You seem to forget that. Now all of a sudden you decide you don't like it anymore, and you think you can just pack and split? That's not right."

"What's not right is this lifestyle." He gritted his teeth. "Make more, want more, buy more. Trying to act white. That's all you fucking care about now, Evelyn. You didn't used to be like this. *I* didn't used to be like this. Sadly, this is what our lives have become."

Evelyn watched in horror as he walked back into the closet, grabbed the two suitcases, and placed them on the floor in the bedroom. He went to retrieve the duffel bag, and it was all she could do to keep from grabbing the suitcases and putting everything back in the drawers and closet where it belonged.

"You're leaving now?" she asked when he came back out. "Right this minute?"

He sighed. "I was going to tell you this tonight and leave later in the week, but I figure I might as well go now."

She swallowed hard. "But . . . where will you stay?"

"I rented an apartment in College Park, but I can't move in until Wednesday. I'll just stay in a hotel until then."

He hastily changed into a fresh white T-shirt and picked up all the bags, then paused and looked into her eyes. For a split second Evelyn thought she recognized the old Kevin. The one who *saw* her when he looked at her. The one who listened to what she had to say when she spoke. The one who genuinely cared about her feelings.

Then in an instant he had brushed past her without another word. She followed him. "Kevin, you can't just walk out. This is wrong."

She paused and watched as he moved down the stairs. He obviously had no intention of listening to her. "Fine!" she yelled, leaning over the banister. She was so tired, so weary of all the antagonism between them. "Go ahead, leave. Bastard! I don't give a damn!"

He crossed the foyer silently, and she grabbed the banister to catch her breath as he walked out and shut the door behind him. She straightened her shoulders, pulled herself erect, and willed her breathing to slow down. *One, two, three,* she counted to herself.

Twenty minutes later, she realized that the sky had gone dark and that she was still gripping the banister so tightly her fingers ached.

Chapter 7

"I think you're making a terrible mistake taking Otis back, Valerie," Beverly said as they sat on the covered patio having lunch together on Monday afternoon at Phillips seafood restaurant on the Baltimore Harbor. Valerie had delivered the news to Beverly over the phone the previous night. After giving it a lot of thought she was going to give Otis another chance. Beverly couldn't believe what she was hearing, but she had resisted the urge to call her best friend stupid, dumb, an idiot, and a whole lot more. Instead, she insisted that they meet face-to-face during their lunch breaks the following day.

Beverly had decided to drive to the restaurant, even though it was only a mile from her office at the *Baltimore Sun* to the harbor. Parking at the harbor wasn't a huge problem as long as you were prepared to pay to park in a lot. And driving would allow her more time to stay at the office and continue editing the feature article she was working on about the musicians who would be appearing at the Merriweather Post Pavilion in Columbia, Maryland, for this summer's concert series. Editing the annual feature about the concert was one of Beverly's favorites tasks at the *Sun*. The series always attracted some of the biggest names in music, such as Roberta Flack, Jill Scott, Sheryl Crow, and Duran Duran, and this year would be no exception.

"You don't need to act desperate," Beverly added after the waitress placed a bowl of steamed littleneck clams in front of her and a plate of crispy calamari in front of Valerie. Valerie was wearing a white cotton short-sleeved shirt, and Beverly could detect the faint outline of a bruise on her friend's upper arm where she had hit the wall when Otis shoved her. Valerie was light-complexioned, and Beverly could tell that the bruise had looked much worse when it first happened. It was appalling to think of her friend being hurt by the man in her life.

"I'm not acting," Valerie said. "I'm forty-one years old and I've been single for more than twenty years. I *am* desperate." Valerie had gotten pregnant and married—in that order—right out of high school, so she postponed college for a couple of years. By the time Valerie and Beverly met at Hampton University, Valerie was divorced and living in Newport News, Virginia, with her parents, who were helping her raise her baby daughter, Olivia. Although Valerie had done a good job with Olivia, who had graduated from college and gotten married herself about a year ago, life as a single mom hadn't left Valerie with much time for a social life of her own. And a part of her resented that.

Valerie took a generous sip from her beer. "I'm so tired of being alone I don't know what to do, and I ain't ashamed to admit it."

"I don't get it," Beverly said. "You have a lot to offer." Even if her friend was a little kooky and dressed like a hippie, with long flowery skirts and cotton blouses, she had recently dyed her hair a striking jet black. She had a nice job as an artist at a graphic design firm. "You're attractive. You're artsy. You're fun to be with. I could go on and on. You don't have to settle for some asshole who smacks you around like this." Beverly gestured toward the bruise on Valerie's arm.

"How many times do I have to tell you that he did not hit me? Otis never hits me." Valerie flicked her wrist as if to brush the bruise aside. "This is nothing. It's almost gone. And I know he didn't mean it. He just got a little emotional. I was needling him, so in a way it's my—"

"Hey," Beverly said, snapping her fingers in Valerie's face. "Cut the bull. This is me. He shoved you and you fell. Your arm is black and blue. That's violence, in my book."

Valerie slapped Beverly's hand out of her face. "He didn't really hurt me. And he apologized yesterday."

"If he didn't do anything wrong, what's he apologizing for? Huh? You're making excuses, girlfriend, and you know it. Even before this happened, I didn't think Otis was right for you."

"Aha, now we get down to the real deal. You just don't like him. Well, why not? He's always been nice to you. He has a good job as a programmer."

"So what? A lot of men have good jobs," Beverly countered. "That doesn't automatically mean that they're good men."

"Oh? Where are all these gainfully employed men hiding, Bev? Please share. 'Cause I'm having a real hard time finding 'em. That's why when I get one, I want to hold on."

"I admit it's not easy to find them. I never said it was easy. But they're out there. I got one."

"Yeah, thanks to me."

Beverly frowned. "What's that supposed to mean?"

"I'm the one who introduced you two. Or did you manage to forget that?"

Beverly nodded, surprised at the bitter tone in her friend's voice. She was only trying to help. "No, of course I remember."

"You're one of the lucky few, Bev. You got yourself someone who looks good, works good, and *is* good. And I admit, I'm jealous at times."

"Don't be, Valerie. Just find *yourself* someone who looks good, works good, and is good. Otis always struck me as the chauvinistic type. You know, cocky, arrogant, condescending. The 'you're my woman, you better behave yourself' type."

"He's forty-eight years old and he can be a little hot-tempered and old-fashioned at times," Valerie said. "But he's really sweet to me when he wants to be."

"So was O. J. Simpson to Nicole, no doubt."

"Ouch! That's not fair. Otis is working on his temper."

Beverly scoffed.

"And our charts are beautifully aligned, you know. Our moons are really compatible. There are a few problem areas, mainly with Venus, but at least I know about them and I can deal with them. I can make this work, Bev, trust me. I just need to be patient with him." Valerie leaned in close to Beverly. "And did I ever mention that he's hot as hell in bed?"

"Only about a hundred thousand times since you met him."

Valerie giggled. "I can't help it. There's something about a dark-complexioned brother with a shaved head that gets me going. I cannot lie. I get wet just thinking about him going down."

"Valerie, please. I'm trying to eat here."

Valerie laughed and put her finger to her lip. "Okay, I'll shut up." She picked up her beer glass and drained it.

It upset Beverly to realize that her best friend was so blind to this dude. Beverly was convinced that he was bad news, a poster child for dangerous men who mess up women. "I just don't understand why all it takes is a little sweet talk and some good loving from a brother to turn us into pitiful pushovers."

Maybe she had become too self-righteous now that she had a good man, Beverly thought. She could definitely remember when she wasn't much more clear-eyed or levelheaded about men herself. Still, she wanted so much more for her best friend than what her friend seemed willing to settle for. Beverly shook her head with sadness.

Valerie reached across the table and patted Beverly's hand. "I know you have my best interests at heart. But you don't have to worry about me. I can take care of myself. I told Otis that if he touches me in anger one more time, that's it. I'll find me somebody else."

Beverly smiled thinly. "I hope you really mean that. I don't want it to come to that, but if it does and you don't walk away, I'm going to kick your ass myself."

"Deal." They slapped a high five across the table. "How is Julian these days? I haven't talked to him since he left last month to take that new job at the video game design firm out there near Baltimore."

Beverly smiled broadly for the first time that afternoon. "He's good. He loves it there. We're good. What can I say?"

"Say a little prayer of thanks that your best friend introduced you to him. The brother is one in a thousand—heck, one in a million."

"Amen. We definitely agree on that much."

"So he makes video games now?"

Beverly nodded. "He animates the scenes and characters in the games."

"Sounds exciting."

"He works his butt off, but he's happy there. And when a man is happy he makes his woman happy."

"You Jordan women definitely got it going on in the man department," Valerie said. "You and Julian, Evelyn and Kevin. It even looks like Charmaine finally got her act together too."

"Tyrone seems good for Charmaine," Beverly said. "I'm so happy for her. It took her a while to get it right, but she did. And it might take you some time, but you will if you don't . . ."

Valerie held her hand up and Beverly paused. "Hey, knock it off, okay?" Valerie said. "I'm perfectly happy with the man I've got, thank you."

Beverly made a motion and zipped her lips shut. "Fine." She

wasn't going to push anymore. But obviously it didn't take much to make Valerie happy, Beverly thought sadly, if she was content with Otis. Still, she would keep those thoughts to herself for now. Valerie had made up her mind, and no amount of talk was going to change it.

That didn't mean that Beverly had given up trying to talk some sense into her best friend. She wouldn't give up until she thought Valerie was safe. She would just wait for a better moment to bring it up again.

For now Beverly wanted to enjoy a fine seafood lunch and chat about pleasant things until it was time to head back to the office. They had a glorious view of the boats in the Baltimore Harbor on a sunny afternoon, and Beverly couldn't wait to sink her teeth into one of Maryland's famous crab cakes.

"Have you been able to get over to the bridal salon for your fitting?" Beverly asked as the waiter placed their entrees on the table.

"I called and set something up for this evening as soon as I get off work." Valerie signaled the waitress and ordered another beer.

"When did you start all this drinking?" Beverly asked after the waitress walked off.

"It's just beer."

"I've never seen you drink more than one at lunch."

"So? I'm having two now. What's the big deal?"

"Are you driving back to the office or walking?"

Valerie waved her hand. "Oh, brother. I'm driving, but I'll be fine."

Beverly knew that this was Otis's doing. Valerie hardly touched liquor before she met him. But Otis was a regular beer drinker, and now Valerie was drinking more and more of it. Not that there was anything wrong with that, she supposed, if you didn't overdo it. "I guess you know what you're doing."

The waitress placed the beer in front of Valerie. "Of course I do. Now, how are Evelyn and Kevin doing?"

"They're good."

"They seem to have a fabulous relationship," Valerie said. "They're about the only couple I know that hasn't ended up in divorce court. In fact, now that I think about it, they may be the only couple that has stayed married for so long, at least that I can think of. They're definitely the only couple I know with both people still in their first marriages."

"I admit they're my ideal," Beverly said, nodding. "They give me hope that marriage can work."

"Any idea what their secret is?"

Beverly shrugged. "You hear all these theories about successful married couples, but it's got to be much harder than it looks, since so few manage to stay together. And even more black than white married couples end up in divorce. Did you know that?"

Valerie frowned with surprise. "No, although it's not hard to believe."

"Evelyn is like a rare species when it comes to marriage," Beverly said.

"Kevin seems like a doll and that always helps," Valerie said. "I've only been around him a few times at your family's get-togethers, and he's always so sweet. You ever ask Evelyn why she thinks they've survived all these years?"

"Not really. Maybe I should."

"I'm sure that having a man who is willing to work with you is important," Valerie said. "Kevin seems like he'd be good at that. Julian too."

"No doubt that's important." Beverly gave her friend a 'Why don't you follow your own advice?' look.

"What?" Valerie asked innocently when she realized what Beverly's look meant. "I told you, Otis and I are fine. He's going to work on his temper, and we're gonna live happily ever after. You'll see."

"I hope you're right," Beverly said. But I doubt it, she thought wryly as she bit into her crab cake sandwich.

Chapter 8

As Evelyn listened to Cathy, one of her longstanding clients, talk about her man problems, she realized that she had made a huge mistake. And in her mind's eye, she could see herself smacking her own forehead. Bam! She had completely forgotten to get back to the caterer she hired for Beverly's surprise bridal shower. The affair was Saturday after next, little more than a week from today, a Wednesday. Everyone would be there—her mom and sisters, Beverly's friends and coworkers—and she really needed to finalize the menu. It was funny when and how these things hit.

Cathy's husband had walked out on her some five years earlier, after nearly twenty-five years of marriage, and Cathy had sunk into a deep depression and stayed there for several years. She had started dating again only a few months earlier and now viewed every man she met as possible future husband material. Instead of relaxing, having fun, and trying to get to know a man on the first few dates, Cathy was attempting to figure out if he would make a good spouse.

She was doing it right now with Ted, a man she met a few weeks earlier and had gone out with only twice. Evelyn was trying to persuade Cathy to enjoy the freedom to explore and meet new people that the end of a relationship often ushered in, without obsessing about remarrying. She reminded Cathy that she wasn't planning to have any more children now that she was well into her forties. And that she had been through a wedding once—the dress fittings, florists, caterers, bridal showers, and all that stuff. She didn't need those things again.

That was when Evelyn remembered that she had completely forgotten to call the caterer back for Beverly's bridal shower. When Evelyn had offered to host the surprise shower, her life wasn't in complete disarray as it was at this point, with Kevin leaving this past weekend. Thank God she had hired a caterer instead of planning to prepare all the food herself. That would have been more than she could have handled, given her current mental state.

She grabbed the notepad she kept on a small glass table next to her armchair and discreetly jotted a note to herself: *Call caterer—urgent.* Then she listened as Cathy, wearing a floral print sundress and seated on a small couch across from Evelyn, talked about wanting the security and comfort that comes from knowing that someone will always be there for you.

"I miss so much about being married," Cathy said. She was twisting a lock of her shoulder-length blond hair, a habit she had whenever she felt anxious. "Like having someone I can tap on the shoulder when I'm feeling horny." Cathy chuckled. "Someone I know is attracted to me and free of diseases too, by the way. And yes, women in their late forties get horny."

There was a time when Cathy's blunt sense of humor would have made Evelyn laugh herself. But not now. Not today. Given what she was now going through in her own marriage, all she could manage was a weak smile. It felt familiar and yet so strange to talk about divorce with a client, now that she and Kevin were separated and her own future was so precarious. A part of Evelyn wondered if she would begin to view divorce differently now.

"You don't have to tell me that women in their forties have

those feelings," Evelyn said, thinking with dismay about the many months that had passed by since Kevin had touched her intimately. She quickly shook the personal longing from her head and focused on her client. "We're about the same age, you know."

Cathy's pretty blue eyes brightened. "Really? I always thought you were in your early forties at the most. You look so young." Cathy laughed good-naturedly. "It's not fair. You-all age so beautifully."

Evelyn smiled. "I'm not surprised that you have these feelings. You're still a healthy woman. And being around a man whom you find attractive is reawakening the feelings within you."

Cathy nodded eagerly.

"But do you feel that you need to be in a marriage to deal with them?" Evelyn asked.

"Not really. I'm not *that* old." Cathy laughed again, and this time Evelyn joined her. "I could get it on with a man without marriage," Cathy continued. "I guess what I really miss is having someone I know will be around to the end, at least until one of us croaks. For that, you need marriage or something close."

Evelyn nodded with understanding. "You're talking about lifelong companionship or a partner who is always ready to share intimacy or whatever else whenever you are. Can you be sure you'll have that with marriage?"

Cathy frowned with thought and the wrinkles around her eyes deepened. "Obviously, I didn't have those things toward the end of my marriage, even though I didn't realize it at first." She shrugged. "That doesn't mean I couldn't have them with someone else in the future."

"Sounds like you think marriage would be different the second time around."

"Maybe. Well, yes, I do."

"Why would it be different?"

"I could meet a better man. Someone who wants a lifelong commitment just as I do."

Evelyn nodded again.

"Not that my first husband didn't want those things in the beginning," Cathy continued. "I'm sure he did. I know he did. At least I think he did." Cathy sighed. "But he changed, you know? We both did. People change all the time, I guess, and I have no way of knowing if this man I'm seeing now would change on me. Or anyone else I might meet, for that matter. At least I'm older and wiser now, as well as the men I meet, so we should be smarter about these things." Cathy paused, and Evelyn waited, as she could see from Cathy's expression that she was turning things over in her head. One of the tricks Evelyn had learned as a therapist was that sometimes the best thing you could do was wait and see where the client was going.

"Do second marriages have a better success rate?" Cathy finally asked. "I know the success rate for first marriages is lousy. But what about second marriages? It seems they would have a better success rate, since you learn something from the first."

"Actually, no, they don't."

Cathy looked shocked.

"Sorry, it's true," Evelyn said. "People don't always learn much from their first marriages. They tend to repeat the same old patterns."

Cathy frowned. "Really? You mean if they marry a jerk the first time, they turn around and marry another jerk? How stupid."

Evelyn smiled. "Or they marry someone with the same incompatibilities. But that doesn't mean that *you* can't learn something and do better next time. You can break the pattern."

"I definitely don't want to end up in divorce court again. It was nasty, a horrible experience for me." Cathy shuddered visibly.

"There's probably only one way to be absolutely sure that won't happen again."

Cathy frowned briefly, then blinked with enlightenment. "Oh, you mean don't get married again in the first place?"

Evelyn nodded.

"You're telling me that marriage always has pros and cons."

Evelyn nodded again. "So does being single. There are different kinds of risks or different pros and cons, as you put it. It all depends on what you prefer. Some prefer the freedom that comes with being single. But the downside is loneliness, and it can be a big downside when you're an older woman. Not to mention the risk of all the STDs out there."

"Tell me about it."

"Not that you can't catch things when you're married, but ideally it's less of a concern then. If you go for marriage, you'll have someone to share things with, from bills to lovemaking and everything else. But that comes with the risk of losing it all and being hurt or maybe being trapped in a bad marriage that you can't walk away from so easily. In the end, it's about knowing yourself—your strengths and your vulnerabilities, your hopes and dreams—so you can make smart choices."

The more Evelyn listened to herself talk, the more she realized how much she wanted to stay married. The alternative didn't sound too appealing for a woman her age. She tried to sound impartial as she counseled Cathy, but it was harder to do that now, given what she was going through in her own personal life.

As soon as Cathy left, Evelyn moved to her desk and picked up the phone, not to call the caterer but to call Kevin once again. She would get to the caterer in due time, but she had been trying to reach Kevin since Monday, the day after he left, and she was tired of waiting for him to call her back. She wanted to hear his voice, and she didn't even know his whereabouts. Was he still in a hotel, or had he moved to the apartment today as planned? It was utter nonsense that she had no idea where her husband was.

She dialed his cell number. How ironic, she thought as she

waited. The only way she could get in touch with her husband was through his cell phone. She listened as it rang and rang until finally his voice mail greeting came on. She twisted her lips impatiently until the greeting ended, then left yet another curt message for him to call her and slammed the phone down.

How could Kevin walk out and not even bother to get in touch for three days? She felt like some desperate twenty-year-old calling her man again and again and praying that he would call her back. She hadn't gone through crap like this in decades and she hated it. She was too old for such nonsense.

She still had some good old-fashioned pride left in her. She would wait it out. If she gave Kevin some time, he would get in touch sooner or later. They had been together for so long. He needed her more than he realized. He needed his life with her more than he knew or was willing to admit. All his talk about trying to act white was foolish nonsense. Kevin had always been just as eager as she had to improve their lives, to have nice things for themselves and their children. With patience on her part, he would come back to his senses and back to her.

Or would he? What if he didn't come back to his senses? What if he enjoyed his time away from her? What if he met some other woman while he was away? Worse yet, what if he had already met another woman? Evelyn didn't think he had, but could she be sure? No, she couldn't.

"Oh, God," she muttered. She tapped her fingers on the desk and took a deep breath. "Calm down," she said softly. Don't allow yourself to wallow in negative thoughts just yet. Kevin was about to turn fifty. Most likely, he was going through the male change of life. It was surprising, since Kevin had always been so stable, so rock solid, but turning fifty could freak anyone out, even someone as rational as Kevin. Maybe even more so with someone like Kevin. He was likely regretting all those years of being so sane and serious about everything. Now he wanted to let it all loose and have some fun.

She glanced at the telephone, willing him to call her back. If he did, she could tell him that she understood what he was going through, that he didn't need to dump his wife to find fulfillment. They could talk things over and it would be good for him. After all, she was a psychologist.

Maybe she would try to reach him at Blockbuster. She had never gotten his number there, thinking the job was a stupid fad that wouldn't last. That was obviously a big mistake.

She was about to call directory assistance for the local Blockbuster when her desk phone rang. She almost fell out of the chair when she saw Kevin's number on the caller ID.

"You called?" he asked when she answered, his voice filled with more than a hint of irritation.

Evelyn almost sputtered. He acted like he was doing her a favor by returning her call. What gave him the right to treat her like some random slut off the street chasing after him?

She had planned to talk to him calmly and rationally, despite the fact that she had every right to be thoroughly pissed about his behavior. But that plan had flown straight out the window the moment he called, copping an attitude with her.

"What is going on with you, Kevin? You walk out on me and don't even bother to get in touch. What the hell am I supposed to do?"

"I thought it would be best to give us a few days to chill and, you know, clear our heads, given how upset we both were when I walked out on Sunday."

"So are you planning to walk back *in* any time soon?"

"I need more time to think things over, Evelyn. You should do the same."

"What am I supposed to be thinking about? Will you please tell me that?"

Silence.

"I'm waiting, Kevin. What the hell am I supposed to be thinking about?" She didn't mean to shout, but she couldn't help it. He was turning her life inside out.

"You should try to calm down," he said.

"*I* don't need to do anything. *You* need to tell me what you expect me to do while you're doing all this damn thinking. 'Cause I don't need to do any thinking. I know exactly what I want. I want us to be a family just like we've always been."

"I hear you."

"Then what are you going to do about it? And what do I tell people until you decide?"

"I can't answer that," he said calmly, too damn calmly, as far as she was concerned.

"God, Kevin. You sound so cold. What's gotten into you?"

"It's not just me," Kevin said. "We've both changed. We've grown apart. If you think about it, you'll see that."

"*I* haven't changed. *You've* changed."

"Fine, Evelyn. If you can't see it, you don't want to see it. 'Cause any way you look at our lives recently, we've grown apart. We want different things. I woke up one day and realized that I couldn't care less about legal briefs and depositions or even about my clients. I don't give a damn about the house or the lawn or driving a luxury car. All that shit disgusts me now. I don't need it, don't want it. The question is, are *you* willing to give those things up?"

Evelyn was silent. She didn't know what to say to that.

"I didn't think so," Kevin said.

Evelyn swallowed. Kevin was right about one thing. He had changed—a lot. But was this permanent? Could they work through it and perhaps find a middle ground? He didn't seem to think so, but she wasn't ready to give up on him or on them yet. "Are you saying you want a divorce? That you want to give up on us without first trying to work through this?"

"I'm not saying anything now," he said. "I know it's not fair to ask you to give all that up, and I really don't expect you to. But

I need to clear my head and think about what I can realistically live with."

"And you need to do your thinking away from me. Right?"

"It's better that way, Evelyn."

He seemed determined to have this time away from her, and fussing about it wasn't going to get him to change his mind. "How long do you think you'll need?"

"All I can say is that I'll call you at some point."

She sighed. "Can you give me something a little more definite? It's frustrating to be completely shut out like this."

"It will be soon," he said. "More than that I can't say now. I need to clear my head."

Your head, your head, your head. Was that why he had shaved it? To clear out all the memories of their lives together. That was what she wanted to shout. But she didn't, simply because she knew it wouldn't do a bit of good. "Fine. Where are you staying?"

"The Wynfield apartments in College Park."

"Apartment number?"

"Just call me on my cell if you need to reach me."

"Honestly, Kevin, do you have to be so secretive?" Her lips tightened. "Fine, I'll call you on your cell."

"Good. Anything more?" he asked.

Of course there was more. She had a million questions for him, but it was hard to express her innermost thoughts to someone who so obviously didn't want to be bothered with her. "That's it. Oh, wait. Have you talked to Andre and Rebecca? Have you told them anything about this yet?"

"I haven't talked to them since I left the house. I'll probably call them before the week is out."

"Maybe, um, maybe you should hold off telling them until we decide what we're going to do. This will come as a shock to them. It might even affect Rebecca's studies."

"Fine. I can go along with that."

Evelyn let out a sigh of relief. "Thank you."

"I'll call you soon."

She listened as he hung up, then stood and looked out the window behind her desk. It was hot out and the streets were slick from several thunderstorms they'd had since Monday afternoon. The heat she could do without, but they had needed the rain desperately. After a multiweek dry spell, the flowers and shrubs in her yard at home were starting to dry out. The wet weather should do a lot of good toward replenishing everything.

If only she could figure out how to replenish her marriage. Or was it just too hopelessly dried out? How had it come to this? The distance between the two of them, the heated disagreements. They had always argued from time to time, but where there was once fire and passion now there was only bitterness and resentment.

She would wait for his stupid call and she would try to be patient about it. She didn't have much choice. She hated the feeling of waiting in the dark until he was ready to bring the light. She hated that he had the upper hand in all of this. It was demeaning and exasperating beyond belief. But she had to swallow her pride, her feelings, her convictions—all of that and a whole lot more—if she wanted to try and save her marriage. For now the best thing to do was to get on with her life, just as she would have told Cathy and all her other clients.

She sat back at her desk, picked up the phone, and dialed the caterer's number. As soon they finished discussing the details for the buffet menu, she opened the bottom desk drawer and removed her lunch and that morning's copy of the *Washington Post*. She opened the bag, took out the tuna sandwich and the apple, and stared at them blankly. Suddenly her lunchtime routine of eating at her desk while catching up on the news seemed dreadfully dull.

She stuffed the sandwich and apple back into the bag and tossed the bag and the newspaper back into the bottom desk drawer. She grabbed her Fendi purse and slammed the drawer shut. She needed to get out of the office for a change of scenery. And she needed something a little more appetizing for lunch.

She had never liked eating out alone, but this was downtown Silver Spring, and there were several sandwich shops between here and the Metro line. She would pop in somewhere for something a little more exciting than a tuna sandwich before her next client was due.

She removed a small mirror from her purse and checked her hair, then grabbed her suit jacket from a hook on the wall and left the office.

Chapter 9

Evelyn buttoned her linen suit jacket neatly as she waited for an elevator to take her down from the sixth floor to the lobby of the office building. One of the two elevators stopped and just as she was about to enter, a couple stepped out of the other elevator. The three of them smiled at one another briefly, and Evelyn entered her elevator and pressed the button for the lobby.

That was when she heard her name being called.

"Evelyn?"

She frowned and stuck her hand between the elevator doors just before they shut. They popped back open, and Evelyn stepped out to face the man she had just seen alight from the opposite elevator, standing there in front of her, the woman slightly behind him.

"Evelyn Jordan?" he said as the elevator door closed behind her.

She smiled slightly and narrowed her eyes. She didn't recognize him, but he was using her maiden name. "I'm sorry, but—"

"McKinley High School," he said. "You graduated in the seventies and you were one or two classes behind me, I think. Reuben Roberts."

The smile on Evelyn's face widened. She remembered the name well. Reuben had been one class ahead of her, and he was a star on the basketball team, very popular with guys and girls alike. Evelyn and every other girl in the school had a huge crush on him. At the time, though, Reuben had eyes only for Belinda, whom he later married when they both finished college.

He had changed a lot, Evelyn thought as they shook hands. She recognized the twinkling brown eyes and long lashes from all those years ago. But gone were the baby cheeks and the deep dimples that had made high school girls swoon. In their place was a devilishly handsome mature face that Evelyn was sure now made grown women look twice.

"I remember you," she said. "It's good to see you, Reuben."

He reached out and they moved in for a quick hug. Then Reuben gestured toward the woman standing behind him, who Evelyn noted was much younger. She was also as beautiful as she was impeccably dressed and made up. Although it had been many years since she'd seen Reuben, Evelyn was pretty sure this woman wasn't Belinda.

"This is a colleague of mine, Carissa Valentine," he said. "Carissa, this is Evelyn Jordan."

The two women shook hands and Reuben laughed.

"I still can't believe it's you, Evelyn. You haven't changed much at all since high school. You look fantastic."

"Oh, I don't know about that. But thank you for saying it. You're looking good yourself."

"Thanks. I remember you had a sister, right? Name is Charmaine?"

Evelyn nodded. "Actually I have two sisters, but you probably never met Beverly, since she's eight years younger than I am."

"No, don't think I did. How is Charmaine? Crazy Charmaine. Yeah, I remember her well."

"She's good. She got married about a year ago."

"Oh? Tell her I said, congratulations. What about you? Married? Kids?"

Evelyn paused for a second, not sure how to respond to the question about marriage. Then she collected herself. There was definitely no need to go into details about her marriage—or lack thereof—with a man she hadn't seen in thirty years. "Yes, we have two children, a boy and a girl. Rebecca is in college. Andre just finished and now lives in Baltimore. How about you, Reuben? Did you have children?"

He nodded. "Two boys, both grown now."

An elevator appeared again, and Evelyn stuck her hand in to keep the doors open.

"It was nice seeing you, Reuben." She nodded toward Carissa. "Nice meeting you."

Carissa smiled. "You too."

Reuben reached out to help Evelyn hold the elevator doors, which were doing that thing they do when they desperately want to close. "Do you work here in this building?" he asked.

Evelyn nodded. "Yes, I have for several years now."

"Cool. I just moved here from downtown D.C. a couple of weeks ago. I'll probably see you around."

"I'm sure."

They let the doors have their way, and Evelyn realized that she still had a smile on her face when she stepped out into the first-floor lobby. She couldn't believe she had just run into Reuben Roberts, easily the most popular guy in the entire high school when they were there. She would have to be sure to tell Charmaine. Or maybe she wouldn't. Charmaine used to tease her relentlessly about the way she got excited whenever Reuben was around.

She opened the door leading onto Georgia Avenue, a busy street in downtown Silver Spring filled with the sights, sounds, and scents of lunchtime traffic. She clutched her bag a little more tightly and headed toward the restaurants. It didn't take long for the smile on her face to fade away as she trudged up the rain-slicked hill, all her recent troubles with Kevin filling her memory.

Chapter 10

Charmaine's suggestion was made with the best of intentions—a nice little family outing to a restaurant for dinner on a Friday evening, with Kenny and Tiffany getting to choose the spot. When she suggested it to Tyrone, she pointed out that it would be a great way to get Kenny and Tiffany to cooperate on something. That was the idea at least.

She should have known better. Kenny stood firmly in the living room in his baggy blue jeans and baseball cap and stated that he wanted barbecue at Famous Dave's. Tiffany, her hands on her hips and dressed in a denim fluff miniskirt and orange cami, insisted on the Olive Garden, which Charmaine found strange, since Tiffany didn't eat pasta or tomatoes. But Tiffany claimed to love the stuffed mushrooms and said she had learned to avoid the things she disliked.

The disagreement between the kids didn't seem so awful at first, as the whole point was to try and teach them to work together and to compromise when they disagreed on something. So back and forth they went, with Charmaine trying patiently to broker an agreement. After nearly thirty minutes of this, neither of them had budged a millimeter. Which was weird to Charmaine because she knew that Kenny liked pasta and Tiffany liked barbecue. Or maybe it wasn't so weird, since what they *didn't* like was each other.

So she got tougher and warned that if they couldn't agree on a restaurant, the adults would pick an alternative. That helped not at all, and Charmaine threw her hands up in despair. It was obvious that this was going nowhere. "We'll do seafood," she decided firmly. "We haven't been to the Crab Shanty since last summer."

Her decision was reasonable and fair, she thought. After all, she had warned Kenny and Tiffany repeatedly as they both stood there with stubborn scowls on their faces.

"Everybody likes seafood, right?" Charmaine said, looking from one to the other.

Kenny shoved his hands in his jeans pockets and shrugged. Tiffany switched her new Furla bag from one arm to the other as she carefully studied her freshly painted orange fingernails.

"We should go to the Olive Garden," Tyrone said suddenly out of nowhere. "We haven't been there in a while either."

"Huh?" Charmaine couldn't believe what she was hearing.

"The Olive Garden this time," Tyrone repeated. "Kenny can choose next time we eat out."

"And might I ask why you made that decision?" Charmaine asked, hand planted firmly on her hip.

"Tiffany is our guest. We'll do what she wants today. There will be plenty of other chances for Kenny to pick where we eat."

Naturally, Tiffany was delighted with this idea and she clapped with joy. Kenny was pissed and flopped down onto the couch, arms folded defiantly across his chest.

Charmaine did not think Tyrone's suggestion was helpful at all. The whole point was to try and get the kids to work together, not to choose sides. Even still, if Tyrone had made the suggestion to go with Tiffany's choice this time and Kenny's later *before* she had chosen seafood as an alternative, she would have gone along with it. But Tyrone waited until she had ruled on the matter to come up with his cockamamie idea. In effect, Tyrone was overruling *her.* In front of Tiffany and her son. Not good. No way, no how.

What the heck was the matter with this man? Whatever it was, Charmaine was losing all her patience with him. It was past nine o'clock by the time he and Tiffany had come home from their shopping spree after leaving the airport last Sunday. They'd had to rush through a meal she had spent hours preparing and they missed out altogether on the videos she had rented for them to watch. But Charmaine had kept her lips zipped, since it was Tiffany's first day there.

That was then, this was now. Charmaine tugged at the sleeve of Tyrone's navy shirt and pulled him into the kitchen. "What's wrong with my suggestion to get seafood?" she whispered, not wanting the kids to hear.

"Tiffany is visiting. We need to make her feel welcome. We can go to Famous Dave's next time we eat out."

"This isn't about the kids anymore. This is about you overruling me in front of them," she said, poking him in the arm. "I don't think that's right."

"I wasn't trying to overrule you. I was trying to solve the disagreement."

"But you *did* overrule me." Charmaine was trying to keep her voice down, but she could feel herself about to fail. "I had decided on seafood after they kept going back and forth and couldn't agree on anything. Then you sided with Tiffany when you came up with this stuff about going to the Olive Garden."

"Look, I wasn't trying to start anything. I was just trying to get things moving."

"Things *were* moving. I had just made a decision."

"How the hell is suggesting seafood helping? Neither of them wanted any damn seafood."

"That's better than siding with Tiffany," she snapped. She paused when she realized that they were both shouting and making absolutely no progress. Her idea to have the kids cooperate and pick a restaurant together had completely backfired. The kids were not getting along any better, and she and Tyrone were arguing with each other. "This is going nowhere," she said. "I think we should pick someplace neither of them suggested. I don't care what—seafood, burgers, whatever. That's fair to both of them."

"I disagree. We go to the Olive Garden today. Then next weekend we can go—"

Charmaine's head snapped back. He obviously was not backing down one inch. Well, neither was she. "*You* can go to the Olive Garden. We won't be joining you."

Tyrone's eyes flashed red in a way that Charmaine had never seen before. "Suit yourself." He stomped back into the family room. "C'mon, Tiffany. Let's go."

Tyrone didn't need to explain to the kids what had happened, since they had no doubt heard most of it anyway. She and Tyrone were being stubborn, but Charmaine was too upset to care. The last thing she wanted was to be challenged in front of Tiffany, a child who had little respect for her authority in the first place. And she didn't think that Tyrone was being at all fair to Kenny.

She watched with sadness as Tyrone and Tiffany marched through the kitchen and left through the door to the garage. It felt as though they had drawn battle lines. But Tyrone's personality was so different when his daughter was around. The wonderful husband and stepfather would vanish and this unreasonable, red-eyed freak would take his place.

She called Kenny into the kitchen and forced a smile on her face when he walked in looking disappointed and puzzled.

"What was that all about, Ma?"

She patted his cheek. "Looks like it's going to be you and me chowing down on some barbecue, handsome."

"Really? Why are we going to separate places to eat? We're family. That doesn't seem right."

"I know, but sometimes families disagree." Charmaine hoped that was all it was—just a temporary disagreement among family members. Surely they would all soon get along much better.

Chapter 11

Beverly had wanted to try The Melting Pot fondue restaurant for dinner ever since she first spotted it at the Wilde Lake Village Center in Columbia a few months earlier. Fondue was all the rage when she was a girl. She could remember Evelyn borrowing the family car and driving Charmaine and her downtown in Washington, D.C., for fondue. Then it fell out of favor. It was good to see it making a comeback, even if only a modest one, because she loved the sauces and was a real sucker for the fruit dipped in milk chocolate.

It was especially cool that she was meeting her sisters here for dinner, she thought as she pulled her Lexus into the parking lot. Once every couple of months they would pick a spot to meet for lunch or dinner. Sometimes their mother or one of their girlfriends would join in the fun. It was a tradition the sisters had started years ago that got maintained or not, depending on how busy they each were. They had picked it up again a couple of years back, when Beverly first moved from Washington, D.C., to Columbia, Maryland, after landing a job at the *Baltimore Sun*.

Beverly loved living in Columbia, a jewel of a community nestled about halfway between Baltimore and Washington, with a rich assortment of progressive people of all races. Although Columbia was no D.C. or even Baltimore when it came to amenities, it still had decent restaurants and shopping and was relatively free of the crime found in the two bigger cities. Many people assumed that all the middle-class blacks outside of D.C. lived in Prince George's and Montgomery counties, but Columbia and parts of the nearby Ellicott City could rival the both of them when it came to diversity.

The only problem was the skyrocketing prices of real estate. Not long ago, housing out here was a lot cheaper than it was in Washington and Baltimore, but all that was changing as more people discovered the area and its ideal mix of features and serenity. Beverly was glad she had bought her town house before prices skyrocketed. Charmaine had also moved to Columbia from Prince George's County when she got married about a year ago.

Beverly parked her car next to Charmaine's Honda Accord and smiled as she thought about her date with Julian last night while she walked through the lot and past the bank drive-through. Julian had to work that Saturday afternoon, and she hoped she hadn't worn him out by insisting they go at it twice last night and again this morning. But she couldn't help it. The man really stirred her passions.

She walked through the door of the restaurant, and the waitress escorted her to the table where Charmaine was already seated, looking sexy as usual in a colorful print sundress with a low-cut halter top. Beverly sat down across from her.

"Sorry to be late," Beverly said. "I had a scorching hot date last night."

Charmaine pointed at her watch with deliberate exaggeration. "Last night? What's that got to do with anything now? It's five o'clock."

"I said it was a scorcher," Beverly said slyly. "Those always last until the following morning with Julian. I didn't get to sleep until around noon."

Charmaine rolled her eyes skyward. "What did you two lovebirds do? Besides screw."

Beverly laughed. "What else is there? I don't know what it is exactly, but it seems the older I get, the hornier I get. Does that change after forty? Everyone assumes it does."

Charmaine shook her head vehemently. "That's a myth. My forties have been some of my most passionate years."

"Really? Why do you think that is?" Beverly asked.

"Fewer hang-ups, less inhibited."

"Must be, 'cause I can't seem to get enough of Julian. Don't get me wrong now. That's not all we do. We also talk—a lot. Actually the talks are starting to take up more and more of our time together. We're getting to be so much like an old married couple that it scares me sometimes."

Charmaine smiled. "I bet. What's he up to now? Waiting for you to get back home?"

Beverly shook her head. "I wish. He had to go in to work."

"On a Saturday?"

Beverly nodded. "For a couple of hours. Then he and two of his co-workers were going to the golf course to hit some balls."

"Now that's dedication," Charmaine said as she took a sip of her drink.

"He loves it, but yeah, he's in a very competitive field. Video games are so hot now. Plus, not many black people work in the field, so he's trying to fit in and prove himself. In fact there are only two other black professionals where he works."

Beverly paused and watched as Charmaine fiddled absentmindedly with the slice of lime in her margarita. Charmaine wasn't her usual full-of-fun-and-laughter self. She obviously had something else on her mind. "And then we climbed up on the roof, stripped naked, and screwed while standing on top of the chimney."

Charmaine blinked. "Huh?"

Beverly laughed. "So I finally got your attention."

Charmaine twisted her lip when she realized what was going on. "Not funny."

"Well, what are you thinking about? How are things with you and Tyrone? And Tiffany?"

Charmaine scrunched up her nose. "We were doing okay until last night. That was awful. This morning wasn't much to get excited about. You could have sliced the chill in the air with a knife."

"Good grief. What happened?"

"I only want to have to say this once, so let's wait for Evelyn to get here." Charmaine looked back toward the entrance. "By the way, where is she? She's never late anywhere."

"I was going to ask you the same thing. She's usually the first to arrive."

"Maybe she's stuck in traffic, since she's coming all the way from Silver Spring," Charmaine said. "Or maybe her brand-new Benz broke down."

"Don't be so hard on her," Beverly said. "You're just jealous."

"You're right. I am."

As if on cue, Evelyn strode into the dining room and rushed to the table, hastily fastening the jacket buttons to her off-white pantsuit. A strand of her normally picture-perfect hair kept falling across her forehead, and she brushed it back.

Beverly frowned. It was so unlike Evelyn to be anything but ultra cool.

"Sorry to be so late," Evelyn said as she slid into her seat.

"Traffic?" Charmaine asked.

"Not really. Just . . . stuff. I'm sure you all don't want to be bothered with my issues."

"Yes, we do," Beverly said.

"You mean *you* have issues?" Charmaine added. "I'm shocked, but take a ticket, sister. You're next in line after me."

"Oh?" Evelyn said. "What's going on?"

"Something to do with Tiffany," Beverly said. "Something happened last night. Go ahead, Charm, tell us."

Charmaine crossed her legs under the table and leaned in. She was bursting to get last night's fiasco with Tyrone and Tiffany off her chest. Besides, she suspected that Evelyn's problems were minor compared to her own. Evelyn, with her perfect little suits and her perfect little married life, was probably worried about her vegetable garden getting too much rain lately. Or maybe she had a stain on one of her precious designer bags.

"I blame Tyrone more than I do Tiffany. She's just a child. It's the way her daddy acts when she's around that drives me nuts. God! The man has a split personality if I ever saw one. One minute he's a wonderful husband and father figure to Kenny. The next minute he goes flying off on this crazy absentee-father guilt trip."

"Whoa." Beverly said. "Guilt about what? You always said he was an attentive father."

"He *is* attentive. They talk on the phone several times a week when Tiffany's not here. But he still feels guilty 'cause he doesn't live with her year-round. He tries to make up for it when she's here by turning into this overbearing monster, stepping on everybody else's toes to please her."

"What happened last night?" Evelyn asked.

Charmaine paused and took a generous sip of her margarita as the waitress came by to take drink orders from Beverly and Evelyn. Beverly ordered her favorite, an apple martini. Evelyn didn't usually drink anything stronger than a glass of wine but decided to go for a margarita this time. Charmaine took note and began to think that maybe something more than soaked gardens was bothering Evelyn.

Just thinking about the argument with Tyrone the previous evening made Charmaine's heart pump faster. It was the biggest disagreement that they'd had since they met. They had barely spoken to each other that morning. Then he and Tiffany left around noon to do yet more shopping, and Charmaine dropped Kenny off at a friend's house before coming to The Melting Pot.

"There's always been this competition between Kenny and Tiffany, especially for Tyrone's attention," Charmaine continued as soon as the waitress left. "Tiffany misses her dad no doubt, and Kenny is starved for a father figure. A little competition between them is understandable. So yesterday I suggested that the kids decide on a restaurant for dinner, to try and get them to work together on something that would be fun. But they couldn't come to an agreement, so after a lot of back-and-forth, I suggested an alternative. That's when Tyrone stepped in and overruled me right in front of them. He decided that we would go to the restaurant that Tiffany picked."

"Uh-oh," Evelyn murmured.

"He didn't," Beverly said, shaking her head.

"Yep, sure did. I said no, I don't think so. I explained that it wasn't right to overrule me in front of the kids and that this wouldn't be fair to Kenny, not to mention that it sends the wrong signal to Tiffany. He got mad and they went on without us."

"That's so over-the-top," Beverly said with disapproval. "It sounds like he doesn't even care how it affects Kenny."

"You talked about this problem a little when Tiffany was here last summer," Evelyn said. "I had no idea it was this serious. A lot of absentee fathers have some guilt, but it sounds like Tyrone has it bad."

"I think it's worse than it was last summer," Charmaine said. "Or maybe I'm less patient now. We had only been married about a month then, and I wanted to make Tyrone happy and get to know his daughter. But I'm past the need to please no matter what, thank you."

"Have you tried sitting down and talking to him about it, away from the kids?" Evelyn asked. "It's not good for them to see you two arguing. They will milk that for all they can get out of it."

"Of course I have," Charmaine said, a little exasperated to have Evelyn lecturing her. She was a mother too, and a damn good one at that. She knew what was and wasn't good for children. "I tried to talk to him after Tiffany left last summer, but it was going in one ear and out the other. So I dropped it."

"That's too bad," Beverly said.

"She visited us for only two weeks during summer and another week at Christmas," Charmaine continued. "And I figured I could live with him indulging her for such a short time, you know? Now that she's staying all summer, I can't overlook it. If it was just me, I might, but not with Kenny. Hell no. I worry about what it will do to his psyche."

Evelyn nodded. "You have to speak up and protect Kenny. I'm with you on that."

"No question," Charmaine said.

"At the same time, I can kind of understand where Tyrone is coming from," Evelyn added. "It can be hard on absentee dads. It's natural for him to want to coddle her."

"Up to a point," Charmaine said. "But like Beverly just mentioned, this is way over-the-top. I can't excuse this."

"You still have to try and strike a balance with him," Evelyn said.

"Don't you think I am?" Charmaine said indignantly. "But that's much easier said than done. When it comes to this man and his daughter, it's like he has tunnel vision."

"Just try to be patient," Evelyn said. "That's all I'm saying."

"Maybe he'll come around with time," Beverly said before Charmaine could respond. The talk between her sisters was heating up, and she wanted to try and lower the temperature.

"I hope so, 'cause Lord knows I'm trying to be patient," Charmaine said.

"I'm sure you are," Beverly said.

"It got ugly yesterday, and I do mean ugly," Charmaine said. "We haven't spoken since it happened." Charmaine twisted her lips. "Why do I have such rotten luck with men?"

"Oh, Charm," Beverly said. "You just hit a wall. Tyrone seems like a decent guy. I'm sure you two will work it out."

"That's what I kept telling myself with Clarence," Charmaine said, thinking back on those turbulent days with her second ex-husband. "He was the one I thought I would make it with, but we all know where that went."

"Tyrone is nothing like Clarence," Evelyn said. "And Tyrone is a father. Clarence wasn't."

"That's why I can't imagine that Tyrone won't come to his senses soon," Beverly said. "He knows how important Kenny is to you."

"What I don't understand is why he isn't more balanced with them," Charmaine said. "He's a parent. He should understand that you never favor one child over the other, never. He's such a good father figure to Kenny when his daughter isn't around. They hang out together watching movies at home and go out and shoot hoops. All that goes out the window when she comes to visit, and I don't understand it for the life of me. I just hope to God this doesn't ruin my marriage."

"Whoa, Charmaine," Beverly said. "You aren't thinking of leaving him for this, are you? That's crazy. She's only here a few weeks out of the year."

"That's a bit dramatic, Charm," Evelyn said.

"I'm not about to walk out tomorrow," Charmaine said. "But no one is going to take advantage of my son or overrule me in front of him, even for just a few weeks out of the year. Hell no. That's disrespectful."

Beverly and Evelyn exchanged glances as the waitress brought the drinks. After she had taken their orders, Charmaine turned to Evelyn. "Now tell us what's going on with you." Charmaine wanted to hear about Evelyn's problems, but she also wanted to get off the subject of Tyrone and Tiffany and all this talk about patience. She knew that she would have to tread carefully in the days ahead and not do something she'd later regret. But she also knew that she had her limits when it came to what she would tolerate with Kenny, and no one was going to change her mind about that.

Evelyn carefully placed her drink down and smoothed her hands over the tablecloth. She had been mulling over how much to tell her sisters ever since she left her house. She wasn't ready to admit that Kevin had left until she was sure it was going to be a permanent deal, and she prayed it wouldn't come to that. But she couldn't pretend everything was hunky-dory between them either, when it was probably written all over her face that something was troubling her.

"We're having some problems," Evelyn said softly.

"Who's having problems?" Beverly asked. "Not you and Kevin?"

Evelyn smiled awkwardly. "Yes, Kevin and I, believe it or not. He's been acting strange for several months now."

"This is *Kevin* we're talking about?" Charmaine said with disbelief. "My brother-in-law? The straitlaced, buttoned-up attorney?"

"He's about to turn fifty, isn't he?" Beverly asked.

"In about six months," Evelyn said, nodding. "I think he's having a midlife crisis."

Charmaine smiled thinly. "What did he do? Go out and buy a sports car?"

"I wish," Evelyn said. "It's a lot more serious than that."

"I wondered why he stopped coming to family get-togethers," Beverly said. "But you always told us he was busy."

"I wasn't exactly forthcoming," Evelyn admitted.

"I have to say, I thought something was fishy," Charmaine said.

"The truth is, he started acting like I was asking him to go to a funeral or something whenever I asked," Evelyn said. "So I stopped asking."

"You're not about to tell us that Kevin is cheating on you, are you?" Charmaine asked.

"No, it's nothing like that. At least not that I'm aware of." Evelyn thought that she wouldn't put anything past Kevin these days. But Kevin said he wasn't having an affair, and she was going to believe that until she had evidence otherwise. She was miserable enough as it was. She didn't need to drag more crap into this situation unless it was absolutely necessary.

"Then what is it?" Charmaine asked anxiously.

Beverly listened quietly. She realized that if Evelyn had brought this up, it was probably serious. In all the years Evelyn had been married, she had never discussed any real problems with Kevin. The biggest crisis was when Kevin wanted to start his own law firm, and Evelyn was reluctant to go along with it. Although that whole episode dragged out for months, it never looked to be marriage threatening, and they had worked it out in the end. So if Evelyn was looking a bit disheveled and saying that she and Kevin were having problems, things must be grave. And that made Beverly nervous.

"I'm not sure what's going on with him, to tell you the truth, which is part of the reason I haven't said anything about it," Evelyn said cautiously. "I don't want people to worry about me. I really hoped that Kevin would come to his senses sooner rather than later, but that hasn't happened. In fact he quit his job last fall and turned the business over to his partners."

"What did you just say?" Beverly asked, eyes wide with amazement.

"Damn!" Charmaine said. "You mean he left his law firm? After all the work he put into it?"

Evelyn nodded. "You heard me right." She was determined not to cry, but hell if she didn't feel like it.

Beverly stared at Evelyn, mouth hanging open. She couldn't

believe Kevin would do something so radical. But more than that, she couldn't believe that Evelyn had hidden something this big all these months.

Charmaine whistled. "I thought something was up with you two, but I honestly never expected anything like this. Where is he working now? Another law firm?"

Evelyn cleared her throat. "At Blockbuster." She said it so softly she could barely hear her own voice.

" 'Scuse me?" Charmaine asked, straining across the table to hear Evelyn.

"I said at Blockbuster!" Evelyn snapped in frustration at having to repeat such vile words.

"Get out!" Charmaine said.

Beverly was still silent when the waitress appeared with their fondues. She took a big sip of her martini as her mind raced back over the past months for clues of all this, other than Kevin being a no-show at family gatherings.

"I'm as shocked as both of you are," Evelyn said when the waitress left. "None of it makes any sense whatsoever. He seems to be going through an antimaterialistic life-is-too-short-to-worry phase, and he wants nothing to do with anything middle class. He says that's trying to be white. And last weekend he shaved his head. All of it."

Beverly gasped.

"Un-fucking-believable!" Charmaine said in a whisper so as not to stun the other patrons.

Beverly put her martini glass on the table and took a deep breath. "How are you dealing with all of this, Evelyn?"

"There's not much I can do except try and wait it out. I'm sure it's temporary. At least I hope it is."

"Has he explained to you why he's doing this?" Beverly asked.

"Hell, Beverly," Charmaine said. "He probably doesn't understand why he's doing half this crap himself."

"Charmaine's right," Evelyn said. "Talking to him does no good. He doesn't even make sense most of the time. He's still upset that he let me talk him into updating the kitchen. Claims I spend too much money on frivolous things. That I care too much about appearances and so on."

Evelyn leaned back. She felt better now that she had opened up a bit. It was good to share her woes with her sisters, to get some of the burden she was carrying alone off her mind. Still, she wasn't ready to go all out and admit that Kevin had left her. She hoped he would come back home soon and she would never have to tell a soul.

"Earth to Kevin," Charmaine said, hoisting her margarita glass. "Actually that should be earth to all husbands, period. They're all nuts."

"Don't say that," Beverly said. "They could still work things out. You *do* think you'll work it out, don't you, Evelyn?"

"I'm trying to stay positive. Yes."

"At least you'd be able to make ends meet if your marriage fails," Charmaine said. "Not that it will, but I know that if I left Tyrone I wouldn't be able to afford the house we just bought by myself. We'd have to sell it, and I'd probably have to get an apartment somewhere in—"

"Why in the world are you even talking like that Charmaine?" Beverly interjected. "You just got married a year ago."

"I'm not saying anything is going to happen," Charmaine said. "I'm just being realistic, and it doesn't take much thought to realize that I couldn't afford our house all by myself. I love living here, but it's so damn expensive."

"That's because you have a brand-new mortgage," Evelyn said. "We bought our house so long ago, the mortgage is low now, and I could pay it on my own. But please, I haven't started thinking about those things. And I don't plan to start. This is a phase that Kevin is going through."

"Of course it is," Beverly said. "I'm having a hard time imagining Kevin even acting like this." She shook her head. "Shaving his head. Jeez!"

Evelyn laughed nervously. "I know, I know."

"A lot of men look sexy with shaved heads," Charmaine said.

"I have to admit that it looks good on him," Evelyn said. "It was just a shock to walk in and see him like that when I wasn't expecting it."

Beverly forced a smile on her face. This was all so weird. Kevin, attorney-at-law, now working at Blockbuster. Maybe if he and Evelyn had been married for just a few years, all of this would be less startling. But couples who had been married for more than two decades were not supposed to act this way. Their lives were supposed to be routine and predictable—boring, even.

Charmaine's problems with Tyrone were disappointing, but they had been married only a year, and Charmaine changed husbands about as often as she changed hairdos. Evelyn's problems with Kevin were truly mind-bending.

Beverly smiled wistfully. "And here I am holding you two up as examples when I tell Valerie to dump that bum Otis and wait for someone better to come along."

Charmaine snickered. "You should have known better."

"What's going on with Valerie and Otis these days, Bev?" Evelyn asked. "Is she still with him?"

"Unfortunately, yes," Beverly responded. "She forgave him for hitting her or shoving her or whatever he did."

"She said he shoved her, not that he hit her," Charmaine said.

"Not much difference, in my book," Beverly said. "She has a bruise on her arm too. Let's face it. No man is perfect, but you have to have limits when it comes to what you'll put up with."

"Any time a man puts his hands on you, that's a deal breaker," Evelyn said. "That's crossing a line."

"I would have thought Valerie felt the same way," Charmaine said. "I'm surprised she's putting up with it."

"At one time she wouldn't have," Beverly said. "But lately she's getting desperate because of her age. She really wants to get married again. And soon."

"So she moved the line between what's acceptable and what isn't," Evelyn said.

"Or erased it altogether," Beverly added.

Chapter 12

Beverly opened the front door to her town house to see Julian standing on the stoop, looking handsome as ever in black jeans and a fresh white T-shirt. Dinner with her sisters—and their tales of marital problems—had reminded her how lucky she was to have him. She had rushed home and quickly changed into her favorite pair of cutoff jeans, a pink tank top, and fluffy Ugg flip-flops in anticipation of Julian's visit after he got off work. Now she ran eagerly to him and smothered his face with wet kisses.

"Whoa!" he said, laughing. He dropped his canvas duffel bag as he balanced the Giant Food bags he carried in his arms. "What did I do to deserve all this luscious goodness?"

Beverly smiled and stepped back. "Nothing, besides being you and loving me." She picked up his garment bag. "I'll go put this upstairs for you. What ya got in the grocery bags?"

"Stuff for the Spanish omelet and homemade waffles I'm going to fix up for you in the morning. And the margaritas for tonight."

Beverly smacked her lips. "Yummy, I can't wait for breakfast. And you ask why you get so much goodness."

Julian smiled. "I aim to please. I'm going to put the groceries away and mix our drinks while you put that up." He crossed the dhurrie rug on the living room floor and headed toward the kitchen as Beverly took the stairs two at a time. Julian's coming to her town house and cooking for them was one of her absolute favorite experiences on earth. As exotic as their nights out on the town were, she liked nothing better than slipping into jeans and simply lounging around with her man.

Listening to her sisters earlier that evening as they complained about the ups and downs of married life had tripled Beverly's appreciation of Julian and their special relationship. They had so much in common. They both loved their jobs and worked hard to get ahead in their careers. They both liked to relax around the house with good food and the occasional mixed drink or glass of wine as they shared lively conversation about everything from family to work and world issues.

They sometimes argued, but the disagreements never lasted more than a few hours. And even their differences were complementary. He liked to cook; she could live without it. She found washing and folding the laundry relaxing. He despised those chores. It was beyond obvious to Beverly that they were soul mates.

She knew that there would be problems ahead and difficult moments. There was no such thing as the perfect marriage. But they were both mature and open enough to realize that their differences could be opportunities to grow and learn from each other. Beverly was confident that the special bond she and Julian shared would help them get through anything that might come up in the months and years ahead.

She placed Julian's bag across her bed, then walked down the stairs and into the kitchen, where she slid onto a chair and propped her elbows on the table. She loved watching him at work in the kitchen as much as he loved cooking. And she thought the way the late evening sun slanted through the sheer white curtains on the bay window at that moment was as romantic as a candlelit dinner on the banks of the French Riviera.

She smiled as he deftly sliced a lime and dipped the rims of two stem glasses into a dish of kosher salt. Julian always said that if he hadn't gotten into computer animation he would have become a chef, and it showed in the time and care he took with the details whenever he was in the kitchen.

"How many holes did you-all play?" she asked.

"By the time we got to the course, there wasn't enough time for that. We just went to the driving range and worked on our swings." He stepped back from the counter and imitated a golf swing.

She nodded. "Any new developments on that racing car game you're working on?" Beverly loved her job as an editor at the *Baltimore Sun* covering books, film, and television. She had started working at the newspaper two years ago, after being employed for several years as a reporter at the *Environmental Review* magazine in Washington, D.C. Now, instead of chasing leads for stories out in the field, she worked behind a desk editing articles written by other reporters. Occasionally she would get out and report on a story herself, the last being a feature about costume design on the locally filmed hit cable series *The Wire*. But she did that only when something really grabbed her interest.

Still, she thought that Julian's new job as an animator at Falcon Studios, a small company that made games for video consoles like the Xbox and the PlayStation and for personal computers, was much more thrilling. Video games were so fresh and all the rage among kids, teens, and young adults. The competition for positions at the development companies was fierce, and when Julian landed the job he was ecstatic. He had called her from his cell phone as he walked out of the building to deliver the good news.

With a major game for the Xbox due out in a few months, the company was in the midst of crunch time, and Julian was working weekends and late into the evening during the week. He loved the hustle and bustle, though, and his only complaint was that so few African Americans worked in the field. But that just made him want to work harder to prove himself.

"It's all good. I finally finished several physical poses for a dragon. That was really challenging, since we can't use mocap to record the motions digitally." Beverly smiled broadly and listened patiently. She never thought she'd find smart men who wore glasses and got all excited about complex technical stuff sexy. But Julian's sharp mind was a huge part of his allure, even if her handsome hunk of a fiancé could sometimes talk weird. Just now—although he was dressed in a short-sleeved T-shirt that showed off his muscular brown arms—Beverly had visions of him in a white shirt with pens sticking out of a pocket protector.

"Uh-huh," she said when he paused. "English translation, please?"

"Oh." Julian chuckled as he poured the drinks he had just mixed into the margarita glasses. "Sometimes I forget to turn the geekiness volume down when I leave work."

"Don't worry. I think your inner geek is sexy."

He laughed and took his time to explain motion capture to her in language she could understand. Then they clinked their glasses together. "How was dinner with the girls?" he asked as he took a sip.

"Fun enough."

He frowned. "That's it?"

"Well, they're both having marriage problems. With Charmaine it's maybe not so surprising, since she's on her fourth marriage. But Evelyn and Kevin are going through some stuff. It was a real shock to hear that."

"I don't think I've ever heard you talk about them having problems. Still, all couples do, now and then. It's probably not serious."

Beverly grimaced, unconvinced. "Things are more iffy than

I've ever seen with them. Kevin is acting strange. It's like he's going through some kind of dude menopause."

Julian frowned. "Example?"

"He quit his job."

"Whoa. For real?"

"Yep. He's working at Blockbuster."

Julian whistled sharply. "Sounds like he's burned out or something if he took a job at Blockbuster."

Beverly shrugged. "Maybe. Evelyn didn't go into a lot of detail and I didn't want to push. But yeah, that's a pretty drastic change, whatever the reason."

Julian nodded thoughtfully. "I can't imagine doing something like that."

"And that's not all. He shaved his head. As in bald. You know, naked up there." Beverly pointed to her head.

"Okay, so something *is* going on with him. Wonder what it is."

Beverly shrugged. "I have no idea, but don't you ever get stupid like that on me."

Julian blinked. "What does that mean?"

"You heard me. Don't you ever go getting all weird on me like that. I don't care how old you get."

"Where is this coming from? And what makes you think I'd do that?"

"If it can happen to Evelyn and Kevin, it could happen to anyone."

"It won't happen to us," he said firmly.

"I'm not saying it will, but I'm putting you on notice now." She shook her forefinger at him. "You ain't allowed to do stuff like that after we're married."

"If Kevin really is going through some kind of midlife crisis, as serious as it sounds, it could be chemical or hormonal, you know? Not much you can do about that."

Beverly shook her head in disagreement. "You can do plenty

about the way you handle it. You don't have to be an ass. Women go through physical and emotional stuff when they get older, but we don't pull crazy stunts like quitting our jobs and shaving our heads, do we? I would never do something like that."

Julian was silent for a moment. Then he walked up to her slowly, took her drink out of her hand, and placed both drinks on the kitchen table. He took Beverly by the hands and pulled her up out of her seat and into his arms.

"What do you say we take our drinks upstairs and jump in the shower together. Let me take your mind off all this."

The last thing Beverly was thinking about at that very second was anything having to do with sex. She pushed his arms away. "Stop treating me like a child. You're not even paying attention to what I'm saying."

"No, I'm not."

"So you admit you're ignoring me."

"Yeah, I do. Because this isn't about us. That's Evelyn and Kevin and their stuff. And I'm sorry about it and I hope they work things out and all, but it's not going to happen to us. So there's no point in obsessing about it."

"I'm not obsessing. I'm just talking. There are some valuable lessons for us to learn in this."

"Okay, fine. So we learned something, and you made your point. Can we please move past it?" He put his arms back around her. "Those cutoff jeans you're wearing always turn me on."

Beverly felt her muscles relax as she stood in Julian's arms. He had a point. She was all worked up about something that hadn't even happened to them, and maybe it never would. For all she knew, Evelyn and Kevin could have made up by now.

She allowed herself a small sly smile as she reached up and removed Julian's eyeglasses. "That's why I wore them," she said as she placed the glasses on the table beside her. "That's exactly what I wanted to do."

"Now that's how I like to hear my woman talk." He kissed her on the side of the neck and tickled her behind the ear with the tip of his tongue. She moaned softly.

"What you got on under them shorts?" he whispered. "One of my little thong numbers?"

She reached around, guided his hand down toward her waistline, and whispered back. "Why don't you make it your business to find out?"

"I don't think I'm going to make it upstairs at this point," he said as he undid the button and zipper to her jeans. He eased her toward the countertop. "You good right here?"

"I'm good anywhere," she whispered hoarsely.

He deftly slid her shorts and underwear off and hoisted her up. Before Beverly knew what was happening, he was sliding in. She couldn't even remember when he had shed his jeans. All she could think about was how good it felt and how all her worries had quickly vanished. She wrapped her legs around him and moaned loudly.

They dropped to the floor with him on top of her. Whether it was the drinks, her frustration with the news coming from her sisters, his long day at work, or other things entirely, they both came fast and hard. Beverly trembled and gasped for air, the release as welcome as a cold splash of water on a blistering summer day.

He rolled off her and they lay side by side. He reached out, pulled her toward him, and wrapped his arm around her. She snuggled against his chest. She loved the natural musky scent of his body.

Moments like these made Beverly feel that all was right with their little corner of the world. Julian was so special that together the two of them could conquer anything that might come their way. She knew that the feelings they shared for each other would change over time, but she could look forward to the future with a good man like Julian at her side.

Bring it on, she thought with a smile. Together we can handle it.

Chapter 13

Sunday was church day for Charmaine and her family, and following the service, she decided to have a leisurely soak in the tub. That was something she rarely did, preferring instead to hop in and out quickly. But the previous week had been a rarity in itself, and she needed a moment to relax and reflect quietly. The bathroom was the only room in the house where she could be sure she wouldn't be interrupted.

She leaned back in the tub and thought about Tyrone's behavior on Friday. It had really thrown Charmaine off guard. And when he took off with Tiffany yesterday afternoon with a simple "See you later," this had knocked her silly. They hadn't said much more to each other when he and Tiffany returned home from their shopping spree well after dark. Ditto all through church that morning.

Still, she had arrived home from dinner with Beverly and Evelyn in fairly good spirits and was feeling much more introspective. Even though she didn't like some of the things Evelyn had said about seeing Tyrone's side in all of this, she found herself questioning some of her actions. Had she been understanding, patient, and forgiving enough? Maybe not. And if she wanted her marriage to have a chance, she needed to do and be all of those things.

She sat up straight in the tub and decided that she would get dressed and go down to the study where Tyrone likely was at that moment and suggest to him that they bury their differences from the past couple of days and start fresh. She was willing to forgive and forget if he was.

Before she could even stand up, Tyrone opened the door, marched into the bathroom, and stood in the middle of the floor.

"We're going to the roller skating rink," he said, looking down at her.

Whoa, Charmaine thought. *What was with all the attitude?* "Who's we?" she asked, frowning up at him in puzzlement.

"Me and Tiffany."

Charmaine blinked. He hadn't thought to ask what *she* might have planned for today after church, or what she might have in mind for this evening. There was no family discussion, no husband-and-wife chat, no compromising, no nothing. Skating was likely what Tiffany and Daddy had decided they wanted, and skating was what Tiffany and Daddy were going to get. Everyone else be damned.

"What about Kenny?" Charmaine asked, trying to tamp down the rage building inside her.

"You're both welcome to join us if you'd like," Tyrone said stiffly.

Charmaine gritted her teeth. And she was supposed to be patient with this? She didn't say a word, not trusting herself to speak without exploding. She just sat and stared at the water. How the hell did he think he could just walk in here and tell her what they were going to do after church? Not suggest. *Tell.* And he had the nerve to act as if he was doing her a favor to invite Kenny and her to join them.

During that long pause, Charmaine remembered her sisters' advice, remembered church that morning, and found a smidgen of tolerance from deep within her soul. After all, Tyrone was a good husband and stepfather most of the time. Somehow she had to reach the better part of this man.

She cleared her throat and spoke softly. "Maybe you aren't aware of it, but Kenny isn't crazy about roller skating. Why don't we do something both of the kids will enjoy? Like a movie?"

"I already promised Tiffany that we would go skating and I don't like to break my promises to her."

"Well, what the hell did you go and do that for without even talking to your wife and stepson to see what we wanted? Aren't we supposed to be a family?" Charmaine could feel every ounce of patience evaporating from her pores.

Tyrone sighed. "Why can't you understand where I'm coming from? I only get to see Tiffany a few times a year. When she's here, I like to indulge her. That's what I always did when it was just the two of us. That's what she's used to."

"Well, it's not just the two of you anymore. Don't you get that? We're all part of a family now. And families plan things together. They compromise. It can't be all about one person every day for two months."

"The relationship between you and me is so new for her. She needs time to accept that her daddy is married to someone besides her mom. I worry what too much change to our routine could do to her mentally and emotionally. Maybe I shouldn't but—"

"Do you ever think about what catering to her all the time will do to her mentally and emotionally?" Charmaine interjected. "Or what ignoring Kenny will do to him?"

Tyrone threw his arms in the air. "Kenny is fine. He's with us all year round."

She stood abruptly and reached for her bath towel. That was it. To hell with being patient. She tied the towel around herself and stepped out of the tub. "Did you give any thought to how Kenny feels about having a new stepfather move in on him and his family? Huh? Have you thought about that? He's had to make adjustments too, and I resent that you're so quick to brush his feelings aside."

Tyrone took an angry step toward her. "Don't you fucking tell me I'm brushing his feelings aside. I worked hard to develop a good relationship with him and Russell. Even you said that they've done a good job of adjusting to me."

"Part of the reason they have is that I insisted on it," she snapped back as she walked away from him and into the bedroom. "I insisted that they accept you at our family outings and think of you as a part of us. Tiffany will never make that adjustment if you let her think she doesn't need to accept us. Or let her pretend that things haven't changed in your life when they have."

"I don't have all the answers," he said, following her out of the bath. "I just know that it's hard for her because she's away from home."

"Kids are stronger than you give them credit for, Tyrone. She's tougher than you realize." Charmaine picked up a bottle of lotion from the dresser and applied some to her arms.

"I think I know my daughter," he snapped. "I know what she can deal with."

"Is this about your daughter or is it about you and your guilt?"

He frowned. "What do you mean, my guilt?"

"Oh, come on," she said. "It's obvious that you feel guilty for letting her mother move back to Oakland to be with her family when Tiffany was two and you-all broke up."

"Is that so horrible?"

"No, I just wonder why you didn't move to Oakland a long time ago if you miss her so much."

"It just didn't work out that way."

"Fine, but to put me and Kenny through all this now is wrong. If it was just me, maybe I could go along with it, even though I still wouldn't agree with the way you indulge her all the time. But not when Kenny is involved."

Tyrone stomped toward the door. "Suit yourself. I'm done trying to get you to understand. Like I said, we're going to the rink."

"Do what you want. We won't be joining you."

He walked out and slammed the door, and she stared after him, eyes wide with dismay. She couldn't believe how stubborn and irrational he was being. It was as if an evil force had entered their home, snatched her husband away, and left this strange being in his place.

She grabbed the bottle of lotion from her dresser, dumped a generous amount in the palms of her hands, and sat on the bed to apply it to her legs. All she could think about was the horrible luck she had at picking men. Her first marriage had lasted less than a year. They were both in their early twenties—young and horny—and when the sex began to get dull, so did their lives together. Then came Kenny's father. She had never married him, and he ran faster than a professional sprinter when she told him she was pregnant.

After that it was the lying, mooching waste of human flesh named Clarence. Clarence could be funny and charming when he wanted, and she had stayed with him longer than anyone else. But he couldn't keep a job, and she soon realized that he was lying almost every time he opened his mouth. She ended up kicking his ass out when she couldn't take his trifling ways any longer.

Following her divorce from Clarence she married Oliver, and quickly realized that he had about as much financial sense as a baboon. The man couldn't keep a buck in his pocket, and financial security was important to Charmaine. That marriage also lasted barely a year. She thought she had finally gotten it right with Tyrone. Now she had to wonder.

Evelyn paced the floor of her bedroom in shorts and her gardening shoes as she listened patiently to Rebecca on her cordless telephone. Against her wishes, the night before, Kevin had called the kids and told them about the separation, and Rebecca was taking the news hard. When she had spoken to Andre that morning just before church, he claimed that he could see it coming months ago, and maybe that was the truth, since he lived nearby in Baltimore. But Rebecca was at college several hundred miles away in Atlanta and had been attending summer school there. She was completely blindsided.

When Evelyn arrived home from church and checked her voice mail after changing into her gardening clothes, there were three frantic messages from her daughter asking what was going on. Evelyn had called Rebecca back immediately and now could barely get a word in edgewise. It had been years since she'd heard Rebecca whine like a child. And although Rebecca didn't come right out and say it, Evelyn sensed that her daughter blamed her mom more than she did her dad.

"You can be so rigid sometimes," Rebecca said, her voice thick with frustration. "You want everything to be perfect."

Evelyn listened in silence. Inside she was seething. How dare Kevin go ahead and tell the children about the separation when he had agreed to wait. And on top of that, he had made it seem like the separation was all her fault.

She tightened her lips as Rebecca continued to rant. As soon as Rebecca paused, Evelyn assured her that she had been extremely tolerant as Kevin changed over the past several months. She tried to avoid making Kevin look bad, since she knew that Rebecca adored her father. But it was tough not to cast some blame on the man when he was being a total asshole about their problems every chance he got.

She hung up after she had calmed Rebecca down, then sank into the armchair next to the bed and leaned back on the small silken pillow. It had been a week since Kevin walked out of the house. This was the first time that she had gone for so long without seeing her husband. When one of them had traveled on business in the past, it had never been for more than a few days at a time, and they were in constant contact with each other, calling and e-mailing daily. Even over the past several rough weeks, there had been daily contact, however scant. To go without any contact whatsoever for days at a time left her feeling unbalanced.

As exasperated as she was with Kevin's strange and inconsiderate behavior, she was used to having him around and missed him something awful. Whenever she allowed herself a moment to think what it would be like as a single or divorced woman, a part of her panicked. She had gotten married in her twenties and it was all she had ever known as a woman. She liked being a Mrs. She liked seeing the wedding ring on her finger.

She held her hand out at arm's length and studied the platinum and diamond jewel gracing her finger. She thought about how happy she was when they went to pick it out. She rarely noticed the ring after the first year or so of her marriage. Now it seemed like a treasure chest full of memories.

She lowered her hand and reached back for the pillow. She clutched it tightly in her arms and reminded herself that she had agreed to wait for him to contact her. Of all the things Kevin had done lately, probably the oddest was his reluctance to call. It was as if he had developed a sudden aversion to her. As if he didn't want to have anything to do with her for fear that she would somehow tarnish him. She didn't understand it at all, and it hurt her so much.

If he didn't come back home soon, she would have to start telling family members and close friends that Kevin had walked out on her. She dreaded having to do that. Everyone had always looked up to them as the perfect couple, the ideal husband and wife. They would be shocked to find out it was a big fat lie.

She squeezed the pillow and stared at the phone on the nightstand. Should she give in? Maybe call him just this once? He was her husband. She shouldn't have to act coy or modest with him. She shouldn't have to wait for him to call. She sat up on the edge of the chair and glanced at her watch. It was twelve-thirty. Kevin worked on Sundays but was probably on his lunch break now. Why the hell not?

She bit her bottom lip, grabbed the phone, and dialed his cell number. She slammed the receiver down before the first ring. What the hell was wrong with her? Was she a glutton for self-punishment? Obviously, if Kevin wanted to talk to her he would pick up the phone. That he hadn't done so yet spoke volumes.

She jumped up and paced the bedroom floor. It was pitiful not to be wanted by your husband. She wouldn't wish the feeling on anyone. But she was determined not to be one of those despondent, groveling women, breathlessly chasing after a man who didn't want to be caught.

She had spent all these years helping women get through divorce. Until now she hadn't really understood how utterly devastating it could be. She had seen the tears and the crestfallen faces of women who had lost a loved one. She had heard the whining, fussing, and cussing. But she had never really known the pain until Kevin walked out on her.

She had to do everything in her power to fix this marriage. Kevin had once loved her; maybe a part of him still did. If there was a way back for them, she had to find it.

She snatched the receiver up again and hastily dialed Kevin's number. But she wasn't going to grovel. She was going to be more creative than that. She would tell him that she needed him to help her move some furniture around the house before the bridal shower she was holding for Beverly the following weekend.

In a way this was true. She was expecting almost thirty women for the affair and she wanted to place the dining room table up against a wall to allow more space for mingling. She had planned to get a neighbor to assist her, but this was the perfect excuse to call Kevin without seeming desperate. She thought that if she could somehow get him over here and talk to him calmly in person, it would help both of them get a grip and come to their senses.

She held her breath, closed her eyes and gritted her teeth as the phone rang. One, two, three . . .

"C'mon, Kevin," she muttered. "Answer. Please answer."

She knew that he could see her number showing up on his caller ID if he looked. Would he be cruel enough to ignore her call? Don't do this to me, Kevin, she whispered to herself.

His recorded message came on and she slammed the phone down. Crap! She didn't want to hear a stupid recording. She wanted to hear Kevin. She dialed his number again. Maybe he was having a hard time getting to this cell phone because . . . because . . . whatever. She bit her bottom lip as the phone rang. When his recording came on a second time, she left a curt message, banged the phone down again, and took a deep breath.

As aggravating as this was, she could not let it get her down. Maybe he was on the line talking to one of the children. Or maybe he was working through his lunch break and had his phone turned off. Lots of things could have happened to keep him from answering. It didn't necessarily mean he was ignoring her. Right?

She reached down and undid her gardening shoes. She would stay inside and wait for him to check his messages and call her back. She didn't feel much like pulling weeds anyway.

Chapter 14

Evelyn walked through the revolving doors of her office building, entered the lobby, and shook the rain off her umbrella. She stamped her feet on the carpet to remove some of the water from her heels. What a dreary day, she thought as she passed the stairs and made her way to the elevator bank. Hot, humid, raining.

She had just pressed the button to go up when her former high school classmate Reuben Roberts came bounding down the stairs near the entrance. She smiled as he approached her, tall and handsome, wearing beige slacks, a blue pin-striped shirt, and a denim-colored necktie. He was the first thing she'd had to smile about in three days, when she learned that Kevin had told Rebecca and Andre about the split. Rebecca had called every night since getting the news, but Evelyn had yet to speak to Kevin, who apparently saw no reason to return his wife's calls.

"Good morning," Reuben said.

"Morning," she said. "Although maybe not so good, given the weather. Depressing, isn't it?"

"Not to me. This time of year, I welcome the rain. Cools things off."

She nodded. "That's one way to look at it, I guess."

A newspaper in his hand, he gestured toward the front door.

"I'm going back out to grab a cup of coffee. Care to join me? It's been ages since I saw you, and it would be nice to catch up with each other."

"Um, yes, it would be." Evelyn hesitated and glanced at her watch. It was a kind thought, but Cathy was due for her weekly Wednesday appointment at nine-thirty, less than thirty minutes away. "Unfortunately, I don't really have the time. Got a client coming soon."

"Ah. Maybe another day, then?"

She nodded. "I'd like that. Thanks for asking."

The elevator arrived and she stepped in as Reuben headed out the front door. In truth, she wasn't sure she would have joined him even if she didn't have a client on the way. It would have been nice to hear what he had been up to all these years, but she wasn't exactly in the mood for idle chatter and catching up on old times. Her husband had split and refused to call her. Her daughter was pissed off at her. Talking to an attractive man over coffee would be way more fun than she felt she deserved to have at this moment. Besides, what would she tell Reuben about her life as they caught up with each other? That her husband had just left her?

She got off the elevator on the sixth floor, walked to the door of her office suite, and bent down to pick up the day's *Washington Post*. She unlocked the door and walked down a short hallway past the closed doors of two other psychologists. She entered her own office, dropped her purse and the newspaper on her desk, then sat down and picked up the phone to listen to her messages.

The first was from Cathy, canceling her session that morning due to a bad case of seasonal allergy, aggravated by the rain. Evelyn listened and jotted down notes from two other clients who had called wanting to make appointments. Then she hung up and flipped her computer on.

So she had an hour and fifteen minutes to kill before her first appointment that morning. She could fill the time by catching up on her e-mail and visiting some of her favorite websites. She could take her time reading the newspaper with her morning coffee. Or she could dash across the street and join Reuben. She swiveled in her chair to face the window behind her desk and stared down at the rain pounding the pavement and all the people scurrying in and out of office buildings and shops on the avenue below. *Nah,* she thought. Why go back out in that nasty weather?

She stood, removed the jacket to her black linen suit, and hung it on the wall hook. She walked back down the hallway to the coffeemaker and poured herself a cup of brew, then sat back down at her desk and opened the newspaper. She would read a few articles and check her e-mail until her first client was due.

She had barely gotten through the first paragraph of the lead article before she found her mind wandering back to Kevin and his call to Rebecca that weekend, getting their daughter all riled up. And why hadn't he returned her calls? Evelyn sighed loudly. She hated having all this downtime before her first client. It gave her more time to think, and she knew that if she dwelled on negative thoughts she would get upset. That was the last thing she wanted to do before a client's arrival.

Maybe she should go and have coffee with Reuben after all. It would take her mind off her problems and certainly be more interesting than sitting around fuming about Kevin. She stood up, grabbed her jacket, purse, and umbrella, and left her office.

Within five minutes, she was shaking water off the umbrella and scanning the crowded coffee shop for Reuben. He was tall, so she quickly spotted him sitting at a small table in a far corner. He was sipping from a paper cup and reading the morning newspaper. She wove between the tightly packed chairs and tables and approached him.

He glanced up and a look of pleasant surprise crossed his face. "You changed your mind," he said.

"My client canceled."

"Ah. At any rate, you're here." He stood and pulled a chair out for her.

"I want to get something to drink first," she said as she placed her soggy umbrella on the floor. "What are you having?"

"Plain black coffee. None of that fancy stuff for me. But you look like a latte kind of girl."

She smiled. "Right you are."

He held up a finger. "I'll be right back."

"No, no," she protested. "I can get it myself."

"I don't mind. Really."

"I insist. I'll get it." She walked quickly toward the coffee counter to order. She didn't want this to seem in any way like a date. He was married, as far as she knew, and so was she. They were just two office buddies having a cup of brew before work.

When she arrived back at the table, he folded his paper and once again stood to help her get seated.

"Do you come here for coffee every morning?" she asked as she sat down across from him.

"Most mornings," he said. "Although I've only been working here for a few weeks now."

"Right. You were in D.C. before. Your company relocated?"

He shook his head. "No, just me. I'm a technology consultant, and I decided to strike out on my own."

"Oh, that sounds interesting."

"I like it, but I couldn't afford office space in the city. Not that it's cheap out here in Silver Spring, but it's better than D.C."

She nodded. "Do you live in Silver Spring too?"

"I just got an apartment nearby. Hope to get a condo soon."

She frowned, surprised to hear him say "I." Wasn't he married?

"My wife and I just separated," he said to answer the question on her face.

Evelyn blinked. Reuben and Belinda had been a couple ever

since she could remember. Every girl in high school envied Belinda for her tight hold on Reuben. "I'm sorry to hear that."

"Don't be. We both realize it's for the best. We actually decided to part ways several months ago. We were trying to share the house until the settlement—we have a big place over in Mitchellville and we're selling—and I was living in the basement. But that didn't go over so well when we both started seeing other people, if you know what I mean. So I decided to go on and move out."

Evelyn nodded. The parallels to her own life recently were startling. Although maybe she shouldn't be surprised, given how common divorce was. "I'm still stunned hearing that. You and Belinda had been together since forever."

"That might have been part of the problem," he said, shrugging. "We were so young when we got married, and we're both different now. After the boys grew up and left home, we realized how much we had grown apart. People change. Sometimes they change together, sometimes they don't."

That was certainly true, she thought. People definitely changed, and not always in harmony. For a few seconds, Evelyn toyed with the idea of telling Reuben about what she and Kevin were going through but decided against it. Despite how dismal things looked now, she still had faith that they would get back together eventually.

"Well, I hope you two work things out to your liking," she said.

"I think we will since it's what we both want. We've accepted it. So what do you do in the building? You said you have clients."

"I'm a psychologist."

"Oh, wow. For children? Adults?"

"All of the above, but mainly family and relationships."

He laughed out loud. "Talk about coincidences. You've been holding out on me."

She smiled. "Not really. You and Belinda seem to be working things out pretty well yourselves."

"Belinda and I are actually getting along better since we decided to divorce. But dating again is proving to be, well, interesting, to say the least. It's been a challenge."

"How so?"

"Women are different now than they were twenty-five or thirty years ago. More . . . how can I put it?"

"More forward?"

He cocked a finger at her. "That's the word."

"And you don't like that?" she asked.

"I'm adjusting, but it takes some getting used to. I probably seem old-fashioned to many of them, especially the younger ones."

"Hmm. Then maybe you should try women closer to your own age."

He laughed.

"Seriously."

"You're probably right. Guess that's why they pay you the big bucks."

"Actually, in a way, I'm the very last person who should offer advice about relationships these days."

He looked puzzled. "Isn't that what you just told me you do for a living?"

Evelyn sighed. "Yes."

"But? Seems like there's a *but* coming."

"Isn't there always?" Maybe she would open up to him just a little. It had been her choice to keep most of her troubles from family and friends for now. She wasn't sure how things would turn out and didn't want to burden them. But it was hard not having anyone to open up to and share things with. Reuben was outside her normal circle, and even if he talked, it wouldn't be to anyone in her life. So what difference would it make?

"I'm going to tell you something I haven't told anyone else. Not my friends. Not even my family."

He raised his brow with curiosity. "I'm all ears."

"My husband and I separated a couple of weeks ago. Less than that, actually. Sunday before last."

"Really?" he asked. "Of course you mean it. You wouldn't joke around about something like that."

"No, I wouldn't."

"Are you okay with it?"

"Well, yes, but . . ." She paused. The whole point of sharing this with him was to finally let it all out. "No! I'm *not* okay with it. It's killing me."

"I'm sorry to hear that," he said. "How long were you married?"

"Going on twenty-five years."

He whistled softly. "Almost as long as us. That's rough. Whether it's been two years or twenty or you think you're ready for it or not, divorce is always painful."

"I know. I feel like such a failure."

"I hear you. I felt that way too when I first realized that our marriage wasn't going to work. Actually, we both tried to keep the fires burning for a while, but it just wasn't going to happen. Maybe you'll have better luck, though. It's only been a short time since you separated. Is that what you want? To get back together?"

She nodded. "Very much so. As miserable as we've been the last several months, I'm even more miserable now." She laughed nervously. "But we'll see if that happens. He's going through some kind of midlife thing, and right now it seems that I want to stay together more than he does. It's also hard on the children. My daughter's away at college and she just found out this past weekend. He told her, which I didn't agree with, and Rebecca has been calling me every night since. She's beside herself with worry."

"Yeah, mine had a bad time with it too. Even when they're grown, it's hard for them to think of their parents divorcing. I know it's impossible to believe now, but it does get more bearable for everyone with time."

She smiled thinly. "That's what I always told my clients. Now I'm getting to practice what I preach."

"That could be a bright side. It could help you in your work as a therapist."

"Yeah, maybe *something* good will come out of this mess." She smiled at him. "Thanks for listening. This has been a big help."

"Don't even mention it." He reached into his pocket. "Here's my card. Anytime you need to chat or want some company over coffee, just call. Maybe we could get together for lunch next week."

Evelyn took the card and smiled. She knew that she would probably feel awful again the moment she left the coffee shop and went back up to her office. But right now, after talking with Reuben, she actually felt pretty darn good. In fact she felt better than she had in many months. She had forgotten how a little attention from an attractive, intelligent man could make a woman feel so alive.

Chapter 15

"Surprise!"

Beverly froze in her tracks at the entrance to Evelyn's living room and gasped. Thirty women—from blondes to brunettes and light-complexioned to dark—were smiling at her. A surprise bridal shower! And it looked like everyone was there—family, friends, co-workers.

She looked at the pink and white balloons and the lavish buffet spread of shrimp and Swedish meatballs and all sorts of vegetable and fruit salads. How in the world had Evelyn managed to pull this off, even with a caterer's help? Beverly had thought that there would be no big bridal shower, maybe just a small affair with her sisters and a couple of friends.

"Gotcha good, didn't we?" Charmaine said, laughing gleefully.

Beverly nodded as her mother came up and hugged her. "You sure did," Beverly said.

"You look shocked," Mama said, touching Beverly's cheek.

Beverly laughed and hugged her mother. "That's 'cause I am, Ma."

Evelyn, Charmaine, and Valerie hugged and kissed her on the cheek; then the other women approached and offered their congratulations. As Beverly mingled with cousins and friends, she soon realized that beneath all the joviality something was seriously out of whack with Evelyn.

After everyone had settled down from the initial excitement of her arrival, Evelyn was still fussy and jumpy, rushing around picking up used plates and silverware, sometimes before the user could even set them down. In the hour since the party started, Evelyn hadn't stopped moving for more than a few seconds. That was so unlike her cool eldest sister.

Beverly listened as she and Valerie stood near the window in the living room and Valerie chatted, but her eyes followed Evelyn as she dashed into the kitchen with her hands full of dishes. In less than a minute, Evelyn hurried back out and headed for the buffet table in the dining room, where Beverly noticed her shuffling things around needlessly. Then Evelyn slipped into the living room and picked up used glasses.

"What's wrong?" Valerie asked. "You have this really weird look on your face."

Beverly glanced back toward her friend. "Sorry, it's nothing."

"You sure?" Valerie asked, her voice filled with doubt.

Beverly nodded. She had her suspicions that whatever was bothering Evelyn had to do with Kevin and she would have loved to discuss it with her best friend. But Valerie had a sizable mouth on her, and Beverly figured it was probably best to keep her thoughts to herself for now.

"Is something bothering Evelyn?" Valerie asked.

Beverly blinked. For a second she thought her friend was going clairvoyant on her. Then Beverly realized that Evelyn's behavior likely looked a lot odder than she realized and that others may have noticed it too. "I don't know. I'm not sure."

"She doesn't seem like herself," Valerie said. "She's a lot more jittery or something. Evelyn's usually so composed."

Beverly tried to appear unconcerned. "She didn't have much time to plan the shower. She's busy."

Valerie nodded. "Maybe that's it. I should offer to help out."

At that moment, Beverly heard the front door shut and she looked to see a bald-headed man walk quickly past the living room entrance.

"Was that Kevin?" Valerie asked.

Valerie had taken the words right out of Beverly's mouth. "I think so," Beverly said.

"When did he shave his head?"

"Recently, from what Evelyn tells me."

"Damn, he looks good. I love a man with a shaved head."

Beverly smiled. "Actually, you love any kind of man with any kind of head," she said teasingly. "Don't forget, he's taken."

Valerie rolled her eyes at Beverly in mock disgust. "Like I don't know that. Not to mention that I'm spoken for too. A girl can still look and admire, can't she? No harm in that."

"I was kidding," Beverly said. With a man like Otis she'd probably look and admire other men too, Beverly thought, although she decided to keep that thought to herself. Valerie already knew how she felt about Otis, so there was no point bringing it up.

❖ ❖ ❖

Evelyn stood stock-still as Kevin skipped up the stairs two at a time. So he had decided to show up *now*? When he finally called her back yesterday afternoon, he agreed to come by after work and help her move the table. But then he didn't show up. Not last night, not this morning. Finally, Evelyn walked across the street and got her neighbor to help.

Now he had the nerve to stroll in at two o'clock in the afternoon, an hour after the shower had started, and act like things were normal. Evelyn placed the dirty glasses she had just picked up on a side table and followed him up the stairs, where she found him standing in the middle of the floor in their bedroom.

He had his hands in the pockets of his faded blue jeans and he looked totally uncomfortable in these surroundings.

She stood in the doorway and silently folded her arms across the chest of her tailored navy pantsuit. Sometimes there was no need to say anything. Sometimes a simple disgusted expression could do.

"Sorry I got here so late," he said. "Something came up yesterday after we talked."

"You couldn't have called to say you wouldn't be able to make it?"

"Didn't think to."

He spoke without a single ounce of regret. It was infuriating. But sadly his behavior didn't surprise Evelyn. Not anymore. Nothing he did surprised her now. Her eyes flashed with annoyance. "So why bother to show up here today?"

"I thought I'd stop by to see if you need help with anything else."

She threw her hands up in the air. "The goddamn party is almost over now. And is that the only reason you came? We're probably on the brink of dissolving a twenty-five-year marriage, yet you have no need to talk to me about anything?"

She paused and he stared at the floor in silence. So he still had no words for her? She shook her head with despair. Nothing seemed rational when it came to Kevin anymore. She hardly knew what to say to him. "Honestly, Kevin. No, I don't need any help. You may as well go back wherever you came from."

He ran his hand across his scalp. "I need to pack a few more things while I'm here. You go on and entertain your guests."

So cold and distant. Evelyn couldn't believe how much he had changed. This was the man who had lain beside her and kept her warm almost every night for decades. Now whenever he was around, it felt like an arctic chill was blowing through. She turned to leave.

"Evelyn."

She paused and turned back to face him.

"I know you want to talk, and we will in due time, but I'm not ready yet. Sorry it's taking so long."

She nodded. That was the most considerate thing he'd said to her in months. It wasn't much, but it was better than nothing. "When do you think you'll be ready?"

"Soon."

"Soon, soon. You keep saying that. Do you realize that it's been two weeks since you left, and we've barely spoken to each other?"

"There's a lot to think about. I want to be sure I have things worked out."

"Kevin." She dreaded even asking if there was another woman. He had already said there wasn't, but it was hard to imagine what else could have brought such a drastic and sudden change in him. "Are you seeing someone else? I want the truth."

He shook his head firmly. "No, absolutely not. It's nothing like that."

"Would you tell me if you were?"

He hesitated for a second. "Yes. Yes, I would."

Something about the detached way he'd said it made Evelyn believe him. She realized that if he was seeing someone else, he would have no reservations about admitting it to her, simply because he cared so little about her feelings at this point. Still, Evelyn had a hard time accepting that his attitude was anything more than temporary. He was going through a phase, and she still hoped that he would snap out of it eventually if she was patient enough.

"Rebecca is really upset about all of this," she said. "I wish you hadn't told them."

"After you and I talked, I decided that it was best to be up front. I don't like hiding things from them. She'll be fine."

"I'm not so sure about that. I worry that it's going to affect her studies. Thank God she's coming home in a couple of weeks for Bev's wedding. I can talk to her in person then. We both can."

He nodded silently.

"It would be helpful to us all if you would give an indication of where you're going with this, Kevin."

"And I will."

"I know," she said drily. "*Soon*."

He smiled thinly. "What else can I say?"

"Nothing. If nothing is in your heart, then there's nothing you should say." Evelyn realized that the distant and uncaring expression on his face hurt her but not nearly as much as it had when she last saw him. She might be getting used to this. And that scared her more anything.

She turned on her heels and walked away.

Chapter 16

Evelyn descended the stairs slowly, and Beverly noticed that she looked even more morose than she had before she had gone up. Beverly excused herself from Valerie and went to her sister. "Is everything all right?" Beverly asked softly, even though she knew things couldn't possibly be all right. You didn't walk around looking like you'd just seen death when things were going well.

Evelyn tightened her lips and stared at the floor as Charmaine approached them. "Everything is fine."

"Don't lie to us," Charmaine said bluntly.

"You know better than to try that with us," Beverly said. "We can see right through it."

"It's just . . ." Evelyn paused. She knew she needed to tell them the whole story, despite the fact that it was hard to admit it, even to herself. But she didn't have much choice at this point. Kevin was about to walk down the stairs with a bag in his hand, and the truth would be fairly obvious. She could lie and say he was going on a trip, but she was tired of being deceptive.

She beckoned her sisters into the family room, which was on a lower level next to the kitchen and far away from the crowd. She might as well get this done, and the quickest way was to come right out with the ugly reality. She faced them and squared her shoulders. "Kevin has left me."

Beverly and Charmaine both gasped.

"Oh, my God," Charmaine said.

Beverly covered her mouth with her hand. "Are you serious?" Beverly had figured that something was drastically wrong in the DuMont household but had never suspected this. Not with Evelyn and Kevin.

Evelyn nodded. "He left about two weeks ago. The day after your fitting, Bev."

"Good grief," Charmaine said.

"So when we met for lunch last weekend he had already left?" Beverly asked.

Evelyn nodded again.

"And you never said anything," Charmaine said. "Not one damn word. We sat and talked all that time and you said not one word."

"Sorry, but I was too embarrassed. And I didn't want to burden anyone with my problems. I was so sure he would come back soon and I wouldn't have to. Well, he hasn't. And the truth is, I don't have the faintest idea what he's going to do. He doesn't tell me much of anything anymore."

"Oh, Evelyn," Beverly said. "This is crazy."

"I know," Evelyn said.

"Where is he staying?" Charmaine asked.

"A rental in College Park."

"But why?" Beverly asked. "Why did he leave?"

"I wish I could tell you, but I don't really understand it myself. Like I said last week, it's some kind of emotional thing he's going through. A midlife crisis or something. We haven't talked about it much at all yet. He won't talk to me."

Beverly could hardly catch her breath. She knew this must be extremely hard on Evelyn. Still, she was aware that even the best of couples quarreled, sometimes badly. In the end, they patched things up. Kevin and Evelyn probably needed a break from each other, and what couple wouldn't after more than two decades of marriage? "He just needs some time to himself, Evelyn. He's at that age where he's worried about getting older and he's doubting himself. I'm sure he'll come around eventually."

Charmaine nodded. "I kind of saw this coming, but that's what I'm thinking it is too. A bad midlife crisis. I'm hoping he comes to his senses soon."

Beverly stared at Charmaine. "You saw this coming? How?"

Charmaine shrugged. "The distance between them. I figured something was up. Look, I've been married four times. I've seen it all."

"Well, it's news to me," Beverly said. "I had no idea. How are you dealing with it, Evelyn?"

Evelyn swallowed hard. "I'm not in the best shape, I won't lie. But I'm hanging in there. What else can I do? The ball is completely in his court. I have to sit here and wait to see what he decides to do."

Charmaine shook her head with doubt. "I got plenty of ideas about what else you can do. You might not want to do them but—"

"Charm," Beverly interrupted. "She's been married too long to just walk off at the first sign of real trouble the way you would."

"I'm just saying. I agree she should give him some time, but if he doesn't come around soon . . ." Charmaine brushed her hands together.

Evelyn shook her head. "Bev's right. I have to give him the space he needs and hope for the best."

"You two will work things out," Beverly said firmly. "As long as you've been married, I have no doubts of that. Is there anything we can do in the meantime?"

Evelyn shook her head. "Not really."

"How are the kids handling it?" Charmaine asked.

"Andre seems fine, but Rebecca is having a lot of trouble with it. Now that I think about it, there is one thing you can do for me. Please don't say anything to Mama. Let me tell her later."

"Fine," Charmaine said, nodding. "I understand."

"No problem," Beverly added.

Evelyn let out a deep sigh. "I'm so glad I finally told you all the truth. It's a load off my mind." She smiled.

"That's what we're here for," Charmaine said.

"You bet," Beverly added.

Evelyn touched Beverly's arm. "I'm really sorry this came out now. This was supposed to be a day for you to celebrate getting married, and here I am going through this stuff."

Beverly waved her hand. "Don't be silly. It's hardly your fault."

Charmaine shrugged. "This is life, you know? We sure as hell can't control when these things happen. Men are so unpredictable and sometimes they can be such . . ."

They heard laughter coming from the kitchen, and Charmaine paused midsentence. Beverly listened and then smiled. She would know her best friend's loud cackle from a mile away.

They all walked up to the newly updated kitchen to see Kevin and Valerie standing around the table. Kevin must have just said something hilarious, because Valerie was having a hard time shaking the giggles. The smile faded from Beverly's face when she noticed a black leather duffel bag on the floor next to Kevin and was reminded that he had his own place.

"Hello, ladies," Kevin said. He nodded at Beverly and Charmaine.

"Hello, Kevin," Beverly and Charmaine said in unison.

"Kevin was telling me about some customers that came into Blockbuster last week," Valerie said. "What was it, Kevin? Some teenage guy whose mother caught him watching an R-rated video with his girlfriend and brought him into the store and made him return it. It was so funny."

The three sisters stared at Valerie blankly, obviously not getting the joke.

Valerie waved an arm. "You had to be here to hear him telling it."

"Uh-huh," Beverly said, folding her arms across her chest. Sometimes her girlfriend could be so frivolous, especially after a couple of glasses of wine. Still, Valerie understandably had no clue that Kevin and Evelyn had separated, and it was making for an awkward moment.

"Oh, good luck to you on your upcoming nups, Bev," Kevin said as he bent down and reached for his bag.

"Thanks." Normally, Beverly would have been eager to catch Kevin up on the plans for the wedding. She had come to think of him as a brother, someone who would always be in the family. She couldn't be sure of that any longer and as a result wasn't so sure how to act around him.

"I only met Julian a few times," Kevin said. "But he seems like good people."

"He's very nice," Evelyn added. "Bev's lucky to have him."

Beverly smiled. "I hope you see him again some time soon, Kevin, so you have a chance to get to know him."

Charmaine listened in silence to the small talk but kept her eyes glued on Valerie, who in turn couldn't seem to take her eyes off Kevin. Charmaine knew flirting when she saw it, even subtle flirting, and it looked like Valerie was being a bit coquettish with Kevin, batting her eyelashes and smiling at him like a fool. Charmaine didn't trust any woman besides her sisters around an attractive man.

She glanced at Beverly and Evelyn to see if they were picking up on the signals, but they didn't seem to have noticed anything unusual. Maybe she was imagining things, Charmaine thought, because of what Evelyn had just told them. And even if Valerie was flirting with Kevin, it was probably no big deal. It made Charmaine a little uncomfortable to think that Valerie would flirt with her best friend's brother-in-law, but it wasn't exactly going to start World War III. Valerie and Beverly had been friends for years, and Valerie should know better than to step over the line.

"Well, I'm out of here," Kevin said. He kissed Beverly, Charmaine, and Valerie on the cheeks and split, and the four of them went back to the party. As Evelyn and Charmaine moved off, Beverly thought now was the time to get her friend caught up.

"Kevin and Evelyn are separated. I just found out."

Valerie's eyes widened. "You're kidding!"

"I wish. Unfortunately, it's true."

"I wondered why he had the overnight bag. I thought maybe he was going on a business trip or something, until he told me he worked at Blockbuster, and then I didn't know what to think. When did this happen?"

"A couple of weeks ago," Beverly said.

"That's a shame. Whose idea was it for them to split up?"

"His. And no, Evelyn is not sure what's going on with him. Midlife crisis or something maybe."

Valerie nodded. "That probably explains the shaved head. And why he left his law firm to work at Blockbuster, of all places."

"I know. Crazy, isn't it?"

"Yeah, but it happens," Valerie said. "He's probably searching for the meaning of life. Why he's here on earth. That kind of thing."

"He can do that shit with his wife."

Valerie chuckled. "True. How is Evelyn handling it?"

"She's okay. Not great, but okay."

"I hope she bounces back quickly. She's been married so long that being single will probably be a big adjustment for her."

"Slow down, girlfriend," Beverly said. "They haven't signed any papers, so I wouldn't give up on them just yet. They had a good marriage for a long time. I happen to think they'll work things out."

"You're right. I'm sure they will."

Charmaine walked up and tapped Beverly's elbow. "C'mon, kiddo. Time to open your presents and see how many thongs you got."

Beverly laughed. "You so crazy."

"I can tell you right now that the little number I got you is going to heat your sex life up to the boiling point." Charmaine looked at Valerie. "Can you get us a couple of trash bags out of the kitchen pantry, honey? We need them for the gift wrapping. Then join us."

"No problem," Valerie said. She walked off to the kitchen as Charmaine guided Beverly to the armchair in the living room where she and Evelyn had piled up all the gifts and the guests were gathering around.

Beverly put her hands on her hips just before sitting down. "What makes you think my sex life isn't already at the boiling point, Charm?"

"Well, excuse me if it is," Charmaine said with mock indignation. "You can use what I got you to keep it that way."

"All right, girls," Mama said. "That's a bit too much information. We don't need to hear all that."

"I have to agree," Evelyn said, laughing.

Charmaine gently pushed Beverly down into the chair as Valerie entered the room and Evelyn tied the corny little hat she had made from paper plates and balloons onto Beverly's head.

"The things a girl will do for love," Beverly said as she smiled broadly for the cameras.

Chapter 17

Julian was acting especially amorous that evening when he arrived to pick up Beverly after the bridal shower. As he helped Beverly load up the trunk of his black SUV with her gifts, he kept touching her whenever Evelyn and Charmaine looked the other way or went into another room. Once he got Beverly alone in the kitchen he backed her against a wall and playfully licked her behind the ear. She laughed and shoved him away.

"What the hell is going on with you?" she asked.

He shrugged. "Just wanting my woman, that's all. Can't I want my woman?"

"Of course, just not now." Normally, touching her and eyeing her lustfully was all it took for him to send her into a frenzy. It wouldn't have been all that unusual for them to pull into an almost empty parking lot behind a strip mall on their way to her town house, let down the backseat of the SUV, and get it on with feverish abandon.

But Beverly had her sister Evelyn on her mind that evening. She lingered a little longer than usual at the front door to say good-bye and comfort Evelyn, willing her eldest sister to hang in there.

"You sure you don't want me to stay and keep you company? We can sit up and talk all night if you want."

Evelyn smiled weakly. "Thanks, Bev, but I'm fine, honestly."

"I'm going to hang around a while longer and help her straighten up," Charmaine said. "You go on and be with that man you got waiting for you, girl. Nothing better than new love."

"Charm is right," Evelyn added. "Please don't worry about me."

Beverly hugged Evelyn as Julian slammed the rear door of the SUV shut. "Call me if you need anything, day or night," Beverly said. "I mean that." She blew a kiss to both of her sisters.

Once in the car with Julian, Beverly couldn't stop thinking about the fact that her brother-in-law had left her sister. She hadn't let on just how much the whole thing bothered her at the bridal shower because she could see that Evelyn was having a difficult time with it. But now she found herself trembling uncontrollably.

Julian frowned with concern, reached across the seat, and squeezed her leg just below the hemline of her denim skirt.

"Talk to me, baby," he said. "Something's obviously bothering you."

The warmth of his hand on her leg helped her begin to relax. She let out a deep breath and filled him in on what was happening with Evelyn and Kevin. Julian listened silently and attentively while she poured out her feelings for ten minutes straight, relieved to get it all off her mind.

"Other couples do this kind of thing, not Evelyn and Kevin," she continued. "They were supposed to be different. They were the ones who got it right. At least I thought they were different. I thought they were doing everything right. I . . ."

Beverly stopped talking abruptly when she realized she was just repeating herself. There was nothing more to say.

"They're human and flawed just like the rest of us," Julian said soothingly.

"No, uh-uh. Don't you see? They were supposed to be *better* than everybody else. They were the ones who proved that marriage could work. Even though it might be hard, you could still make it work. Now I don't know what to think."

"I can understand why you're worried about them. I just hope this doesn't mean that you're getting second thoughts about us."

She shook her head no. "I *am* thinking that we need to talk more. We both have to be real clear about what we want out of marriage. And what we don't want."

"We talk about that stuff all the time. We want two kids and we know that we need to get started sooner rather than later, given our ages. We want to live here in Columbia, Maryland, in your town house and later get a bigger place. We're equal partners, et cetera, et cetera."

Beverly sighed impatiently. Did he really understand the gravity, the urgency of her feelings? This was important to her and she had to make sure he got it. "I know we talked some, but it can't hurt to talk more. We don't want to jump into marriage without covering all the bases. It's too important. That's exactly what I told Valerie about Otis."

"Whoa, wait a sec. You aren't comparing us with Valerie and Otis, are you? Gimme a break. He smacks her around. He's a damn thug."

"I don't mean it like that, Julian. I know you'd never hit me or get violent in any way. But we still need to discuss things more. I mean, what is your stance on how kids should be raised?"

Julian hit his forehead. "My stance? My *stance?* Jeez, Bev. You make it sound like we're having a damn political discussion or something. We're engaged to be married! The wedding is in two weeks. Lighten up."

"I wish you wouldn't be so flippant. Charmaine and Tyrone are going through some stuff too, something about their kids. And like you just said, we only have two weeks to talk."

He shook his head adamantly. "Actually, we have the rest of our lives to talk, you know?"

She sighed with exasperation.

"What? I see the way your folks raised you. That's all I need to know. I assumed that we were on the same wavelength about that."

"Well, we shouldn't assume," she said. "That's the problem. We need to put it all out there on the table. What about religion?"

"What about religion? We're both Christians."

"But you're Baptist. I was raised as a Catholic."

He knitted his eyebrows. "And?"

"Which church will we take our children to?"

"Bev, we did talk about this. That much I know. We decided that we didn't care which denomination we practiced as long as it's Christian. Remember?"

"That's fine for us, but what about our kids? Which church are we going to raise them under?"

Julian sighed with resignation.

"Don't get mad at me," she protested. "All I'm saying is that marriage is a big step."

"I hear you."

"We need to talk about these things."

"Baby, we can talk all you want," he said. "I have no problems with that. Talk is good."

"Thank you. We can have a question-and-answer session when we get back to the house."

"No problem. But can it wait until after I ravish you? I've been waiting to get you naked all evening." His lingering hand roamed a bit higher under her skirt.

She smiled. "So I gathered."

By the time they walked in the front door of her town house, Julian's burning passion had ignited her. Before they even got all the packages out of the back of the SUV, she had slipped out of her thong and he had removed his glasses and dropped his black jeans. She fell back on the living room couch and eagerly lifted her skirt above her thighs.

He penetrated her instantly, and they both released deep guttural moans. They needed no foreplay—no kissing, hugging, or fondling—only the memories of all the previous rapturous encounters to send each other to the heights of sexual delight.

It was over in a matter of minutes, and they both lay silent, still intertwined and utterly spent. He eventually rolled off Beverly and landed on the dhurrie rug, and she could hear him trying to steady his breath.

"I'll take that kind of bonding over talking any day of the week," he said.

She rolled her eyes. "You're a dude, you would say something like that." She stood up and reached for her underwear.

He perched up on his elbows in his T-shirt and watched her. "You're gonna tell me you didn't enjoy that?"

"Of course I did. I always enjoy this with you. You know that."

"Just checking. I mean, the way you were squirming a minute ago, I thought so, but now you're popping up and running off. What's with that?"

"I want to get the rest of the things out of the trunk, then go take a shower."

"Uh-huh." Julian sat up on the rug and leaned back against the couch, watching her as she smoothed out her skirt.

She stared down at him. "You going to help me or just sit there looking cute?" she said sarcastically.

He reached for his briefs, hopped up, and slipped them back on. "What's your rush? You don't usually cut and run like this."

"I told you. I want to get my things. You can see everything in the back of that SUV. My stuff could get stolen."

"C'mon, there aren't any thieves out here in the suburbs."

"Thieves are everywhere."

He reached for her hand and gently pulled her into his arms. He pushed a lock of her auburn hair out of her face. "Evelyn still on your mind?"

She inhaled deeply. "It hit me hard."

"I know."

"She told us they were having problems last weekend, but she never said anything about him leaving. My heart goes out to her. It's a shock."

"She probably didn't want to bother you with her marital problems, seeing as how you're planning to get hitched soon."

"I know. Does it ever make you nervous at all?"

"What? Getting married?"

Beverly nodded.

"Some. I just remind myself that it's normal and think about how crazy I am about you. It's a big change, yeah. I've gone almost forty years without getting married. Never really wanted to until I met you. So hell yeah, I get the jitters now and then. You'd probably have to be some kind of freak not to be a little nervous about it. But this is us, Bev. We agree on so many things. We love each other. We'll be fine."

"I wasn't nervous about it at all until recently. I mean, I'm not thinking about backing out or anything, just feeling a little shaky, I guess."

Julian wiped his brow in mock relief.

She smiled. "Seriously, though, this has got me thinking about stuff I didn't before."

"Such as?"

"Evelyn and Kevin were almost the only two people in our generation whose first marriage lasted more than a few years. There may be one or two others, but I can't think of them now. A woman at work has been with this guy for twenty years and they have four kids, but they never actually got married. And my boss has been married about fifteen years now, but it's her second marriage. The divorce rate is even worse for black married couples than it is for white married couples. Did you know that?"

"I do now."

"So yes, I'm wondering what the heck is going on with this marriage thing. Is it, like, we're all selfish brats who cut and run at the first sign of trouble, or is there something wrong with the whole institution of marriage itself? Because something is not making sense, if you ask me, and I want—"

He covered her mouth with his hand. "Beverly, wait. Slow down. You're getting all worked up again about nothing, really."

"How can you say that? This is our life we're talking about here. And my sister."

"I'm not talking about your sister. You know me better than that. I'm talking about marriage in general. Yes, your sister and her husband broke up, and I'm sorry about that. But it has nothing to do with you and me as a couple. I'm telling you, that won't happen to us."

"How can you be so sure?" she asked.

"Because we're madly in love."

"You say that like it's the be-all and end-all," she said. "Like it solves all problems. So were Kevin and Evelyn at one time. I'm sure all these other couples thought they were in love and that their marriages would last forever. It wasn't enough. I mean, they didn't go into it thinking it would fail."

"No one does."

"So why should *we* be the exception? Can you tell me that?"

He sighed impatiently. "What are you getting at here, Beverly? 'Cause everything I say, no matter what, you have a counterargument for it. Are you saying you think we shouldn't get married?"

"No, that's not what I'm saying. I'm just saying we should . . ." She paused when she realized that she didn't know quite what she was trying to say. She just had a gut feeling that all was not well, that they could be getting themselves into something far bigger and more challenging than they realized.

She was trying to give a voice to the feeling, but it was coming out all wrong precisely because she didn't understand exactly what was bothering her or why. It wasn't as if Julian had suddenly done something wrong. Or that she had stopped loving him. None of that had changed and yet everything seemed different. She was thoroughly confused. Or maybe she was just scared.

"We can talk about it later," she said. "I'm a little tired, so let's just get the gifts out of the car now."

She needed time to digest all of this. Chances were that she was making a big deal out of nothing, just as Julian was implying. She would probably wake up tomorrow morning and feel fine.

He took her hands into his. "Okay, but if you're having any kind of doubts about us going through with this, I want to talk sooner rather than later. I want this to work."

"I'm not having doubts. And I want this to work as much as you do."

"I think you'll feel better after you get some sleep tonight."

She nodded in agreement. "As usual, you're probably right."

He let her go and put his eyeglasses on. "Why don't you go run yourself a hot bath? I'll get the rest of the things out of the car."

She smiled at him as he slipped into his jeans and fastened his belt. She wasn't sure why she had doubted this sweet man, even for a minute. Or doubted them together. Julian was good to her and for her, and she couldn't imagine going forward without him. "That sounds fine to me."

He opened the front door and looked back at her. "I love you." He blew her a kiss.

"Love you back."

Chapter 18

Charmaine stepped into her kitchen, arms stuffed full of goodies left over from the bridal shower. She placed the shrimp salad in the refrigerator and the rolls and chocolate cake on the countertop. Then she dropped her shoulder bag onto a chair near the kitchen table and walked into the living room, where she sank down onto the couch. She didn't bother to turn on the lamps even though it was dusk. There was something soothing about sitting alone in the darkness at the end of a long, hectic day.

After all the guests had left the bridal shower, Charmaine had hung around and helped Evelyn tidy up. Then they sat at the kitchen table and chatted for two hours about everything—kids, work, dieting, but mostly marriage and divorce.

"Never in a million years did I think this would happen to me," Evelyn said as she placed cups of steaming herbal tea on the table in front of both of them. She removed her suit jacket and draped it on the back of a chair. Then she sat across from Charmaine, put her feet up on an empty seat, and blew into her hot cup. "Call me stupid, but I thought we would be together forever."

Charmaine shrugged as she kicked off her heels and reached for her tea. "Happens to the best of couples."

Evelyn sighed. "I guess."

"Kevin has really changed," Charmaine said. "You can see it in his eyes, his whole demeanor."

"Tell me about it," Evelyn said. "How does that happen?"

"Don't look at me, 'cause I couldn't tell you. All I know is that men pull stuff like this all the time. Too damn often. Even men like Kevin who seem to have their shit together, apparently. So if you're going to be out there dating again, you'd better get used to it, 'cause trust me, many of 'em are worse than Kevin."

"Girl, please. We don't need to talk about me dating. That's the last thing I want to think about now."

Charmaine smiled. "Yeah, it's early to talk about it. I'm just saying. Maybe you and Kevin will still work things out. Who knows?"

Evelyn nodded. "God, I hope so. I can't even think of a life without him."

"Even though I suspected something was wrong, I was absolutely stunned when you told us he left. I figured whatever the problem was, you guys would work it through. Never in hell did I think one of you would leave."

"We've always had ups and downs, like any couple," Evelyn said. "But this is the first time he's left. I kept it to myself because I didn't want to bother others with my problems."

Charmaine nodded. She suspected that Evelyn's secrecy also had a lot to do with her pride. Evelyn had more than enough of the stuff to go around. For some reason, Evelyn had this need for people to think that she was perfect, that her marriage was perfect, and Charmaine could never understand that.

Personally, Charmaine thought it was silly to hide the truth. She believed in being frank about all things, good and bad. Let it out there. But she had sipped her tea, kept her thoughts to herself, and let Evelyn do most of the talking. At least Evelyn had started to open up, and that was what counted.

Back at home sitting on the couch in the dark, Charmaine

kicked off her heels, hoisted the skirt to her sundress up several inches, and put her feet up on the coffee table. The main level of the house was deserted, but Tyrone's car was in the driveway, so he was around somewhere. If the previous days were any indication, everyone was off doing his or her own thing. Kenny was in his bedroom, where he had recently moved the Xbox. Tyrone was downstairs in his office on his computer, and Tiffany was down there in the recreation room watching television.

It had felt good to sit and yak it up with Evelyn. For once she had exercised patience with her eldest sister and her pretentious ways. Divorce was going to be real hard on Evelyn if it came to that, since marriage was all she had known for so many years. Charmaine had figured that the best course of action, given what Evelyn was going through, was to keep her own mouth shut and just listen for once. She and Evelyn had their differences, but they were still sisters.

So many marriages were crashing and burning these days. Sometimes it was over an affair; sometimes the couple just grew apart or realized too late that they weren't right for each other. On some occasions the man left and on other occasions, the woman. Regardless of the reason, divorce was always a sad, messy affair, especially after a long-term marriage.

Charmaine figured that if she could survive three divorces, her sister could live through one. Evelyn might not believe that now. She was vulnerable and clinging to what she knew. But Charmaine was confident that her sister would be fine. Evelyn was a strong woman, stronger than she herself probably realized.

As difficult as all three of Charmaine's divorces had been, they had taught her a lot about herself—about what she could and couldn't take in a man and what she wanted out of a relationship. Evelyn couldn't see it now, but she'd learn some things about herself too. Upheaval could be a great teacher if you were open to learning the lessons.

That didn't mean that Charmaine was ready to go through another divorce. Hell no. If her marriage to Tyrone went bust, she was never getting hitched again. She would take lovers, might even live with another dude, but no more husbands, ever. This one had to work or she was through.

Someone once told her that marriage was a decision, that you had to *decide* that you were going to stay married and then work your ass off at it. You didn't just fall into happiness and stay there ever after. And if you were foolish enough to believe in fairy tales, then you were just headed straight for divorce court.

As she sat there thinking about her talk with Evelyn and remembering how depressing divorce could be, Charmaine decided to work her butt off to make her marriage work. She would give it everything she had. If things still didn't work out, at least she would know that it wasn't for lack of trying.

She stood and walked barefooted down the carpeted basement stairs. Tiffany's long, lean body was stretched out on the L-shaped sofa. She was wearing a pink knee-length T-shirt and watching a movie on the 42-inch television with the volume blasting.

Charmaine walked over and stood beside the couch. "What are you watching?"

"*Black Snake Moan*," Tiffany said without ever taking her eyes off the screen.

"Isn't that rated R?" Charmaine asked, frowning with disapproval.

Tiffany shrugged. "I've seen it before. No biggie."

Charmaine didn't care if Tiffany had seen it a thousand times before, it was still too mature for a fourteen-year-old. If Tiffany had been *her* daughter, no way in hell she would get anywhere near that movie. But Charmaine had lost that battle with Tyrone the previous summer. Although Tyrone agreed that R-rated movies were wrong for Tiffany, her mother allowed it, and he thought there wasn't much point in disallowing it when she visited them. To Charmaine's way of thinking, that was no excuse for permitting a teen to watch R-rated movies in their home, especially when she was trying to raise a fourteen-year-old son under different rules.

"Uh-huh." Charmaine stood and watched for a few minutes, then slipped out of the recreation room and into Tyrone's office next door. She wasn't even going to mention the movie to Tyrone. That would start an argument, just what she wanted to avoid. She was going to have to choose her battles carefully if she wanted her marriage to have a chance.

"What you up to?" Charmaine asked as she slid up behind Tyrone, seated at his desk. He was obviously watching a film on the Internet, but she was trying to break the chill that had frosted the atmosphere in recent days.

"A political documentary," he said as he pressed the mouse button to pause the film. He turned around in his swivel chair to look at her and smiled. It was an awkward smile, but at least he wasn't scowling at her. Maybe he was ready to mend things too.

"I came to apologize for . . ." She paused when she realized she didn't even know what she was apologizing for. In her opinion, she hadn't done anything wrong. But she wanted to warm the air between them. She wanted things to be the way they were. And to get that, she had to give a little. She scanned her memory over the past several days, back to when it had all started going wrong. "For not being more understanding."

Tyrone nodded. "Apology accepted. I'm sorry it got so far out of hand."

It was kind of painful to apologize when you didn't really think you had done anything wrong. But she was damned if she was going to let a spoiled teenager ruin her marriage to a man who was a good husband most of the time. And if she wanted to save this relationship, someone had to take the first step. She honestly didn't think Tyrone had the foresight or clarity of mind to do it when it came to Tiffany. That left her. "Let's try to avoid letting things go that far in the future, okay?" she said.

"Deal." He reached out and lightly touched her breast through her sundress. It was so unexpected, given that his daughter was right in the next room, and it sent tingles up Charmaine's spine. She laughed softly as his hand slid slowly beneath the dress and up to her thigh.

"Whoa, big guy. You don't waste any time, do you?"

"We've already wasted too much time," he said as he pulled her toward him.

She hiked her skirt up, spread her legs wide, and straddled him. He gave her a long and tender kiss. His tongue traveled slowly down her neck, and he slipped the spaghetti strap to her sundress off her shoulder as he kissed it. She felt him growing harder between her legs, and she gripped the back of the chair and pressed herself against him. He moaned softly and hastily pulled his shirttail from his slacks.

He gently pushed her onto her feet, then stood and shut the door to his office. He sat back down, reached up, and quickly slid her thong down to one foot. She straddled him again and he undid his fly just as a voice came from the other room.

"Daddy!"

They froze. Tyrone shut his eyes. Charmaine swallowed hard and prayed that she had imagined it.

"Daddy, can you come here? The TV's not working right."

Between the two of them, they released enough hot air to melt the snowcap on a mountaintop. Charmaine dragged herself off Tyrone, pulling her thong up and her dress down. He zipped his pants.

"Sorry," he whispered hoarsely. He kissed her lips as he stood.

"Don't worry about it," she said. "I understand."

He paused at the door before opening it. "Can we finish this later tonight?"

She nodded. "You're on."

"Again, I'm really sorry."

"Daddy!"

"Go," Charmaine said. "I'm fine. Or I will be."

They both laughed as he walked out the door.

Chapter 19

Evelyn lit a scented candle and placed it on the edge of the bathtub, then poured a generous amount of gel under the tap. As the tub filled and bubbles began to form, she walked back into the bedroom, slipped out of her nightgown, and wrapped herself in a white terry-cloth robe.

Today was D-day. She was about to launch Operation Tell Me Now. Not next week or next month. *Today.*

But first she had to decide what to wear. She strolled into her walk-in closet and remembered that Kevin loved blue on her. He'd told her that on their very first date, and it had been years since she'd thought about it. In fact the color blue had fallen completely off her radar.

She searched through the closet until she finally stumbled across an old powder-blue St. John pantsuit that she hadn't worn in years. It was funny what you remembered, given the right circumstances, she thought as she selected a sleeveless beige silk top and a long double strand of fake pearls.

She laid the clothes across the bed, then went back into the bathroom and slipped out of her robe. She sank beneath the bubbles and breathed in the sea-scented oil as she leaned back and refined her plan of attack.

Today was Wednesday, one of Kevin's days off. She had called the store where he worked and learned that he stayed late on Tuesday nights and slept in on Wednesday, so she was going to surprise him at his apartment. She was tired of waiting for him to come to her. Tired of letting him have all the control. No longer would she allow him to jerk her about like a rag doll. It was time to take action. She was going to get all dressed up, then park her rump at his place and refuse to budge until he told her exactly what he was planning to do about their marriage.

She had decided yesterday afternoon to make this move after having lunch with Reuben. Spending time with an attractive man just made her miss her husband that much more. After lunch, she had gone back to her office and spent most of the afternoon phoning clients and rescheduling them for later this week or next. Then she telephoned one of Kevin's poker buddies and sweet-talked him into giving her the apartment number of Kevin's new digs in College Park, not far from the University of Maryland. Last night she stopped and bought bagels and cream cheese, one of Kevin's breakfast favorites.

She stepped out of the tub and dressed slowly and carefully, paying close attention to each and every detail. She finished off with the pair of platinum and sapphire earrings that Kevin had given her on their tenth wedding anniversary. She knew not to apply perfume too liberally and to avoid eye shadow altogether—Kevin hated all that.

She stood in front of the full-length mirror next to the bed and checked herself over, from the hair, neatly tucked into place, to the black patent leather sandals and bag. Hmm, she thought. Not bad for a forty-seven-year-old mama. She thought she looked pretty hot. The question was, would Kevin?

No, no, he absolutely wouldn't. She shook her head at herself. He would hate every bit of it, from the fancy suit and shoes to the expensive jewelry. Wasn't that exactly the point he was trying to get across to her? Hadn't she learned anything at all?

She snatched the glittery earrings out of her earlobes and slammed them down on the dresser. She kicked the shiny heels across the floor and ripped the designer suit off. She marched into the walk-in closet, threw on a pair of blue jeans and a white cotton shirt, and slipped her feet into her Pumas. Now she was ready for the new Kevin.

Or was she?

❧ ❧ ❧

Charmaine was typing a draft of a letter for her boss when the telephone rang at nine-thirty that morning. She placed the receiver between her ear and shoulder and kept on typing until she heard Tyrone's breathless voice on the line. Something was dreadfully wrong.

She stopped typing and listened as Tyrone explained that Tiffany had just called him screaming about something that happened at the house and that Kenny had given her a busted lip.

"Wait a minute, Tyrone," Charmaine said. "Slow down. First, is Tiffany all right?"

"What the hell do you mean, is she all right? Her lip is busted."

"I don't mean it like that," Charmaine said. "She's not bleeding or seriously hurt or anything, is she?"

"Not as far as I know. I'm leaving work and on my way there now."

"Well, how did it happen?" Charmaine asked.

"I have no idea. She said Kenny hit her."

"If that's true, it must have been an accident."

"Not according to Tiffany. She said he hit her on purpose when they were playing a game or something."

"I don't believe that for a minute," Charmaine said firmly. "No way."

"Are you saying that she's lying?"

Charmaine hesitated. Careful here, girl, she thought. "Maybe you misunderstood her."

"I don't think so," Tyrone said. "She sounded pretty clear to me. And we both know they don't get along. But I'll get to the bottom of it when I get there."

Charmaine glanced toward the letter she was typing. She wanted to leave the office so badly to see what was going on herself, but her boss needed this draft now. And then she would probably want to make revisions. Charmaine figured she would be lucky to get out of there within the next hour.

"Do me a favor?" she asked Tyrone. "Call me when you get to the house. I'm going to try to get off here, but I'm not sure when I can."

"We don't both need to be there. I can handle it."

Charmaine wasn't so sure about that. In fact she was sure of the opposite. Tyrone would never be able to deal with this impartially because it involved his daughter. The only way to ensure that Kenny got a fair shake would be to get there herself.

As soon as they hung up she dialed the house. Kenny picked up on the first ring.

"Ma, I was just trying to reach you," he said anxiously. "Tiffany has a busted lip."

"I know. Tyrone just called me. What happened?"

"We were playing tennis on the Wii, and I reached back to swing and hit her. I didn't mean it. It was an accident, I swear."

"I know you didn't mean it, Kenny. But I've told you repeatedly to stand far apart when you play on that thing."

"I forgot and then she moved in just as I was swinging."

"Did you apologize to her?"

"Yeah. About a hundred thousand times, but she keeps saying I did it on purpose," Kenny said, his voice rising with anger. "I'm through apologizing to her."

"Calm down. I know you would never do something like that deliberately, okay? Tyrone is on his way to the house. You just explain your side to him, and I'll get there as soon as I can."

"Can you hurry up? He's not going to believe me over her, no way. She's walking around now talking about how her daddy's going to kick my ass."

Charmaine sighed. She wanted to leave so desperately. But there wasn't much she could do other than try and will Kenny to be strong. "No one is going to kick your ass or anything else. Just tell Tyrone your side of it when he gets there. Don't be scared. And if there's a problem, you call me back here. I'll be there as soon as I can, and we'll get it straightened out."

God, she thought as she put the phone down. It was always something. Tyrone had stayed home the first two and a half weeks of Tiffany's visit; today was his first day back to work. Charmaine had wondered that morning as she left for the office how long Kenny and Tiffany would be able to get along without adult supervision before one of them killed the other. Guess she knew the answer now.

She turned back toward the computer and typed as fast as she could.

Chapter 20

Evelyn parked her black Benz in front of the garden-style apartment building in College Park that Kevin now called home, shut off the engine, and paused to calm herself. It was crazy how hard her heart was pounding. This was Kevin she was about to see, a man she had known for more than two decades. Why on earth was she so panicked?

Because he had changed so much, and she wasn't sure what to expect from him. It felt as if she didn't know him at all anymore, and that was frightening. There was a time when she could predict Kevin's reactions with almost perfect precision. No longer. The man upstairs was about as predictable as a boat on a storm at sea.

If she was going to do this, she might as well get going, she thought. Movement would help her shake off the jittery nerves. She grabbed her purse and the bag of bagels from the passenger seat, stepped out of the Benz, and walked across the parking lot.

One good thing to come out of this was getting the jeans and tennis shoes. She almost never wore either unless she was working in the yard. Stylish they were not, but very comfy. She just hoped that Kevin would notice and appreciate her newfound "sluminess" and willingness to bend. She could try to meet him halfway, within reason, if he would just tell her what halfway meant to him. This silence wasn't going to get them anywhere.

She walked up the stairs and found his unit on the second floor. She knocked and stepped back so he would be able to see her clearly through the peephole. The door opened soon enough, and Kevin stood there. The sight of his bald head still jolted her every time. He was wearing a navy bathrobe and black slippers, although it looked like he had been up and about for a while.

"Evelyn," he said, eyes wide with surprise to see her standing outside the door of his new apartment.

"Hi." She forced a smile. "I hope it's not a bad time."

"No." He opened the door wider. "Come on in."

She stepped inside to see a studio apartment that looked almost exactly as she had envisioned it would, furnished sparsely with inexpensive but serviceable rentals. "So this is where you've been hanging out?" she said, walking around slowly.

He nodded. "I know it's not much, but it will do until I make some decisions. Can I get you anything? Something to drink? I don't have much besides water. Think I might have a couple of sodas. It's too early for wine."

"I'm fine." She held the bag up. "Brought you some bagels."

"Thanks," he said, accepting the gift. "I had a pretty big breakfast, but would you like one now?"

She shook her head, and he motioned for her to sit on a dreary gray couch as he sat across from her in a hardback chair and switched the television off with the remote. "So what brings you here at"—he checked his watch—"barely ten o'clock in the morning on a weekday? Don't you have clients?"

"I canceled them. I really want us to talk, and when I called the store they told me that you were off today."

He leaned back, tilting the chair on two legs. She hated it when he did that. She worried that he would fall and bust his head wide open. Normally she would have said something and he would have protested, but not today. She wanted to preserve the peace so they could talk calmly.

"I'm not sure there's much to discuss yet," he said, rubbing his hand across his scalp. "I'm still thinking. But you go ahead. Say what's on your mind."

She clasped her hands. "I don't know where to start, really. It feels strange, talking to you here like this. You keep saying you haven't made any decisions, but I need to know what's going to happen with us sooner rather than later. I need to know what you're planning to do, even if it's just a guess for now. It's not fair to leave me hanging for weeks at a time with no clue whatsoever."

He nodded with understanding. "It's not that I want to leave you hanging. That's not my intent at all. I honestly haven't made any final decisions yet. I just know that I can't go on the way we are, living the lifestyle we have. It leaves me feeling completely empty. It even repulses me." He paused when he saw her flinch. "Sorry, but that's the truth as best as I can give it to you now. You want the truth, right?"

She nodded and he continued.

"I know you think it was crazy to leave the law firm, but it's the best thing I've done lately. I was able to start clearing my head and do more thinking about what I do and don't want out of life. Mostly so far it's what I *don't* want."

"And am I one of the things you've decided you don't want anymore?"

He glanced down at his fingers, then looked directly at her. "I can't answer that yet."

"Truthfully?" she asked. "Or are you reluctant to tell me what you're really thinking? Don't worry about hurting my feelings."

"That's the truth. I haven't made any decisions yet. You'll be the first to know when I do."

"Do you still love me, Kevin?" The question had come out of the blue, and as soon as she asked she regretted it. She could see that it had taken him by surprise. She had a sudden sinking feeling that she might not like his response.

He cleared his throat. "Of course I do. But, you know, if I'm honest with you, not in the way I once did."

"What exactly does that mean?"

"We've shared a lot together. We have a son and daughter who mean the world to me. I have fond memories of a lot of the things we did together as a family. But to be perfectly honest—again, that's what you want, right?"

She nodded slowly.

"I'm not attracted to you in a romantic way anymore."

There it was, she thought. He'd admitted it, and it felt like a stab in the gut. "I see." She closed her eyes and rubbed her forehead with her fingers. Talk about crushed. She knew this kind of an answer was entirely possible, but a part of her had stupidly hoped for the best, that he continued to love her in all the ways that a husband should. How was she supposed to deal with the ugly truth now that he had revealed it?

She opened her eyes and looked at him. He was watching her intensely, waiting for her to respond.

"That hurts. I won't lie."

"I'm sorry."

She bit her bottom lip to hold back the tears creeping up. What was the point in him being sorry? It was what it was. "How long have you felt this way?"

"A couple of years now, I guess. I tried to accept it at first. I told myself that it was normal for my feelings to change, given how long we've been married. And maybe it is normal for some couples. But I realize now that I don't want to live that way, and it's not fair to me or to you to pretend that I feel something I don't."

She was silent. He had just dropped the biggest bomb on her D-day, and she wasn't sure how to react. A part of her wanted to yell and cuss him out. But for what? For leading her on all this time and not being truthful? Maybe. What really hurt was learning that his feelings for her had changed, and he couldn't exactly help that. In her work, she had often heard about this kind of situation, and she knew that getting upset with him wouldn't do a bit of good. If anything, that kind of response could lead to his clamming up again. At least he was finally opening up about his thoughts and feelings.

"I'm glad you're being honest with me," she said. "It's a shock, but I prefer to hear the truth."

"I know you're probably going to tell me that it can be fixed," he said, a hesitant smile on his face.

She smiled in return. "I don't know if I'd use that word. Certainly I don't think we can go back to what we once had. But it doesn't have to mean the end of the road for us. It *is* possible to get passion and feelings back if you work at it."

"I tried to tell myself that for a while, but I eventually realized that it's not just you that my feelings have changed about; it's the whole lifestyle we live. I want to change my life in ways that I know you couldn't deal with. That's what I've been agonizing over."

"What do you want to change?" she asked.

"The whole upper-middle-class suburbia thing we're living. It was fine for a while, when we were raising the kids. But there's so much more that I want to see and do while I can still stand up straight."

"But you don't have to be divorced to do those things."

"I'm not talking about making temporary or small changes. Or even taking a long trip. I'm talking big, permanent change, Evelyn. I see myself moving to New York City or Atlanta or even overseas somewhere in Africa. I don't see myself ever coming back to the McMansion and the suburban manicured lawn. I couldn't practice law because I'd be moving from place to place, living cheaply and simply. I would certainly come back here to visit the kids and my mom, but that's about it. Could you give all this up and live like that?"

Evelyn blinked hard and stared at him for a moment. She had wanted honesty, and boy, was she getting that. She realized now that Kevin had changed at the core in more ways than she had imagined. When and how did this happen? "That *is* drastic."

"You know what they say, be careful what you ask for. You asked for the whole story."

Yes, she thought. And he had really put it all out there. She sighed deeply. She needed a moment to digest it. "Do you mind if I have that glass of water now?"

"Sure." He stood. "I'll be right back."

He went off to the kitchen area, and she walked around the main room of the tiny studio apartment. He had placed lots of photographs of Rebecca and Andre around the room and even a small one of her on a side table. Everything else was foreign to her—chairs, couch, tables. It felt as if a stranger lived here, not her husband.

She stopped and looked out the lone window in the room. And was that what he had become? A stranger? Was the man she had known and loved all these years lost forever? She couldn't answer that now, but she had to begin to consider it no matter how much it pained her.

At least they were talking, and she knew that she had to be careful not to act like a fool as he opened up to her. Although Kevin seemed to be fairly sure that their marriage was over—and she realized more than ever now that he might be right about that—she wasn't ready to give up yet. She had seen this countless times in her therapy sessions: one spouse wanting to call it quits, or at least thinking he or she did; the other clinging to the last thread of hope. She had also seen couples bounce back from the brink of divorce and restore their happy marriages. It didn't happen often, but it did happen. She was no good as a therapist or as a wife if she didn't give their relationship her very best effort.

Kevin returned, and as Evelyn accepted a plastic glass of water from him, she realized that he looked far more relaxed with her than he had in months. It was probably a relief to him to finally get all of this out.

"Why didn't you share this with me sooner?" she asked as they both sat back down.

"I wanted to, believe me. But I didn't really understand what was happening at first. I just knew that I was feeling uneasy. It was only when I began to make changes in my life—leaving the law firm, getting rid of the designer suits—that I started to realize why I felt so bad. By the time I moved out earlier this month, it was clear to me that I needed to make major changes, but I wasn't sure I could go through with it. I'm still not sure I can pick up and run off the way I just talked about. A part of me wants to, but it's a huge change."

"You said something interesting. When you left your previous law firm and started your own ten years ago, were you starting to feel all of this then?"

"I think that was the beginning," he said. "I didn't understand what it was then. I just knew that I wasn't very happy. I thought starting my own law firm would solve the problems, but it didn't."

She nodded.

"So there you have it," he said.

"Sounds like you want to make changes but haven't made up your mind just how many yet."

"Pretty much," he agreed.

So the door was still open, she thought, even if only by a crack. There was still a possibility of saving their marriage.

"Tell me," he said after taking a sip of his water. "What are your thoughts about all of this?"

They were talking truth, right. She wasn't going to hold back, either. "Basically, I think you're being a selfish bastard and very inconsiderate of me and the kids."

He nodded. "Fair enough. So that—"

"Hold on," she said, interrupting. "I'm just getting started. You could have let me in on what was going on a heck of a lot sooner, even if you were only guessing, rather than leave me in the dark for months on end. Not understanding why you were doing these things bothered me more than anything. I mean, I knew something was horribly wrong, yet I had no clue what it was."

"I was trying to spare your feelings until I knew more."

"It didn't work."

"I see that now."

"So where do we go from here, Kevin? What do we do?" A voice in her head wanted to know why in the hell was she asking him that. Shouldn't she be telling him it was over, given that he had so little left to give? But she wasn't ready to do that. She wanted her marriage to work.

He fiddled with his glass. "Like I said, I'm still trying to figure that out."

"We should see a counselor."

"Maybe," he said, his voice full of reluctance. "Give me some time to think about that."

"How much time?"

"Not much."

"I need something more definite," she insisted. "This isn't just about you, you know."

"Okay, I'll call you this weekend and we'll talk then."

"And you'll be ready to make some decisions?"

"Yes."

"Good. Just be sure you call." She placed her empty glass on the coffee table and stood. "Are you still planning to come to Beverly's wedding?"

He stood up after her. "Oh, yeah. She's like a baby sister to me. I wouldn't miss it for anything."

Evelyn wanted to ask if they could go together, but she didn't want him to think she was pushing. Then she thought she was acting silly. She had known this man for ages. She shouldn't be afraid to ask him something so simple. "Rebecca is coming home for the wedding. We could all go together."

"Rebecca told me she was going to be here, and I told her I'd see her at the wedding. Let's leave it at that for now."

"What's the big deal about us going together? It's not like I'm asking you to move back in. Just . . ." Evelyn paused and reminded herself not to be pushy. "Never mind. That should be fine. I'll wait for your call this weekend."

They walked to the door, and he kissed her on the cheek as he opened it. She left without another word between them, and he shut the door behind her.

She paused at the bottom of the stairs. She had just been reminded of what it felt like to be rejected by a man. You'd put your feelings out there and he'd slapped them away. She hadn't felt that since dating before she met and married Kevin. This sickening feeling was further motivation to do everything in her power to avoid becoming single again.

Chapter 21

As soon as the clock struck noon, Charmaine rushed out the door of her office and ran down the back stairs to the building's parking lot. It was kind of hard to gather speed in one of her trademark skintight skirts and a pair of four-inch heels. She had to take lots of baby steps and probably looked like a fool. That was what she got for trying to look so cute all the damn time.

But this situation with Kenny and Tiffany was urgent, and Charmaine really didn't care much about her appearance at the moment. Her boss was in the middle of preparing a big budget report, and she hadn't been able to get away from the office until her lunch hour. She had to come right back to work after her lunch break.

She tossed her shoulder bag onto the passenger seat of her Honda and sped off. This mess with Kenny and Tiffany had to happen now. Thank God she worked and lived in Columbia and could get home in ten minutes. The house line had been busy every time she'd called just before she left the office, and she couldn't get through to Tyrone or Kenny on their cell phones. What the hell was going on over there? She prayed that everything was all right and that she wasn't about to walk into World War III.

She wove in and out of traffic, trying not to drive too fast, until she pulled up to the house. The first thing she saw was Tyrone's SUV parked in the driveway. She entered the garage, quickly jumped out of the car, ran up to the door, and shoved her key into the lock. The door swung open, and Kenny sat at the kitchen table holding his cell phone to his ear. He covered the mouthpiece. "Where you been, Ma?"

"I couldn't get off work. I tried to call you on your cell phone just before I left the office, but if you're on the phone, how do you expect me to reach you?"

Kenny said good-bye to the person on the other end of the line and hung up. "I thought you would call the house if you couldn't get through on my cell."

"That phone line has been busy all morning too."

"Oh, crap. That bitch probably been on the line running her fat mouth."

Charmaine reached out with an open hand and popped her son upside the back of his head. Kenny yelped. "Ouch!" he said, jumping up and rubbing his head. "What you do that for?"

"Don't you cuss like that around me, and don't you ever let me hear you calling her names again. You know I don't like that." She grabbed Kenny's shoulder and steered him into the living room. The room was rarely used, so it was the best place to talk in private. She directed Kenny to the couch and sat next to him. "Where's Tyrone?"

"Downstairs in his office."

"And Tiffany?"

"Up in her room."

Charmaine nodded. "Now tell me what happened between you and her this morning."

"Like I said, we were playing tennis on the Wii and I reached back like this"—he swung one arm back to demonstrate—"and hit her in the mouth. It was an accident."

"Didn't I tell you to be careful on that thing?" she asked.

"I know. I forgot."

"Uh-huh," Charmaine murmured. Kids! It was always something. "Why do you think she's saying you did it on purpose?"

Kenny shrugged. "She's lying. I know that much. Tyrone believes her, of course."

"What did he say to you when he came in?"

"He asked me why I hit her. Said I shouldn't have done that."

"Really? Did he say anything to her?"

Kenny shook his head. "He thinks it's all my fault. Why doesn't he believe me?"

Charmaine folded her arms across her chest. This was starting to look ugly, and she dreaded having to confront Tyrone about it. But she had no choice. She couldn't let him and his daughter walk all over Kenny. "I'll go talk to him. You go on up to your room and watch television or something."

"You believe me, don't you, Ma?"

She touched his cheek. Although his voice sounded defiant, his expression was crestfallen. She knew his feelings had been hurt deeply. "Of course I believe you, Kenny. I know you'd never harm her or anyone else on purpose. Tyrone doesn't know you as well as I do. That's why I need to talk to him."

He smiled slightly. "Thanks, Ma."

Kenny stood and walked off, and Charmaine went to find Tyrone, willing herself to be levelheaded about this. It would do no good to start ranting and raving, no matter how much she was tempted to do so. "You attract more flies with honey than with vinegar," she muttered under her breath, repeating the old line over and over to herself.

She walked down the stairs and entered Tyrone's office without knocking. At the sound of his door opening, he wheeled around in his swivel chair to face her. She stood several feet away, her arms folded tightly across her waist, and spoke with studied calmness. "Kenny tells me that you think he hit Tiffany on purpose. That true?"

"That's what Tiffany said. I believe her."

"That's ridiculous, Tyrone. Kenny wouldn't harm a fly deliberately. You should know that."

"Tiffany wouldn't lie," he said firmly.

"Neither would Kenny when he has no reason to."

"He might if he's done something he knows was wrong."

"He didn't do anything wrong," she countered. "It was an accident."

"If you really believe that, then you must think that Tiffany made up a lie about him."

"I don't know what she's doing," Charmaine said. "But they have a huge rivalry going on."

"Yeah, which explains why Kenny hit her in the first place."

Charmaine scoffed. "You've known Kenny for a year now, Tyrone. Do you honestly think that he would hurt her on purpose?"

"I know my daughter doesn't make up stuff like that."

Charmaine bit her bottom lip. This wasn't going well at all. She was going to have to be blunt to get through to this man. "She's a teenager, Tyrone. All teenagers lie."

He shook his head. "What you're accusing her of is more than just a fib. You're accusing her of lying to get someone else in trouble. My daughter would never do that."

"Well, I know Kenny would never hit her on purpose. And the Wii is famous for accidents just like this, with people standing close and swinging their arms all around." Charmaine waved her own arms to demonstrate. "Why is that so hard for you to see?"

He frowned deeply. "You're asking me to believe that my daughter would make up a vicious lie about Kenny. I can't accept that."

"She's a damn teenager and they lie!" Charmaine was losing her cool and she knew it. But she couldn't stand the way Tyrone was so blind when it came to his daughter.

He jumped up out of his seat, eyes flashing. "Fuck this. If you can't discuss this without losing your goddamn temper and calling my daughter a liar, there's no point talking."

"Hell yeah, I'm losing my temper. You're accusing my son of hitting a girl, his stepsister. He would never do that in a million years!"

Tyrone huffed and puffed as he brushed past her and headed toward the doorway.

"Fine," Charmaine yelled after him. "Run off if you want. That's not solving a damn thing."

He turned back to face her, his face flush with fury. "As far as I'm concerned, it *is* solved. You think my daughter is a vicious liar. I don't want her in this kind of environment, and I won't have it."

Charmaine blinked. Her voice dropped a level. "What does that mean?"

"What do you think it means? I'm packing our bags, damn it."

Charmaine's eyes grew wide. "What?"

"You heard me."

"But . . . where are you going?"

"To my mother's house until you come to your goddamn senses. I don't think Kenny is a bad kid by any means, but what he did was wrong." Tyrone walked up to Charmaine and pointed his finger in her face. "And you need to admit it and straighten him out instead of babying him and trying to blame it all on Tiffany."

Charmaine squared her shoulders and glared at him. "No, *you* need to stop babying Tiffany. And who the hell do you think you are sticking your fucking finger in my face?"

Tyrone threw his hands in the air and stormed off.

"Go ahead, run away. Just like you always do when someone challenges you," she yelled as she chased him. "You know what? I'm glad you're leaving. And you can just stay gone, for all I care. You can . . ." Charmaine paused when she realized that she was yelling at thin air, since Tyrone had disappeared up the stairs. So much for staying composed, she thought, but the man had insulted her son and she wasn't having that, not from Tyrone or anyone else.

She walked back into his office and sank down into the swivel chair. Dear God, what had just happened? Was Tyrone really packing his bags and going home to his mama, all over a squabble between their kids? Charmaine thought about going up to talk to him again, to try and reason with him once more. But they had just had their biggest argument ever. A dogfight if ever there was one. She suspected he needed some time and space to cool off. She knew she did.

Chapter 22

The telephone rang, and Beverly placed her bowl of cereal on the kitchen table and muted the volume on the small TV with the remote control. She put the receiver to her ear, then quickly yanked it about six inches away. The way Charmaine was yelling on the other end, Beverly thought she would go stone deaf.

To make matters worse, she could barely understand anything Charmaine was saying—something about an argument between her and Tyrone, and Tyrone's going off somewhere with Tiffany. Given how upset Charmaine sounded, Beverly worried that Tyrone had split—as in separation, as in divorce—and had taken Tiffany with him. Beverly prayed that she had misunderstood as she waited for Charmaine to simmer down.

As soon as the screaming on the other end of the line stopped, Beverly put the receiver back to her ear. "Okay now, Charm, I could hardly understand a word you just said. Did you . . . ?"

And then Charmaine was off again, screeching and cussing up a storm.

"Hush!" Beverly yelled into the mouthpiece. "Will you please shut up so I can figure out what the hell is going on with you?"

That did the trick. Charmaine gasped loudly at Beverly's

outburst and finally zipped her trap long enough for Beverly to get a word in. "Now tell me exactly what happened. Softly, please. I can't understand a damn thing with you shrieking in my ear. Did you say Tyrone left you?"

"Sorry," Charmaine said more softly. "That's exactly what I said. He left and took Tiffany with him."

"You mean as in, you know, separation? Y'all had a fight or something?"

"Yeah. A really bad one."

Beverly whistled. Whoa, this was big and ugly. Now she understood why Charmaine was so distressed. "When did he leave?"

"On Wednesday."

"That was three days ago. Why are you just telling me now?"

"I was so damn mad at first, I could hardly talk. I can still hardly talk about it without getting pissed. Bastard!"

"Okay, settle down."

"I was starting to calm down and then he just called and got me upset all over again," Charmaine said with irritation. "Said he was coming to get more of his things this afternoon."

"Where is he staying?" Beverly asked.

"At his mother's."

"Where does she live again? P.G., right?"

"Right."

"Well, what did you do this time, Charm?"

"Excuse me?" Charmaine said. "Why does it have to be something *I* did?"

"I'm just kidding, girl. Relax."

"Don't mess with me, Bev. Not now. People always assume it's my fault when something goes wrong in my relationships."

"Well, you have had a lot of them, you know."

"So? I don't take a lot of crap. Doesn't mean it's my damn fault."

"You're absolutely right, Charm," Beverly said. "I was just trying to lighten things up. My mistake. Tell me what happened."

"It's a long story. Actually it's not a long story, it's just fucking incredible. I still can't believe we're arguing over something so silly." Charmaine paused and took a deep breath. "Kenny and Tiffany were playing games on the Wii after we went to work, and he hit her accidentally. He busted her lip pretty bad, but it's probably already healed. He apologized, but she went and told her daddy that Kenny punched her on purpose and he believes her."

"Really?"

"Of course. He believes everything she tells him."

"But Kenny would never do that," Beverly said.

"*I* know that and *you* know that," Charmaine said. "I tried to tell him that. But if Tiffany says he did it deliberately, he's going to believe her. And why is Tiffany lying like this? I don't understand that."

"She probably doesn't like the fact that Kenny gets to spend more time with her dad than she does. That's normal."

"Yeah, but that's no reason to go telling lies on Kenny. He's never done a thing to hurt her."

"She likely believes what she's saying. She doesn't see Kenny in the best light to begin with, so it's not a huge leap for her to think he'd try to hurt her."

Charmaine's voice lightened. "Maybe you're right. I hadn't thought about it like that. When did you get so damn smart about kids? You don't even have any."

Beverly chuckled. "Oprah, Dr. Phil, magazines. When you don't have your own, you have a lot of time to read and learn about them. Anyway, I'm surprised that Tyrone is acting so emotional and one-sided about it."

"He loses his sanity when it comes to her. Why, I couldn't tell you. He just does. I shouldn't be all that surprised. The signs were there when she visited last summer and over the

Christmas holidays. I should have paid more attention then, but by the time I met Tiffany, we were already married."

"Are you saying you wouldn't have married him if you knew what you know now?"

"I don't know," Charmaine said. "Maybe, maybe not. I tell you, he's crazy when it comes to that girl."

"I think you're blowing this out of proportion, Charmaine. I really do."

"He's accusing my son of doing terrible things and he won't listen to reason. When he called just now, he had the nerve to ask if I had come to my senses. Puh-leeze! He's the one who needs some damn sense knocked into him. I'm thinking of calling my divorce lawyer Monday morning."

"What?" Beverly asked incredulously.

"You heard me."

"Why don't you wait a few days and try talking to him again once both of you have had more time to cool down?"

"I don't need to cool down," Charmaine insisted. "I don't like anybody accusing my son of being violent, especially with a girl. I put a lot of time and work into raising a decent, loving young man and I think I did a pretty good job."

"You did a great job," Beverly said.

"Thank you. I don't want it ruined by someone falsely accusing him of doing bad things, especially someone I hoped would be a father figure to him. Who knows what this could do to Kenny's psyche? As much as I care about Tyrone, Kenny is just a child. I have to put him first no matter what."

"I agree with everything you just said, Charm. No one is going to argue with you on that. I still think you should wait a bit before you do something drastic that you could regret later. It's hard blending two families. Try to be patient."

"I will keep all of that in mind as I noodle on this over the weekend, but I'm not sure we'll ever be able to come to an agreement. Who knows, he might decide to call it quits himself. But thanks for listening. I actually feel a little better after getting some of this off my chest."

"Good," Beverly said. "So I'll see you at Ma's tomorrow after church?" Family and friends were gathering at their parents' house for a pre-ceremony celebration before Beverly's wedding the following Saturday.

"Yeah, I'm going to pick Russell up at Clarence's and bring him with us, plus I got a ton of stuff to bring but I'll get there."

"Want me to help?" Beverly asked.

"No, indeed. You're the guest of honor. Let us do the work."

They hung up and Beverly shook her head with disbelief as she went back to her juice and cereal. She really hoped that Charmaine and Tyrone could work their problems out. Charmaine had already failed at enough marriages. Thank goodness she and Julian wouldn't have to deal with trying to blend families. They would be able to have children together, which should make everything a whole lot easier.

She picked up the remote just as the phone rang again. A glance at the caller ID told her that it was her mother.

"Hi, Ma."

"Hi, Bev. Look, I just got off the phone with Vanessa at the bridal salon. Did you know that Valerie still hasn't picked up her dress yet?"

"No, I didn't. She keeps telling me she's going to go and pick it up. Just yesterday when I talked to her from work, she said she was going to get it as soon as she got off."

"Well, she hasn't," Mama said. "You need to call her and see what's going on. Vanessa said they have to close the shop this afternoon for repairs and they won't open again until next week on Wednesday."

"Maybe Valerie went to pick it up yesterday like she said she was, and the dress still needed more alterations, so she left it there."

"Vanessa said she never came by."

Beverly frowned. "I'm not sure what's going on with her. She's usually so dependable. Okay, Ma, I'll call her right away."

They hung up, and Beverly dialed Valerie's home and cell numbers, but her friend wasn't answering at either. How strange, Beverly thought as she left messages on both lines. Still, Valerie was pretty reliable when it came to calling her back, and Beverly was fairly certain she would hear from her soon. Valerie might be wacky at times, but she loved to talk on the phone. Beverly turned the volume back up on the television and picked up her cereal bowl.

Julian was out on the golf course, and Beverly planned to relax as much as she could until they hooked up later that evening for dinner and a movie. Next Saturday was the big day, and she and her mother had a million things to wrap up all week long, from the caterer on Monday during her lunch hour to the rehearsal and dinner on Friday evening. Beverly was really looking forward to vegetating all day long and recharging her batteries for the upcoming week.

An hour later, Beverly hadn't heard back from Valerie, which was more than a little strange. She tried calling again but still no answer on either line. She turned the television off and called the salon to learn that they were closing at two o'clock that afternoon to begin storing their inventory before the painting and repairs that would start on Monday.

"If you want to be sure to have the dress for your wedding, I would pick it up today," Vanessa warned. "We plan to open again on Wednesday, but I can't guarantee that or even that we'll open again before next Saturday."

Beverly didn't want to take a chance that Valerie wouldn't get her dress before the ceremony, so she decided to drive to Baltimore herself to pick it up. She was a little annoyed with Valerie for ruining the only day she had to rest until her wedding, but what else could she do?

Chapter 23

Two hours later, Beverly was in her Lexus speeding down I-95 from Baltimore. She was wearing black jeans and a bright blue off-the-shoulder top. The bridesmaid dress, covered with clear plastic, was hanging on a hook over the backseat.

Beverly had dialed Valerie's phone numbers repeatedly on her way to and from the bridal salon and gotten no answer. It was so unlike Valerie to be unreachable for hours on end, and Beverly was mildly worried. So she had decided to drive straight to Valerie's apartment near downtown Silver Spring rather than wait for her to call. That way she could also check on Valerie.

Fortunately, years ago they had exchanged house and car keys, partly for this very reason. If one of them ever got locked out or got into some kind of trouble, the other could gain access to their car or residence. Neither had ever used the keys, and it had taken Beverly several minutes to remember where she had stored Valerie's. She finally found them tucked away at the back of her bottom dresser drawer.

She pulled up in front of Valerie's apartment building, her cell phone ringing and ringing as she tried to reach Valerie. She spotted Valerie's maple-red Volvo parked in the lot, yet her friend was still not answering her phones. Beverly was more than mildly worried now. She noticed that Otis's car was not in the lot, so Valerie might have gone somewhere with him. But even that didn't make complete sense. Why wouldn't she answer her cell phone?

Beverly pulled quickly into a vacant space next to the Volvo, then jumped out, the dress flung over one arm, and ran to the building. It was a mid-rise, eight stories high, with a locked main entrance. Beverly fumbled with the set of three keys that Valerie had given her while holding her purse and the dress on her left arm, all the while trying not to think of the horrible things that could have happened to her friend. She was more than a little nervous about entering Valerie's apartment alone. After all, who knew what she might find?

But concern for her friend outweighed her fear, and she pushed the glass front door open and walked briskly through the lobby toward the elevator bank. She pressed the up button and stepped back, trying to steady her nerves as she waited. One of the elevator doors opened, and she ran inside, nearly bumping into a couple exiting. She pressed the button for the fourth floor, and as she rode up alone she realized that she was gritting her teeth. She took a deep breath and made a point to relax her jaw.

As soon as the elevator door opened, she darted out and ran down the hallway to Valerie's unit. She fumbled again with the keys until she found the right one, unlocked the door, and stepped into the large front room of Valerie's one-bedroom apartment.

Valerie had heavy burgundy drapes on the windows and the room was dark. As Beverly groped for the wall switch to turn on a lamp, she heard a faint noise. As best she could tell, it was a squeak, and Beverly narrowed her eyes and listened, trying to figure out exactly what it was and where it was coming from. Valerie had a black cat, who always ran and hid when company came. But it had never made such a strange sound before.

Beverly paused just inside the door without flipping the light switch, at a loss for what to do. A part of her wanted to flee, get the heck out of there. What if an intruder was making the noise and she caught him? But that just meant that Valerie could be hurt, and concern for her best friend won out. She stepped cautiously into the dimly lit room and headed toward the sound.

She realized that the noise was coming from Valerie's leather couch, which sat in the middle of the living room floor, its back facing the front door. She also noticed some garments flung across the couch. She was trying to make out what they were when she stumbled over something on the floor. She gasped and started to look down to see what had tripped her up just as a head popped up from behind the couch.

Beverly immediately recognized Valerie, her dyed black hair disheveled, her mouth hanging open. Beverly also realized that her friend was naked and had this strange startled expression on her face. Beverly could understand the startled part. It looked like Valerie had just been caught in the act with Otis, and no one liked to be caught having sex—at least no one rational. But there was something more in Valerie's face, something that Beverly couldn't quite understand.

She was backing away with embarrassment and trying to understand the odd expression on Valerie's face when a man with a shaved head popped up from behind the couch. Beverly froze. The man she had just caught in the act with Valerie was *not* Otis.

It was Kevin, Evelyn's husband.

For a second, all three of them looked as if they had just seen a spaceship land in the middle of the living room floor.

Kevin ducked as Valerie scrambled up off him and reached for the skirt lying across the back of the couch. Beverly stared at the empty space where Kevin's head had once been and swallowed hard. She thought her eyes had to be playing a nasty trick on her and that it really *was* Otis who had ducked behind the couch. After all, both men had shaved heads. Then she looked at Valerie, hastily slipping into her skirt, and saw the look of utter shame on her friend's face. That look could mean only one thing. Beverly's eyes were not playing tricks on her.

Beverly thought she was going to be violently ill. She covered her mouth and backed up, and again tripped over the object on the floor. Only this time she landed flat on her rump. She realized that the thing that had her stumbling about like an idiot was a black leather duffel bag.

Kevin's black leather duffel bag. Evelyn's husband's duffel bag. In her best friend's apartment.

By the time Beverly scrambled back up with the dress and her purse, both Kevin and Valerie were off the couch. Valerie was buttoning her white shirt, and Kevin was grabbing his jeans off the floor.

"Oh . . . my . . . God!" Beverly yelled.

"Bev," Valerie said as she smoothed her jet black hair down. Valerie kicked something red on the floor, and Beverly realized that it was Valerie's thong just before it disappeared under the couch. "What . . . what are you doing here?" Valerie asked. "How did you get in?"

"I . . . I . . . how?" Beverly couldn't get more than a few words out. She could barely breathe. Was this for real? Her best friend and her brother-in-law had just jumped up off a couch and both of them were naked. Now they were standing there together in front of her looking guilty as sin.

"Why are you here, Beverly?" Valerie repeated. "How did you get in?"

Oh no, Beverly thought. Even if Valerie had forgotten that Beverly had a key to her apartment, she wasn't going to make Beverly feel guilty for letting herself in.

"You bitch!" Beverly screamed. She threw the bridesmaid dress onto the floor. "What difference does it make how I got in? How could you do this?"

Valerie looked down.

"Don't give me that silent crap," Beverly said. "Not now. Shit! Any other time, I can't get you to fucking shut up."

"I have nothing to say."

"Too bad," Beverly said. "'Cause I'm just getting warmed up. Are you really so desperate that you have to sleep with my sister's husband? Never mind what this does to me. How the hell could you do this to Evelyn? Hasn't she been good to you all these years?"

Valerie just stared at the floor, so Beverly turned her ire on her brother-in-law. "And you, Kevin. I don't even know what to say to you."

"If I tried to explain this to you, you would never understand," he said.

Beverly glared at him. "You're right, I wouldn't. No one understands what's gotten into you lately. You're not the man my sister married. Frankly, you disgust me now. Both of you do."

"We didn't plan for this to happen," Kevin said. "We talked and one thing led to another and . . ." His voice trailed off as if he knew there were no words to explain this. "I'm sorry you had to walk in and see it."

"Oh, I bet you are sorry, but only because you know I'll tell Evelyn."

"If that's what you feel you have to do," Kevin said. "I don't think it's wise, given her fragile emotional state now, but . . ." He shrugged.

"You don't even care if I tell her, do you?" Beverly pointed her finger at him. "You know what? You're crazy. And you two deserve each other. I hope you both rot in hell."

"Bev, I'm sorry," Valerie said. "I don't know what else—"

Beverly held her hand up to stop Valerie. "You know what? I don't even want to hear your excuses now."

"I know there's no way to explain this," Valerie said. "I just—"

"I said, save it, bitch," Beverly interrupted. "I don't ever want to see or hear from you again." She threw the keys in her hands at Valerie. Valerie ducked out of the way, and Beverly turned and kicked Kevin's duffel bag. It was heavy and didn't move much, so she unzipped and lifted it, turned it upside down, and shook until the contents spilled onto the floor.

"Hey!" Kevin shouted as he flew around the couch toward her. "What the fuck do you think you're doing?"

Beverly dropped the bag and ran toward the front door. Then she remembered the dress. She was damned if she was going to let Valerie keep that dress even if there wasn't much she could ever do with it. Beverly snatched the dress from the floor, then ran out and slammed the door shut behind her, drowning out Kevin's protests about his shaving cream and underwear being scattered all over the floor.

She didn't bother with the elevator. Instead she ran through the hallway, down the four flights of stairs and out to the parking lot. It wasn't until she reached her car that she paused to catch her breath. She leaned against the Lexus, her head spinning wildly as she tried to steady herself.

Was all that for real? Had she actually just caught her best friend and her brother-in-law screwing? She shook her head. It felt like she was having a nightmare.

But she wasn't. Beverly had always thought that Valerie had a crush on Kevin, but she never, ever believed her friend would go this far. She thought Valerie was better than that. And despite all the changes Kevin was going through, Beverly would never have imagined that he would betray Evelyn this way. How could she have been so mistaken about two people she thought she knew so well? At times like this, she hated the idea of sex. It made people do wacky things just to feel good for a few moments, things they knew were wrong or deceitful.

She fumbled in her shoulder bag for her car key. As she inserted it in the lock and opened the door, she realized that her hands were trembling. She climbed in, tossed her purse on the passenger seat, and closed her eyes. How was she ever going to face Evelyn and tell her about this? Evelyn was having enough trouble trying to adjust to the changes in Kevin and to his leaving her. Now she had to know that he was cheating with Valerie. Beverly felt guilty herself in a way, since Valerie was her friend.

Beverly gave Valerie's red Volvo one last evil glare. Her mind flashed back to the time she had almost slashed a cheating boyfriend's convertible top, and for a second she was tempted to run over and key Valerie's car. But she had grown past that kind of foolishness. That would only make things worse. Hell, that wouldn't be a whole lot smarter than Valerie's stupid decision to sleep with Kevin.

What she had to do now was get up the nerve to drive to Evelyn's house and deliver the bad news.

Chapter 24

As Beverly knocked on Evelyn's front door, she almost hoped her sister wouldn't answer. Then she wouldn't have to tell her about Valerie and Kevin, at least not now.

No such luck. Evelyn opened almost immediately. And not only that, she looked more upbeat than she had for weeks. She was smiling broadly and was dressed in a chic salmon-colored pantsuit, obviously on her way to or from somewhere.

"Beverly!" Evelyn said with surprise. "I didn't know you were coming by."

Beverly realized that she had been so wrapped up in trying to figure out how to give Evelyn the heartbreaking news about Kevin and Valerie that she completely forgot to call Evelyn on her cell phone and tell her that she was on the way over. Beverly had toyed with the idea of calling Charmaine and asking her to meet her at Evelyn's house to help break the news. But she had decided against that. Evelyn should be the first to hear this.

Beverly stepped into the house and forced a half smile across her lips. "I should have called first. You're going out?"

"I was on my way to the mall. Nordstrom is having a handbag sale, and you know how I love handbags. You should come with me."

Beverly shook her head sadly. "No, not today."

The smile faded slowly from Evelyn's face. "Come on in and sit down," she said, and led Beverly into the kitchen. "Obviously something's bothering you. I'll make some tea, and we can talk about it."

Beverly sat down at the kitchen table and watched as Evelyn walked to the stove to put on the kettle for tea. Evelyn was probably the last woman on the planet who still used a kettle to make hot tea. Beverly was tempted to tell Evelyn not to bother, to just sit down and let her say what she came to say. But she was so nervous, she relished the extra few minutes that making tea would provide. On one hand, Beverly wanted to get this over with. On the other, she dreaded having to tell at all. But what else could she do? There was no way in hell she could live with herself if she didn't tell Evelyn what she had just seen.

Evelyn placed dainty white teacups and saucers on the table in front of each of them and sat down across from Beverly while waiting for the water to boil.

"So what is it?" Evelyn asked. "Is Julian all right? This isn't about the wedding, is it?"

Beverly nodded. "He's fine. We're both fine. I came to tell you something else."

Evelyn raised her brows in anticipation.

"I just left . . ." Beverly paused and cleared her throat. "Um . . ."

Evelyn glanced down at Beverly's hands on the table. It was unlike her baby sister to be wringing her hands. Something must be dreadfully wrong. "What is it, Beverly? I just talked to Ma, and she and Daddy were fine."

"No, it's not them."

"Then what is it? Just come out and say it."

"It's about Kevin."

"Oh. I was over there earlier this week, and we had a good heart-to-heart talk. He really opened up to me for the first time in, I don't know how long. Said he was going to call me this weekend so that we can . . ."

Beverly held a hand up to stop her sister. "Evelyn, I just saw him."

"Saw him where?"

Beverly swallowed. God, this was as hard as she thought it would be. This was going to turn Evelyn's world completely upside down. It would likely be the worst news Evelyn had ever had, and Beverly hated being the one to deliver it.

"What is wrong with you, Bev?" Evelyn asked. "You have this weird look on your face. You're scaring me."

"I saw him at Val's apartment and . . . they were . . . they were, you know."

Evelyn stared at Beverly blankly.

"Getting it *on*."

Evelyn continued to stare at her sister in silence for a moment. She had heard the words, but she wasn't sure what they meant. She had an inkling, but she wasn't going to allow herself to go there on just a hint. "What do you mean, Bev? Getting *what* on?"

Beverly was silent, and Evelyn noticed that she actually looked to be in physical pain, as if she was having a real tough time saying what was on her mind. *Getting it on. Getting it on.* The words echoed in Evelyn's head. She didn't like the sound of that. No, she didn't like the sound of that at all.

The kettle pierced the silence with a loud whistle, and Evelyn stood abruptly. Her leg bumped the table, and the cups rattled in their saucers.

"What are you trying to say, Beverly?"

Beverly stared at her fingers as the whistle grew louder. "They were having sex," she said, raising her voice to be heard over the kettle. "I walked in on them and they were having sex." Beverly exhaled loudly. There, she had said it. And now she wanted to cry.

"You . . ." Evelyn paused and touched her forehead. "You saw them together?"

Beverly nodded. "I'm so sorry."

Evelyn laughed nervously. She didn't know why but she found the thought of Kevin and Valerie screwing horribly funny. *Kevin and Valerie fucking?* She held her belly and laughed out loud. Before she knew what was happening, her laughter had morphed into sobs and she was crying hysterically.

Beverly stood and moved close to comfort her. She wanted to turn the damn stove off, the kettle was so loud now. But Evelyn needed her more.

"Oh, my God," Evelyn said as she rested her head on Beverly's shoulder. "Why would he do this?"

"I don't know." Beverly rubbed Evelyn's back soothingly. "I don't know why either of them would do this."

Evelyn sank back down into her chair and plucked a napkin from the holder. She sniffed and blew her nose loudly. "Tell me what happened. Tell me everything. Did you talk to him?"

Beverly turned off the stove, picked up the teakettle, and poured water into both of their cups. She placed the kettle back on the stovetop and sat down. Evelyn took a sip of tea, and Beverly noticed that her lips were quivering.

"Ma called this morning and told me that the bridal salon wanted someone to pick up Valerie's dress because they were going to be closed this afternoon and next week for repairs. I couldn't get Valerie on the phone for hours, so I drove out to Baltimore, got the dress myself, and took it to her apartment. We had exchanged keys years ago, in case one of us got locked out, and I used her key to let myself in." Beverly paused and closed her eyes at the memory. "They were in there on the couch. I thought I would pass out."

"You walked in on them, right in the middle of it?"

Beverly nodded. "I didn't see much since the back of the couch was facing me, but yes. They were both undressed."

Evelyn turned up her nose. "That's sickening. What did Kevin say?"

Beverly smacked her lips and rolled her eyes. "That it just happened. That's what they both said. And he didn't seem that worried when I told him I was going to tell you."

Evelyn threw her hands in the air with finality. "That bastard. Why Valerie, of all people? If he doesn't give a damn about how I feel, he should realize that this doesn't hurt just me. It hurts you, Andre and Rebecca, our whole family. But no, the only person he thinks about anymore is himself."

Beverly was silent. What could she say?

"And what's gotten into Valerie?" Evelyn asked.

"I have no idea," Beverly said, shaking her head sadly. "We've been best friends since college. I can't pretend to understand what she was thinking."

"I'm actually more surprised about Valerie doing this than Kevin. I don't put anything past that man anymore. But you and Valerie have been so close for so long. I would never have thought she'd do this to you."

"In a way, I feel like this is partly my fault," Beverly said.

"Of course it's not your fault."

"If Valerie wasn't my friend, this wouldn't have happened."

"Get that idea out of your head, Bev. In no way, shape, or form is this your fault. This is Valerie's doing. And Kevin's. Stop blaming yourself."

Beverly sighed deeply. "I hear you. What are you going to do about him?"

Evelyn shook her head with despair. "Nothing right now."

"Nothing?" Beverly repeated.

"You heard me."

"You have to do *something*," Beverly protested. "At least call him and cuss him out."

Evelyn shook her head firmly. "That's silly. What good will that do?"

"Not much. You're right. Then I guess it really is over between you two after this, right?"

Evelyn hesitated. “That’s the million-dollar question,” she said. And one she couldn’t answer yet.

“You can’t seriously still be thinking of trying to work it out with him after this, can you?” Beverly asked.

“I don’t know what to think,” Evelyn said. She leaned her elbow on the table and rubbed her forehead. “I don’t even want to try to figure anything out now.”

Chapter 25

"Is Evelyn here?" Charmaine asked as she stepped across the threshold and into her parents' house. She was holding two cake dishes, and Kenny and Russell followed with several Safeway bags full of beverages, chips, and homemade cookies. "I didn't see her car outside."

"Not yet," Mama said as she took one of the cake dishes from Charmaine. Daddy went to the door to help Kenny and Russell with the grocery bags. "She said she was coming, but I wouldn't be at all surprised if she doesn't after what happened yesterday."

"Isn't it awful?" Charmaine said. "Beverly called around mid-night and woke me to tell me that she had walked in on Kevin and Valerie."

❖ ❖ ❖

The night before, Charmaine had been sulking in bed, bone weary after a long day baking for the party and feeling miserable about Tyrone's departure. But she was so startled at the news that she had bolted straight up out of bed and yelled, "What? You're lying."

"No, I'm not," Beverly had said. "You heard me right."

"That bitch! Just because Evelyn and Kevin are having problems doesn't mean it's open season on Evelyn's man. If I ever see Valerie's sorry ass again I swear I'm going to kick it back to Africa."

It was only when Kenny came running into the room wielding a baseball bat that Charmaine realized how loudly she was shouting. She mouthed the word *sorry* and waved him back to bed.

"Stop talking trash, Charmaine," Beverly had said. "That would only make things worse. Evelyn wants to let it be and it's her call."

Charmaine had nodded on the phone. Beverly was right, but she was still aching to put a hurt on that woman.

"I guess this means Valerie isn't going to be the matron of honor in your wedding, then," Charmaine had spit out, her voice full of irony.

Beverly had scoffed. "Hell, no. That's one reason I'm calling. I wanted to ask you to do it. Evelyn is going through so much now."

"No problem," Charmaine had said. "You know I will."

❖ ❖ ❖

Charmaine placed the rum cake on the countertop amid the baked chicken wings and all the other dishes that her mother had prepared for the festivities that Sunday. "Where's Beverly?"

"Downstairs with Julian," Daddy said. He and the boys placed the bags on the counter. Then Kenny and Russell went on down where the party was happening as Daddy emptied the groceries.

"How is she doing?" Charmaine asked. "She was pretty upset when I talked to her last night."

"She still is," Mama said as she stood at the counter crumbling blue cheese for a second batch of her homemade dip.

"I don't doubt it," Charmaine said. "Somebody needs to knock some sense into that crazy woman. Don't let me get my hands on her."

"Who?" Daddy asked. "You mean Valerie?"

"Yeah," Charmaine said. "Bitch."

"Charmaine," Mama said sternly. "Sometimes you talk like you just stepped out of the hood."

"Sorry, but this kind of dirty double-dealing gets on my nerves. I suspected something was up when I saw her talking to Kevin at Beverly's bridal shower. She was all up in his face, flirting and carrying on with him. But I never thought she would go this far."

"She was a friend of your sister's for the longest time," Daddy said, shaking his head with regret as he removed several packs of soda from the shopping bags and placed them in the refrigerator.

"Be careful what you say to Beverly when you go downstairs," Mama said. "She's upset enough. I don't want you getting her even more riled up. This is supposed to be a happy time for her, and it will be even if I have to go down there and take you over my knee."

Charmaine laughed. "You're right, Ma. I'll behave." After all, it was her parents' house, Charmaine reasoned. And Mama was right. It was six days before Beverly's wedding, and this was supposed to be a party. But if she ever ran into that whore Valerie, she was going to give her a piece of her mind. And maybe the palm of her hand.

"How are you?" Mama asked. "And Tyrone, where's he?"

"He's still at his mama's house."

Ma sighed deeply. "I don't know about you girls. You all take marriage too lightly, if you ask me."

"You're probably right," Charmaine said as she looked around at party trays full of chicken wings, chips, and celery sticks. She picked out a potato chip and dipped it into the batch of blue cheese dip that Mama had already whipped up. She didn't want to get into a debate about marriage and divorce with her mother.

They were of different generations and would probably never agree. “Mmm, this dip is delicious. Do you have everything you need up here?”

“I’m fine,” Mama said. “I have more than I need for fifty people. You can start taking some of this stuff downstairs if you want.”

“Who’s here already?” Charmaine asked as she lifted one of the food trays and a bowl of dip.

“Your Aunt Jenna and Uncle Willie. And Aunt Alma is here with Judy and Vern and their boys. And Sylvia and Jamie. But it’s still early and I’m expecting a lot more as people get out of church.”

Charmaine made her way down the stairs to the big room in the basement where her aunts, uncles, and cousins were gathered around watching Daddy’s sixty-inch plasma television. Beverly and Julian already had a game of Bid Whist going at a table in the corner with cousins Sylvia and Jamie.

“Hey, Charm,” everyone said at once. Charmaine waved and placed the veggie tray on a table. She hugged her aunts and uncles, then walked over to the card table and pulled a chair up behind Jamie.

“I pass,” Beverly said as she placed her cards on the table and folded her arms across her waist.

“You passed last time,” Julian teased. “That the best you can do? ’Cause I could use some help here, baby.”

“If I don’t have anything decent, what do you expect?” Beverly asked stubbornly. “I’m not going to bid if I keep getting crummy hands.”

Charmaine could tell from Beverly’s tone of voice and the glum expression on her face that she was still quite miffed.

“Five low,” Julian said, upping Sylvia’s bid of five.

“Six,” Jamie said. “Might as well go for it.”

From what Charmaine could see of Jamie’s hand, he had no business bidding a six. He had not a single ace or joker and would likely never make his bid unless he struck gold in the kitty or his partner. "Some things never change," Charmaine said, laughing.

Jamie hid his hand from her and tossed her a warning glance with his eyes. "What you talking 'bout?"

"I'm just saying," Charmaine said.

"I got this one in the bag," he said to Sylvia.

"Right," Sylvia said wryly. "Just like the last time when you bid a four and couldn't even make that." Sylvia rearranged the cards in her hand and glanced at Charmaine. "Did he tell you about him and Imani?"

Charmaine frowned. Imani was Jamie's wife. Although she rarely showed up at the family gatherings, they had been married about ten years and had two school-age children. "No. What happened?"

"We're getting a divorce," Jamie said, never taking his eyes off the cards as he arranged them.

"You're kidding!" Charmaine said.

Jamie shook his head. "Nope."

"I'm sorry to hear that," Charmaine said.

"Don't be. It's been a long time coming. We kept putting it off for the sake of the kids. But it's not worth it, the way we get along. Or don't get along, is more like it."

"Who has the children?" Charmaine asked.

"Right now we're sharing custody. I got an apartment near the house, and they go back and forth. The one thing we do agree on is trying to make this as easy as we can on them."

Charmaine looked at Beverly. "Did you know about this?"

"He just told me."

Charmaine shook her head. "I thought you two were keepers."

Jamie shrugged. "We grew apart. She was getting more and more religious, and I don't want to go down that path. That ain't me."

"So it was religious differences?" Beverly asked.

"Mainly," Jamie said.

"That doesn't sound like a reason to divorce," Beverly said.

"It is when you get as involved as Imani did. That's all she ever talks about, and she's always preaching and praying. If she was here right now, she'd be asking you where you go to church, and if you say you don't, asking you why not. Then she'd get to telling you what she does in the church, blah, blah, blah. It never ends."

"That can get on your nerves if you're not into it," Charmaine said.

"It would get on mine too," Sylvia added.

"But you don't divorce over something that gets on your nerves," Beverly said. "It's not like infidelity or serious financial problems."

"It's just as bad, if you ask me," Jamie said.

"You can't be serious!" Beverly asked, brows lifted in disbelief.

"I'm very serious," Jamie responded.

Beverly shook her head in disagreement. "This attitude is exactly what's wrong with us."

"What are you getting at, Beverly?" Julian asked.

"Our generation doesn't take marriage seriously enough. We break up over any little thing that goes wrong instead of trying to fix it."

"She's got a point," Charmaine said. "We do divorce faster than our parents' generation did. Look at me. Divorced three times, and that's just for starters."

"Come to think of it, where's Tyrone?" Jamie asked, looking around.

Charmaine shrugged. "At his mother's house last time I talked to him."

"Huh?" Sylvia and Jamie stared at Charmaine with open surprise.

"He packed his things and left with his daughter a few days ago."

"Uh-oh."

"What happened?"

Charmaine waved her hand. "I don't want to get into that now, 'cause I'm not even sure what's going on. Get back to me in a few weeks when I know more."

"You know, this just proves my point," Beverly said. "You and Tyrone are fighting about what? His daughter? So she's a little spoiled and he indulges her. That's nothing to split up about. Talk it over, work it out."

"That's easy for you to say, Bev," Charmaine said. "You weren't there. You don't know how unreasonable Tyrone can be."

"Whatever," Beverly said. "I still can't imagine how it would be worth separating over. His daughter lives in California. She's not even here most of the year. Everyone is too damn quick to head to divorce court, if you ask me."

Charmaine waved her hand with impatience. She didn't come here to get into an argument with Beverly about marriage. She had already taken things too far, given what she had promised her mother, even if Beverly was making it difficult to keep her word.

"The way I see it, our generation doesn't tolerate bad marriages like our parents did," Sylvia said. "They put up with a lot of crap, and most of them were miserable, which is why I never got married."

"Why do you assume they stayed in bad marriages?" Beverly asked. "Maybe some of them stayed and worked their problems out. Maybe they compromised and learned how to get along with each other instead of bolting at the first sign of trouble."

"Not my parents," Sylvia said. "They just tolerate each other even now."

"I think it's both," Jamie said. "Some might work things out, but a lot of them just stick with the bad relationships. And I'm not about to do that. At first I tried to be patient with Imani, but she got more and more into Jesus. The day she got down on her knees and started praying for forgiveness right after we made love was the day I said, 'Lord, I'm out of here. I can't take any more of this.'"

Sylvia slapped her thigh and laughed. Charmaine and Julian chuckled. Beverly shook her head with resignation.

"Why on earth was she praying after sex?" Charmaine asked.

"Something about God not wanting us to make love unless we intend to make a baby, and I insisted on using a condom 'cause she stopped using birth control. We can barely afford to take care of the kids we got now. I'm telling y'all. She's not the same woman I married."

"That sounds something like what happened with Evelyn and Kevin," Charmaine said.

Jamie and Sylvia stared at Charmaine, eyes filled with surprise. "What happened with Evelyn and Kevin?"

Charmaine realized that she had slipped. She zipped her lips shut. "Oops, let her tell you when you see her. I've already said too much."

Sylvia shook her head. "Good Lord."

Jamie shrugged. "Sometimes people change."

"Or go off the deep end," Charmaine added.

Julian slammed a winning jack on the table, and Jamie threw his cards down in disgust.

"Not again," Sylvia said with despair at the loss.

Beverly looked across the table at Julian smiling as he gathered the cards to deal next. He looked so comfortable. He fit right in with her family.

So had Kevin at one time, Beverly thought. And look what happened to him. It was as if someone had snatched the old Kevin away, leaving a total stranger in his place. And even if your spouse never went off the deep end like Kevin, what was to keep him from pulling a Jamie on you, ready to walk at the first sign of trouble, even a little trouble? Maybe the only person you could really count on forever after was yourself.

"Ah, man," Julian exclaimed with disappointment as he looked at his new hand. "I hope you got something decent over there this time, Bev."

Beverly picked up her hand and saw a bunch of eights, tens, and jacks. She and Julian had played cards together many times before, but Beverly never realized that winning was so important to him. It was really starting to grate on her.

"You want to take my place, Charm?" Beverly asked. "I've had enough."

Charmaine blinked. Not because Beverly was tired of playing. It was the sharp tone in her sister's voice. Beverly was obviously still seething about catching Valerie with Kevin, but this attitude of hers was a bit much. Beverly wasn't the only one on earth having a tough time, or even the only one in this room. Tyrone had left just a few days earlier, but you didn't see her pouting and being a pain in the ass. Jamie was in the middle of a divorce, and for all anyone knew, Sylvia had her own issues going on too.

Sometimes you had to suck it in and leave your misery at home. Especially at a party in your honor. Charmaine had a mind to tell her sister exactly that, but she had made a promise to her mama. She would have words with Beverly another time. For now she would try to make nice.

"You sure you don't want to stick it out?" Charmaine asked.

"Quite," Beverly responded.

"Quitting on me, huh?" Julian asked playfully.

Charmaine wanted to shush him. Was he really that clueless as to Beverly's bad mood? Hadn't he learned to read the signs?

"What kind of way is that to treat your man, baby?" Julian added.

Obviously he had *not* learned to read the signs, Charmaine thought. Hardly surprising, since men could be a little thick about these things.

Beverly jumped out of her seat. She knew that Julian was

teasing her, but she was in no mood for joking around and found his words annoying. "It's just a stupid-ass card game," she snapped, glaring at him. "You don't have to take it so damn seriously."

A hush fell over the table as Beverly and Charmaine switched chairs and everyone else stared at their cards.

"Sorry," Julian said softly after a few moments. "I was only kidding. Didn't mean any harm."

"Sometimes you kid around too much," Beverly said. She stood. "I'm going up to see if Ma needs any help."

Beverly walked off, and as soon as she was out of hearing distance, Charmaine leaned across the table toward Julian. "Want me to go slap some sense into her?" she whispered conspiratorially.

Julian chuckled and shook his head. "Nah. She's got a lot on her mind."

"Yeah, but that's no excuse for being a whiny little brat," Charmaine said. "She's not the only one around here with problems."

"It's fine," Julian insisted. "We'll work it out."

Charmaine nodded. "I'm sure you will." But was she really? Given Beverly's history of breaking up with her fiancés at the last minute, Charmaine was tempted to warn Julian not to be overconfident. But she decided against it. Beverly had never gotten this far with either of her two previous engagements. Charmaine could see that despite Beverly's tantrum just now, she and Julian had a strong, loving relationship. It could withstand a temporary setback. Hopefully.

Chapter 26

Evelyn never showed up for the pre-wedding celebration and their mother was worried.

"This isn't like your sister at all," Mama said as she, Beverly, and Charmaine washed, dried, and put away the dishes after the guests had left. Julian, Kenny, Russell, and Daddy were in the basement picking up trash and putting furniture back in place. "I'm really worried about what this is doing to her spirit," Mama said.

"She probably just wanted to stay home and have some time to herself," Beverly said.

"That's what I'm worried about," Mama said. "She tries to be so independent, and this isn't a good time to go it alone. She should be here with her family."

"This is going to be rough on her, Ma, but she'll get through it," Charmaine said. "If I got through three divorces, she can get through this. If it comes to that. We don't even know if it will yet."

"I know that," Mama said. "And I don't mean any harm by this, but it's not the same for her as it was with you, Charmaine."

Charmaine pretended to be taken aback. "Well!"

"You know what I'm trying to say," Mama said. "I'm sure it was hard on you too, but Evelyn has been married for so many years to the same man."

"I know," Charmaine said. "I was just trying to lighten things up a little."

"That's just it, Charmaine," Beverly said. "This is nothing to kid around about. Evelyn is devastated, and you're joking around."

Charmaine paused from putting a glass bowl in a cabinet and glared at Beverly. "Damn, girl," she snapped. She placed the bowl on the countertop and cocked a finger at Beverly. "You need to chill, for crying out loud."

Beverly tossed the dish towel across her shoulder and placed her hands on her hips. "*I* don't need to do anything. *You* need to get serious for a change."

Mama held up a wet hand. "Girls, please. That's enough."

"I'm tired of her attitude," Charmaine said. "She was fussing at everybody downstairs. I know she's hurt about Valerie, but what the hell did I do for her to be jumping on me? And poor Julian. She was all over him too."

Beverly turned back to drying the dishes. What *was* she getting on Charmaine's case for? Or Julian's? She honestly couldn't figure that out. She just knew that a lot of people were getting on her nerves. Was it because of what she had seen when she walked into Valerie's apartment? Probably. Unfortunately, realizing that that was likely the source of her bitterness didn't make her feel much better.

Still, she needed to try and climb out of this funk. Her family had done nothing wrong.

"Sorry, Charm. I'm upset, yes, but I didn't mean to take it out on you."

Charmaine shrugged. "Apology accepted."

"Why don't we go over to Evelyn's when we leave here and check up on her?" Beverly said.

"Good idea. I just need to drop Kenny and Russell off at the movie theater in Columbia first."

"Then I can ride back to the house with Julian and get my car," Beverly said. "I'll meet you at Evelyn's."

"If you want, I can stop by and pick you up after I drop the boys off," Charmaine offered. "There's no need to take two cars."

"Sounds good to me."

"That's better," Mama said. "It makes me much happier to see you two working together instead of arguing with each other."

❖ ❖ ❖

Little more than an hour later, the three sisters sat around a table on the patio at Evelyn's house, sipping chardonnay and munching on rum cake left over from the party. It was a warm June evening, but Evelyn hadn't gotten dressed all day long and she was still wearing her white silk pajamas. Beverly had changed into cutoff blue jeans, and Charmaine into siren red shorts.

"Have you talked to Valerie at all since this happened?" Charmaine asked. She kicked off her flip-flops and put her feet up on one of the spare lawn chairs as she looked across the table at Beverly.

Beverly leaned back and looked out over the lawn. She felt peaceful now, sitting and relaxing with her sisters under the glow of the summer moonlight. Certainly she was much calmer than she had been since walking in on Valerie and Kevin the day before.

But no, she hadn't talked to Valerie, and she shook her head adamantly. "I don't care if I never see that bitch's skanky face again."

"Want me to call her and ask what the hell she was thinking?" Charmaine asked. "I'll probably end up cussing the whore out."

"That's why I haven't contacted her," Beverly said. "I'm so pissed, I know I won't give her a chance to say much of anything. What in the world could she possibly say, anyway, to explain what she did?"

"That was some nasty shit she pulled," Charmaine added as she took a sip of wine.

"I don't think I've ever been so hurt in all my life," Evelyn said. "I've been fuming all day, wondering how Kevin could do this to me. I don't see why you all put all the blame on Valerie. Kevin was just as wrong. Hell, he's even more wrong as far as I'm concerned."

"I don't blame just her," Beverly said. "I know Kevin was being an ass. But why do you say he was more at fault than her?"

"Because he's a husband," Evelyn said. "And a father. Yes, Valerie is guilty of betraying you, and me to a lesser extent. But Kevin broke his marriage vows to me, the ones he took before God. Valerie didn't break any vows to anyone. And I've always believed that when a man cheats on his wife, he's also cheating his children. The separation alone has been hard on Andre and especially Rebecca. How do you think they'll feel to find out that Kevin has slept with another woman? That he betrayed their mother? All I've heard is what a bitch Valerie is. What about what a bastard Kevin turned out to be?"

"Amen to that," Charmaine said.

"Preach on, sister," Beverly said.

"Kevin and I may be separated now, but we're still legally married," Evelyn added, getting warmed up. "Even if we had already signed the divorce papers, he had no right to mess around with my sister's best friend. All the women in the world, and he picked Valerie? That was just plain mean."

Beverly nodded. "Okay, I get it. Well spoken. Kevin's betrayal is far worse when you put it that way. Still, I'll never be able to forgive Valerie or trust her as long as I live. Him either, but she was my best friend since college. We talked to each other almost every day."

"I get that too," Evelyn said.

"I hear what you're saying about Kevin," Charmaine said. "But I think Valerie makes me so mad because men always do this kind of thing. They think with their dicks instead of their brains. Sometimes it seems like they can't help themselves. But I expect a lot more from a girlfriend who was as close to Bev as Valerie was."

Evelyn scoffed. "I don't buy that 'boys will be boys' crap. I just don't. First, they're not boys. They're men and they should be able to control themselves better. We buy into the bad-boy myth and let these grown men get away with murder. We're ready to scratch the other woman's eyeballs out but barely say anything to the man, *our* man, the one who cheated on us. That's wrong on so many levels."

"I agree," Beverly said. "Why do you think we do that?"

"Because if we really hold our man accountable for cheating on us, we might have to break up with him. We don't want to do that, so we tell ourselves that the other woman is responsible and that it wasn't really his fault. Poor baby, she tempted him and he couldn't help it. But now that I've caught him and he knows I'm aware, he'll never do it again. Bull."

Charmaine nodded thoughtfully. "If I can just keep all the other *bad* women away from him, everything will be all right from now on. Then we get all possessive, watching their every move like hawks. You got a point, Evelyn, I admit."

"We have to realize that it's the man who broke the bond of trust that we had with him," Evelyn said. "Unless she's a close friend, the woman doesn't owe us a damn thing."

"You've been doing a lot of thinking today," Beverly said.

"I had to. Last night after you left, I thought I was coming unglued. I couldn't stop crying and I literally felt sick. This morning when I woke up I didn't feel much better. Kevin and I had what I thought was a heartfelt talk just days ago, and I was waiting for him to call this weekend to talk about patching things up. And then this happened. My God! It felt like a door had been slammed in my face. And I won't lie. I fantasized about driving over to Valerie's place and whipping her ass good."

Beverly chuckled at the thought of Evelyn trying to whip anyone's butt. "You?"

"Hell yeah. I fell into the usual trap of thinking that she was the one who had ruined any chances of us getting back together. Then I realized that *he* had screwed things up for us and that what I really need to do is move on, get that man out of my life." Evelyn flicked her fingers contemptuously.

"So it's over for you two?" Charmaine asked.

Evelyn nodded. "Oh, yes. I was trying to save the marriage, but that takes both people in the relationship. I can't do it alone."

"I agree," Charmaine said.

"This is all so confusing," Beverly said.

"What is?" Evelyn asked.

"Marriage. Divorce. How does this happen with a man like Kevin? He seemed like a good husband."

"I wish I could answer that," Evelyn said. "I can't."

"Did he change?" Beverly asked. "Or was this in him all along?"

"It's in all men, if you ask me," Charmaine said.

"I hope you're wrong," Beverly said as she thought about Julian. "What you're basically saying is that all men are dogs."

"Hmm," Charmaine murmured, then took a generous sip from her wineglass.

"Don't do that," Evelyn said, kicking Charmaine under the table. "You're going to scare her and that's the last thing we need to do less than a week before her wedding day."

"I'm just trying to be honest," Charmaine said. "I really do believe it's in all men to cheat. Every last one of them. In some of 'em, it's buried down deeper, but it's still there. That doesn't mean they all do it—some need more motivation than others."

"Do you think it's in all women too?" Beverly asked. "Because I know I would never do something like that."

"Sisters are wired different," Charmaine said. "We need more motivation or temptation than men do, as a rule. There are exceptions, but most women who cheat are desperate for love or affection. Men just want to get it on."

"I don't like thinking it's in my man's nature to cheat on me and that I have always got to be on alert," Beverly said.

Charmaine shrugged. "It is what it is. As long as you marry a decent man and keep him happy in the sex department, you should be fine."

"You're saying that the responsibility for a man not cheating falls on *my* shoulders?" Evelyn said with doubt. "And that I have to be ready to put out whenever he wants it. That's the most ridiculous thing I ever heard."

"Men aren't as evolved as women are. So yeah, you have to take some of the responsibility for keeping him from straying."

Beverly shook her head incredulously. "Give guys a bit more credit than that, Charm." If what Charmaine was saying was even remotely true, it was depressing, Beverly thought. That meant that what happened to Evelyn could happen to any woman, including her, and Beverly didn't want to think that.

"I really would like to," Charmaine said. "But men have been cheating on me since my first boyfriend in high school. Then I got smart about it."

"And started acting like a slut?" Beverly teased.

Charmaine rolled her eyes at Beverly. "No, I learned to spot men who are less likely to cheat. Then I make sure they're satisfied in every way."

"Speaking of high school," Evelyn said. "Guess who I ran into."

"Who?" Beverly asked.

"You remember Reuben?"

"Reuben Roberts?" Charmaine asked.

Evelyn nodded.

"Get out!" Charmaine exclaimed.

"Who's Reuben Roberts?" Beverly asked.

"He went to high school with me and Charm," Evelyn said. "Tall, slim. Played basketball."

"Is he still hot?" Charmaine asked.

"Yes, he's still attractive," Evelyn said. "Maybe even more so, since he's filled out nicely, in the way older men often do."

"Oh, I think I remember him now," Beverly said. "Y'all used to talk about how fine he was all the time."

"Yep, that's him," Charmaine said. "Where did you run into him, Evelyn?"

"At the office. He works in my building. Just moved there recently. We had coffee a couple of weeks ago and lunch last week."

"Ooh, nice," Beverly said.

"Not so fast," Charmaine said. "He got married right after college, if I remember right. What was her name?"

"Belinda," Evelyn responded. "But they split up recently. That's one reason he moved out this way."

"It figures," Beverly said. "Can *anybody* stay married these days?"

"It ain't easy," Charmaine responded. "What's Reuben been up to?"

"He's a tech consultant and he's branching out on his own. He has two boys, both grown, and I'm having dinner with him on Wednesday."

"Wow, you're not wasting any time," Beverly said.

"Nope. He called this afternoon and asked. I thought, why not? Here I am lounging around in my pajamas feeling sorry for myself because of a husband who doesn't give a damn about me. Why shouldn't I go out and have some fun? No crime in that."

"You should fuck him," Charmaine said.

"Charmaine!" Beverly laughed. "What the hell's wrong with you, girl?"

"I don't pay her any mind when she talks like that," Evelyn said, waving Charmaine off.

"I'm serious. It would do you a world of good. That's what I would do. Hell, yeah."

"I don't doubt it," Evelyn said. "But you're not me. We don't think of sex the same way. I didn't even sleep with Kevin until we had been dating for a couple of months, and believe it or not I've been faithful to him all these years. For you, Charmaine, sex is like brushing your teeth."

"Hardly. I'm definitely a one-man woman. I don't sleep around, but I will get it on with someone once in a while if I'm attracted to him and we're both unattached. I bet it's been a while since you and Kevin slept together. Right?"

Evelyn shrugged.

"You know I'm right," Charmaine said. "And you're a single woman now. Or almost. If you're feeling it for Reuben, go for it."

"But I'm not feeling that."

"Uh-huh," Charmaine said doubtfully. "You're denying your feelings, is more like it."

Beverly laughed. "Sometimes it's hard to believe we're sisters. We're so different."

Charmaine smiled. "True. But that's what keeps things interesting."

"Now *that* I can agree with," Evelyn said.

"Seriously, though, you should think about what I said," Charmaine added. "Free your mind and do something purely for yourself. I bet when you're having lunch with Reuben that Kevin is the furthest person from your mind, isn't he?"

Evelyn laughed as she thought about how true that was.

"See?" Charmaine said, smiling in triumph.

"I admit that being around Reuben is refreshing," Evelyn said. "But sleeping with him at this point is out of the question. It's way too early. Besides, I'm still legally married."

"To a cheater," Charmaine said.

"We haven't even begun divorce proceedings."

"When are you?" Beverly asked.

"I'm going to contact a lawyer this week. I have to after this."

"When you're ready call me," Charmaine said. "I'll hook you up."

Beverly sipped her wine and sighed deeply as she listened to her sisters discuss the pros and cons of various divorce attorneys. All she could think was that she fervently hoped she never ended up needing one.

Chapter 27

After leaving Evelyn's and picking up Kenny and Russell from the movies, Charmaine entered the house and went straight up to get ready for bed. It had been a long couple of days and she was tired. She climbed between the sheets and flipped the television to the Food Network.

When Charmaine was honest with herself, she realized that Kevin's cheating on Evelyn had unnerved her more than she cared to admit. Yes, she believed all men had it in them to cheat. They were a different kind of beast. Yet she also believed firmly that as long as she picked a good enough man and fulfilled his needs in every way—emotionally, sexually, mentally—he wouldn't stray.

But with Tyrone staying at his mama's, his emotional and physical needs weren't being taken care of—at least not by her. And that was a prescription for marital disaster. Unless she wanted to end up like Evelyn, she needed to patch this thing up with him ASAP.

She picked up the phone on the nightstand and dialed Tyrone's cell number. It was late, after ten o'clock, but this was important. When he didn't answer, Charmaine dialed his mother's house and got Anne, Tyrone's mom, on the line. Charmaine had never gotten along well with Anne. Tyrone was a bit of a mama's boy, and Mama expected her son's woman to treat him like Moses coming down from the mountaintop, which went against every fiber of Charmaine's being. Pleasing her man emotionally and sexually was one thing, catering to him like a servant was another. Tyrone was perfectly capable of pitching in around the house since both of them worked. So Charmaine wasn't at all surprised by the cool tone in Anne's voice when she realized that it was her daughter-in-law who was waking her up.

"Sorry to disturb you, Anne," Charmaine said. "Can I speak to Tyrone?"

"He's not here."

Charmaine frowned. Where would he be so late, when he had work tomorrow? "What time are you expecting them back, if I may ask?"

"He didn't tell me, but he might have told Tiffany. Hold on and let me ask her."

An alarm went off in Charmaine's head as she waited for Tyrone's mother to return to the phone. So Tyrone was out and Tiffany wasn't with him? Where the hell was he? And who was he with?

"Charmaine," Anne said when she came back to the phone, "Tiffany said he went to meet a friend at a bar and grill."

"I see," Charmaine said. She didn't want to push too much by asking who this friend was and whether it was a man or a woman. Besides, Anne was unlikely to give up the information readily even if she knew. Charmaine cleared her throat. "Can you have him call me when he gets in?"

"It will probably be pretty late by the time he gets back. I might be asleep."

"Can you leave a message where he'll see it, then?" Duh!

"I guess I can do that."

Charmaine slowly placed the receiver back into the cradle. This was exactly the kind of thing she was talking about at Evelyn's house tonight. Let your man stray too far and you might not be able to rope him back in before some bitch got her claws into him. Tyrone might be out with his buddies. Then again, maybe not. By letting him go, she had left the door wide open for another woman.

She was going to have to make it her business to catch up with Tyrone tomorrow and have a good long talk with him. It would be hard to find him since he moved from one building to the next as an electrician and kept his cell phone turned off while working. But find him she would. If this marriage was going to work, it was time for them to move beyond the nonsense.

❧ ❧ ❧

Evelyn kicked off her slippers and slid beneath the bedcovers, still wearing the same white pajamas she'd had on all day. She pulled the blanket up to her chin and squeezed her eyes shut, trying to blot out all thoughts of those two people together. But it was impossible, and the vision of Kevin and Valerie having sex with each other literally made Evelyn feel nauseated. It was gross enough to think of him being with another woman, but the thought of him with Valerie, someone she knew so well, was disgusting. If she lived to be a hundred years old, she would never be able to wrap her mind around the idea of the two of them together naked.

Yet in a strange way he had done exactly what was needed to knock some sense into her head. Kevin had obviously decided that their marriage was over a long time ago. He was just biding his time until *she* realized it. Well, she had. She didn't need any more signals from the bastard. She understood with complete clarity that it was over between them and that she had to start planning a life without him.

And poor Beverly. This had been devastating for her too, for different reasons. Evelyn could remember when Beverly and Valerie were in college together and Valerie would sometimes come to the Jordan house to stay during school breaks. The two of them would run giggling up to Beverly's room and talk and laugh until the wee hours of the morning. When they weren't together, they were yakking it up on the phone.

After college, Valerie got a job in Washington, D.C., and moved here with her daughter Olivia. Over time the relationship between Beverly and Valerie had evolved as they started spending more time with the men in their lives. Yet through everything, they had always had each other for consolation and advice.

And Kevin, her husband, had come between all of that history, all of that friendship. Evelyn shook her head. There was a time when Evelyn didn't understand women who always put guys down, dogging them, calling them names. Whenever women talked that way around her, she would remind them that there were good men out there. You just had to look. And she would point to Kevin as an example.

So much for that.

She still believed there were at least a few good guys left. She had to for Beverly's sake. Beverly had yet to get married and try for happily ever after. Even if the dream turned out to be a nightmare for Beverly too, Evelyn thought every woman should experience marriage at least once. And for all she knew, Beverly could be a first among the Jordan sisters. Beverly could get this thing called marriage right.

The telephone rang and Evelyn glanced at the digital clock on her nightstand. It was nearly eleven o'clock. Who could that be? She leaned over to peer at the caller ID, and it delivered a shock. Kevin. *Now* he called? All this time she had prayed that he would contact her and he hadn't. Now that she didn't care to speak to him, what does he do? She rubbed her eyes to clear her head and braced herself for whatever he was about to throw her way.

"Yes?" she said coldly into the mouthpiece.

"Evelyn? How are you doing?"

Evelyn moved the phone a foot from her face and stared at it in utter disbelief. If this wasn't so incredibly unbelievable she would crack up laughing. She brought the phone back to her ear. "Look, I know you're not calling to chat with me, Kevin, so please, just get on with it. I'm tired." *Bastard.*

"Fair enough," he said, clearing his throat. "Um, I suppose you talked to Beverly?"

She didn't utter a word. What the hell did he think? He understood how close she was to her sisters. Or maybe not. Obviously he didn't understand the bond of trust that was needed between husband and wife. So why should she expect him to understand the bond between siblings? Still, that comment didn't deserve a response. Let him figure it out or stay ignorant.

"Okay, well, actually, I wanted to apologize for . . . for what happened. I know you'll have a hard time forgiving me, and I don't expect you to right now. I still thought I owed you an apology. So I'm sorry."

"Well, guess what, Kevin? You're wrong. I won't have a hard time forgiving you. Know why? 'Cause I ain't even going to try."

He cleared his throat. "Fair enough. I understand."

"No you don't or else you wouldn't have done this," she said, her voice rising. "Out of all the women you could have picked if you wanted to cheat on me so badly, you had to pick Beverly's best friend."

He sighed deeply but said nothing.

"You're despicable."

"You're right."

"Why her, Kevin?"

"You and I had separated," he said. "And she was going through some stuff with her ex-fiancé. We were both lonely. We were both there."

"Is that it? You were lonely and she was convenient?"

"That's about the size of it," he said.

"Still no excuse."

"It meant nothing."

"Not to me, it didn't," she said. "I honestly don't even know who you are anymore, Kevin."

He sighed. "I believe that. Sometimes I'm not sure I know myself."

A part of her wanted to feel sorry for him. He was obviously as confused as anyone, even more so. She thought to suggest that he seek out a therapist to talk about what he was going through, but she was so angry with him that she couldn't bring herself to be helpful in any way.

"Is that all you called for?" she asked. " 'Cause I've got things to do. Like falling asleep while watching television and erasing you from my thoughts."

He chuckled softly. "Yeah, well, I wanted to get some tools out of the garage this week, but I can't find my key to the house."

"Come by one evening after I get off work and I'll give you another one."

"I'm off Wednesday," he said. "How is that?"

"Not Wednesday. I have plans."

"If you're working late, I could stop by your office and pick up the key around five or six o'clock."

"I'm not going to be at work then," she said.

"Oh. Might I ask where you'll be?"

"I'm meeting someone for dinner."

"You mean a date? With a man?"

He said it like it was a miracle that she would have a date with someone. Asshole. "Is that so hard to believe? Just because you don't find me attractive doesn't mean no man can."

"I never said I didn't find you attractive. Why would you say that?"

"Because that's pretty much what you said. You said you weren't attracted to me romantically anymore."

He smacked his lips impatiently. "That's different. Who is this dude?"

"An old friend from high school I ran into a couple of weeks ago. You don't know him."

"How can you date while we're still married?" he asked, his voice filled with surprise.

"You're joking, right?"

"You hear me laughing?"

"Well, you know what?" Evelyn said, laughing at this ridiculousness. "I'll do whatever the hell I please. You'll just have to come another day for the key."

"Wednesday evening is the only time I can make it this week."

"Suit yourself," she said. "Come around ten or eleven. I should be home from my date by then." She smiled. She loved rubbing those words in.

"That's pretty late for a dinner date to be over."

"Do you want your tools or not?" she asked.

"Are you sleeping with him?"

"Excuse me?"

"Are you sleeping with this dude?" Kevin repeated louder.

"I can't believe you just asked me that after what you've done. You really have some nerve. Give me one good reason why I shouldn't hang this phone up right now."

"I couldn't blame you if you did. I hope you don't because—"

"I didn't think you had one," she said just before she slammed the phone down as hard as she could. He wasn't even worth a good-bye.

She climbed out of bed, walked to the window, and stared down at the lawn. It was one of those deep dark nights when she could barely make out the silhouettes of the trees and shrubbery at first, and then slowly her eyes adjusted and everything stood out with perfect clarity.

❖ ❖ ❖

Beverly sat on the edge of her bed in her teddy and reached for the telephone on her nightstand, then snatched her hand back. She had promised Julian that she would call him as soon as she got back from Evelyn's house. He had to work late most of the following week, and they wanted to spend what might be their last night together before the wedding on Saturday.

Yet she had been home for more than an hour and couldn't bring herself to pick up the phone. She had done everything else—changed into her bedclothes, checked her e-mail and phone messages, brushed her teeth—but kept putting the phone call off. She had so much on her mind with all that had happened yesterday with Valerie, Evelyn, and Kevin. She honestly didn't think she would make very good company that night anyway.

Who she really had a mind to call was Valerie. She had a thousand questions. Did she think about how her actions would hurt so many people? Did she have feelings for Kevin or was she just being mean? How long had she had these feelings and why didn't she talk things over before doing something so crazy? And on and on and on.

But she figured it would be better to wait a few days, until she'd had time to cool off. Sometimes she thought she would never cool off enough to call Valerie.

She pulled the covers back and climbed into bed just as the phone rang. The caller ID showed that it was Julian. She smiled and picked up.

"Hi, there," she said.

"Hey, you. Thought you were going to call me when you got in so I could swing by."

"I know. I was just about to pick up the phone."

"How long you been back?"

"About an hour, I guess."

"K. So should I come now?" he asked.

"Um, maybe not tonight, Julian. I'm really, really tired. I need to get some rest."

"I've been there before when you were tired."

"Not this tired," she said. "I won't be good for much of anything besides sleeping."

"Then we won't do anything besides sleep. Maybe we can talk a few minutes before we doze off. I know you got a lot on your mind."

"I don't think I have the energy to do much talking even. I would probably drift off to sleep before you even get here."

"Damn, you really are tired."

"Yeah. That's what I said, isn't it?"

"Why you getting all testy with me?" he asked. "Just like at the family get-together. You sure you're just tired? You're not mad at me or anything, are you?"

"No. Why would I be mad? You haven't done anything."

"I don't know. Maybe you're in a 'all men are dogs' phase."

Beverly frowned into the phone. Where was this coming from? "When have you ever known me to be like that?"

"Don't all women get like that once in a while?" he asked. "Especially when they've been around other women."

"Not me," she said firmly. "I don't even know why you'd say that."

"Sorry, just trying to understand what's up with you. That's all."

"Like I said, I just need some rest," she said. "What's the big deal about that?"

He sighed. "Nothing. Let's leave it at that and I'll call you tomorrow. Maybe we can see each other one night this week if I can swing it at work."

"Sounds good. Love you."

"Love you back."

They hung up and Beverly switched the television on and off again almost immediately. Something didn't feel right. She couldn't remember a time when she hadn't been anxious to see

Julian no matter how tired she was. Many a night he had let himself in with his key, found her asleep in bed, and quietly slipped in beside her. She would wake up in the middle of the night and snuggle up to him.

But she hadn't wanted that tonight. And rather than talk to Julian about all that was on her mind, she wanted to be alone with her thoughts and feelings. For some reason, the whole episode with Valerie had left her feeling odd around Julian and she wasn't sure why.

Was it trust? Had the Kevin and Valerie thing left her doubting that men could be trusted? Any man? If Kevin—who until very recently was one of the most reliable and honest men she had ever known—could mess over Evelyn so badly, was any man a hundred percent trustworthy? If Kevin could do this to Evelyn, a woman he had been with for more than twenty years, could she be sure that Julian would never do it to her?

Chapter 28

Charmaine finally caught up with Tyrone on Monday evening. After work, she parked her Honda outside his mother's house and waited until he drove up in his SUV. Wearing his leather electrician's tool belt, he hopped out and entered the house.

Charmaine exited her car and crossed the street. She wasn't exactly looking forward to seeing Tyrone's mother. But once Charmaine made up her mind she was going to do something, she wasn't about to let anything or anyone—including Anne—get in her way.

She walked quickly to the front door and knocked firmly. Tyrone answered almost immediately and he looked genuinely surprised to see her. He also looked pleased—or at least not displeased—and that Charmaine took as an encouraging sign.

He stepped aside to let her in. Being so close to his rugged scent reminded her instantly how much she missed him. She was glad she had worn one of his favorite outfits—a snug-fitting black dress with a wide fire-engine-red belt. Her toenails peeked out of her sandals and matched the color of the belt.

"You're looking good," he said as he shut the door and admired her openly.

"Thanks," she said, smiling.

"Come on in. I'll get us something to drink and we can talk."

She followed him into the living room, and Anne and Tiffany came out from the kitchen to see who was at the door. Anne was wearing an apron and holding a large spoon. As usual, Anne was wearing too much makeup, trying to look younger than her seventy-something years. Charmaine had always thought that Anne was an attractive woman and didn't need so much makeup. Tiffany was looking as cute and stylish as always. Both Anne and Tiffany's expressions seemed to fall flat when they saw who their guest was.

"Oh, hello, Charmaine," Anne said coolly.

Charmaine nodded. "Anne, how are you?"

"I'm fine."

"Hi, Tiffany," Charmaine said.

Tiffany gave a weak wave. "Hi."

Anne looked at her son. "Tyrone, Tiffany and I are almost done. Dinner will be ready in about ten minutes."

"Thanks, Ma," Tyrone said. He looked at Charmaine. "Do you want to stay for dinner?"

Charmaine shook her head quickly. "Oh, no, thanks. I really need to get back and get something on the table for Kenny. But thanks for asking."

"Sorry to hear that," Anne said, not sounding sorry at all. "But I certainly understand."

Anne and Tiffany walked back to the kitchen, and Charmaine could have sworn she'd heard two big sighs of relief.

"I really wanted us to talk in private," Charmaine said.

Tyrone nodded. "Why don't we go for a walk up the block or something?"

"Sounds good to me."

Tyrone removed his tool belt and placed it on a shelf in the front hall closet and they walked out the door.

"Nice evening," he said as he moved around her to get to the outside, near the road. "Not too humid."

"Beautiful," she agreed.

They strolled in silence for a couple of minutes, both in deep thought. "How did it get to this point?" Charmaine asked, suddenly blurting out loud what she was thinking. She had practiced what to say while waiting in the car and just again as they walked silently beside each other. In the end, she realized that all the rehearsed words sounded phony. This was her husband. They needed to get real.

He shrugged sadly. "I'm not sure. It's unfortunate."

"Do we really want it to be like this?"

He shook his head. "I don't. There's nothing I want more than for us to get back together."

She smiled with relief.

"But . . ."

Uh-oh, she thought. Here it comes.

"I can't let Tiffany live in a situation that's uncomfortable for her. Even if it's only for part of the year."

"I wouldn't expect you to. Honestly."

"After what happened with Kenny, it wasn't the best of situations for her," he said.

Charmaine knew that she needed to tread carefully here. No way was she ever going to believe that Kenny had hurt Tiffany deliberately. Neither was Tyrone going to believe that Tiffany was lying to him. Charmaine had come to believe that the truth probably lay somewhere between the two versions. Kenny had been careless when they were playing, and Tiffany just didn't trust her stepbrother.

But Tyrone was too blind to see that. And she hadn't seen things much more clearly herself for a while. Now she realized that if she wanted this marriage to work she had to have her eyes wide open. She had to see not only his faults but also her own. And they both had to find a way around them.

"Look, Tyrone, we're not going to agree on what happened between Kenny and Tiffany. You see it one way, I see it another. The irony is that neither of us is completely right or handling this right."

He smiled thoughtfully.

"They're both good kids," she continued. "And they can move past what happened and get along in the future if we lead the way. The question is, are we up to it?"

"I agree that Kenny is a good kid, and any man would be proud to have him as a son. I never said or thought otherwise. I want him and Tiffany to be friends."

"Then we have to encourage it and stop taking sides. We're the adults here."

"That may be easier said than done," he said. "There are a lot of differences in the way we see things when it comes to them, and I'm at a loss as to how to overcome the differences. Believe me, I've given it some thought."

"I don't have all the answers, but I'm willing to try harder to see your point of view if you try to see mine."

"That sounds fair now, but will it work?"

She smiled. "That's the tricky part. We have to try, though. We owe it to ourselves and to the kids."

He thought for a minute, and she could see that he was turning things over in his head. She hoped he would come around. She had done her part and reached out with an offer to meet him halfway.

Finally he shoved his hands in his pockets and looked at her with a half smile. "Let's do it," he said. "We have to find a way to make this work. Tiffany and I will move back in on Wednesday after I get off. That'll give us a day to pack."

"Sounds good to me," she said. "I miss having you both at home."

He put his arm around her. "I missed you and Kenny too. I'm glad you came by and we talked."

"So am I."

"We're good together," he said. "I've always believed that. It'd be a shame to let a couple of teenagers ruin what we have."

"I couldn't agree more."

Chapter 29

Beverly had finally decided to confront Valerie. She wanted to get the talk with Valerie out of the way to clear her head before her wedding day, and she wanted to do it in the flesh rather than by telephone or e-mail. She needed to see her friend when they had what Beverly figured would be their last talk together.

She felt that she had calmed down enough to meet with Valerie without blowing her top. And all day at work on Tuesday, she rehearsed what she would say and how she would say it without losing her cool.

"Why did you do this, Valerie? I thought you were my best friend. What were you thinking?"

She practiced the words and the mild tone she would use as she drove to Valerie's. Julian was working overtime all that week to make up for the days he would be off next week while they vacationed in Bermuda on their honeymoon. They had decided to hook up for dinner on Friday evening as the last time to see each other before the wedding.

She pulled into the lot outside Valerie's apartment building and sat in her car for a few extra minutes. Valerie's red Volvo was parked there, so Beverly knew she was in. All that remained was to be sure she was ready to do this. It was going to be hard, one of the hardest things she'd ever had to do. In all their years as friends, she and Valerie had never argued about anything more serious than where to go out to dinner together.

Beverly grew teary-eyed as she thought about their friendship coming to an end. Tears were the last thing she wanted at this moment, and she immediately opened the car door and hopped out. No need to get sentimental now, she thought as she locked the car. Their friendship was over the minute she'd caught Valerie and Kevin together. Valerie certainly wasn't thinking about their friendship when she decided to spread her legs.

She slipped through the main entrance as someone else exited, took the elevator to Valerie's unit, and knocked. It took a while, but the door finally swung open and Valerie stood there, still dressed in the long skirt and cotton blouse that she had probably worn to the office. If Valerie was surprised to see Beverly, she didn't show it. She opened the door without saying a word and stepped aside.

Beverly walked in and they stood facing each other in an awkward silence for a minute. Beverly was trying to get out the words that she had rehearsed, but she was surprisingly nervous. It felt like she was standing in front of a stranger rather than a friend.

Finally, Valerie spoke up. "I wondered if you'd come by," she said. "I tried to call you a few times."

"I know. I wasn't ready to talk to you."

"That's what I figured. Come on in and sit down." Valerie gestured toward the couch, the same couch where Beverly had walked in on Kevin and Valerie just days ago. Beverly was having trouble getting the memory out of her head. She didn't want to sit on top of the scene of the crime. She kept her heels planted firmly where they were.

"I'll stand," she said. "I'm not going to be long. I have a couple of questions and then I'm out of here."

Valerie crossed her arms defensively. "I'll try to answer if I can, but I don't—"

"Why, Val?" Beverly blurted out. "Why the hell would you do something so goddamn stupid? Are you really so desperate that you have to go and screw my brother-in-law? Huh?" Beverly paused, more so to catch her breath than to allow Valerie a chance to speak. So much for not getting ruffled, she thought. But how could she stay calm when she was spit-raving mad?

Valerie shook her head sadly. "I don't know what got into me. I admit that what I did was stupid."

Beverly scoffed. "No kidding. Which one of you started this whole mess? You or Kevin?"

"Um, I don't know if you could say one or the other of us started it." Valerie shrugged. "It just happened."

"Excuse me? *Excuse me?* You didn't just open your eyes and find him lying on top of you, Valerie. One of you had to start flirting or something first."

"We both did. Really. I mean, we first talked at your bridal shower. That was when we realized that we have a lot in common, the same taste in movies and books. He's getting into New Age things, which I've always been interested in."

"Did you exchange phone numbers at the party?"

"E-mail. He asked for my address. He said he wanted to send me links to some interesting New Age websites. I offered to do his astrological chart and e-mail it to him. It was innocent then. Just helping each other out."

"If it was so innocent, why didn't you tell me that you exchanged e-mail addresses with him? You never said a word at the party or ever."

"I think I forgot about it," Valerie said.

"You think you forgot?" Beverly said with contempt. "How could you forget that so fast? You're lying."

"I'm not lying. I didn't think it was important because I never thought he would get in touch with me after the party. I thought he was just being friendly."

"So tell me how the hell it went from being friendly to fucking in one week?"

Valerie swallowed hard but said nothing.

"Figures," Beverly said. "For once in your life, you have nothing to say."

Valerie smacked her lips.

"Did he e-mail you first?" Beverly didn't know why, but she had this bizarre need to understand just how this came about.

Valerie nodded. "Yes."

"And you still never said anything to me."

Valerie looked down toward the floor. "I know."

"Why not?"

"I . . . I just didn't."

Beverly sighed with exasperation. "Go on."

"I got the information to do his chart, and we e-mailed back and forth for a few days. At some point I realized that he was flirting with me."

"And you flirted right back, didn't you?"

"Not at first, but well, I guess so."

Beverly rolled her eyes to the ceiling. She was tempted to smack Valerie upside the head, but if she did that she would never get the full story. "Go on."

"We agreed to meet for coffee on Saturday afternoon. But I . . . I never expected it to go so far."

"Oh, come on."

"Seriously. I expected to give him his chart and explain it to him. That's all."

"Is that why you kept all of this from me?"

Valerie clenched her teeth silently.

"Kevin is a dog." Beverly continued. "And you, you're a fool for going along with it. You knew what you were doing with him was dead wrong. I thought you had more integrity than that, Valerie."

They stood in silence for a couple of minutes, each lost in her own thoughts. Two lifelong friends standing only a few feet apart, yet they could have been miles away from each other, given the huge emotional distance between them.

"I don't get it," Beverly said, shaking her head with despair. "I just don't get it."

"I don't know what came over me. I've always thought Kevin was hot and I let him get the better of me."

"So you were being a selfish whore? Is that it?"

"Stop calling me names, Bev. Can't you talk to me without trashing me?"

"Well, excuse me. *Bitch!*"

"Fuck you, then," Valerie said.

Beverly didn't know what came over her, but before she knew what was happening she had slapped Valerie hard across the cheek. Valerie winced as her eyes grew big with shock, and Beverly was horrified that she had allowed herself to lose so much control. Then Beverly realized that she felt more relieved than she had since walking in on Valerie and Kevin. She felt vindicated. She felt good!

Valerie grimaced and touched her cheek. "I don't believe you hit me!"

"I don't believe you fucked my brother-in-law."

"You have every right to be pissed off at me, Beverly. What I did was wrong. But in my defense, Kevin and Evelyn were separated when this happened, and he insisted that they—"

"He's still Evelyn's husband," Beverly interrupted.

"But he insisted that they weren't going to get back together."

"What the hell difference does that make? Even if they were already divorced or had been divorced for ten years, you had no right to screw him. All the men out there, and you had to mess with my family, Valerie. That's just wrong."

"I wouldn't have done it if he and Evelyn hadn't split up. Or if Kevin had said he was going back to her."

Beverly couldn't believe that Valerie continued to try to rationalize this to herself. But maybe she shouldn't be surprised. Something wasn't right in this woman's head. "It's unbelievable that you would try to justify what you did. And what the hell is going on with you and Otis? Where is he?"

"He's still around, only we're not as tight since he shoved me."

"You know what you are, Val?"

Valerie looked at Beverly and waited.

"Pitiful. That's what you are. You're so desperate for a man that you'll do anything. You've stopped caring about anyone's feelings but your own."

Valerie sneered. "You have some nerve talking about hurting someone's feelings. What about *my* feelings? God, you can be so annoying at times."

Beverly frowned. "What are you talking about?"

"You really have no idea, do you? Or at least you pretend not to."

"What? What did I do?"

"If it wasn't for me, you wouldn't even be getting married on Saturday."

Beverly blinked. What on earth was Valerie getting at?

"Yeah, I'm going there," Valerie continued. "You walk in here all self-righteous about me hurting you. Do you fucking realize how much you hurt me? No, of course not. You're too stuck on yourself."

Beverly was stunned. Where was all of this coming from? "How did I hurt you? Are you talking about Julian?"

"Who the hell else would I be talking about? You always pretended not to know, and I went along with it because of our friendship. But how could you not see that I had feelings for him from the very beginning? All you had to do was open your eyes. You didn't want to know the truth because you wanted him for yourself."

Beverly's mouth dropped open. "You never ever said anything about any of this. When you introduced him to me, I asked if you were into him. You told me no."

"Any idiot could have seen that I was lying. But no, you were too selfish to see it. So I waited and hoped you would break up with him, like you did with all the other fiancés in your life. Only it didn't work out that way this time." Valerie laughed with scorn.

"I thought you were in love with Otis," Beverly said. "You were going to marry him."

"When I realized that you and Julian were serious, I convinced myself that I was into Otis. That didn't last long. He's a brutal, male chauvinist ass."

Beverly stared at Valerie and shook her head numbly. "I had no idea. Is Julian aware of your feelings?"

Valerie hesitated a second. "You should ask him that."

Whoa. Something about that reaction didn't sit too well with Beverly. Valerie made it sound like there was something between the two of them that she wasn't aware of.

Beverly backed toward the door slowly and silently. She'd had enough torture from this woman for one evening. She wanted to get out of there. She put her hand on the knob and opened the door without saying a word. Enough had already been said.

She turned, flew down the stairs, and jumped into her car. She paused as she sat behind the steering wheel to catch her breath. Why on earth would Valerie make a comment like that? Beverly had enough faith in her relationship with Julian to be sure that nothing was going on between him and Valerie now. But what about in the past, before she met him or during the early days of their relationship?

Beverly realized that she was seriously doubting Julian for the first time since they had met; she didn't like the feeling one bit. She banged the steering wheel. Men! Talk about agony and ecstasy, ups and downs, highs and lows. One minute it was total bliss with them, the next pure hell. Sometimes, Beverly thought she should just run off and live alone in the woods with the plants and animals, become a hermit, and swear off men altogether.

It was just as her sisters had said—desperate, lonely, horny women would always be out there, ready and willing to pounce on your man at the first opening. If the men would keep their zippers shut, it wouldn't be such a huge problem. But so many of them didn't.

Was Julian one of those who would keep his zipper shut, even ten, twenty, or thirty years from now? Or would he be like the others?

Chapter 30

The doorbell rang just as Charmaine finished placing a bottle of chardonnay and two of her best wineglasses on the kitchen table. That had to be Tyrone and Tiffany, ready to move back in and start fresh with open hearts and minds—she hoped. She tugged her new skirt down over her hips and walked quickly toward the bottom of the stairs leading up to Kenny's bedroom, where he was playing games on his Xbox. Charmaine wanted them both to welcome Tyrone and Tiffany back home.

"I'll be down in a few minutes," Kenny yelled.

"No, you'll come now," Charmaine insisted.

Kenny appeared at the top of the stairs. "What's the rush? They'll be here for a while."

Charmaine smacked her lips and pointed to the lower landing near her feet. "I'm going to count," she said. "If your feet don't appear in the spot where I'm pointing when I get to three, there will be no Xbox for . . ."

Kenny's feet appeared on the spot before she could finish, but it was obvious that he wasn't exactly thrilled about this reunion. "Tyrone and I are working very hard to make this family work," she said. "And I expect you to cooperate. Understand?"

Kenny shoved his hands into the pockets of his knee-length shorts and nodded reluctantly. Charmaine opened the door to see

Tyrone standing there holding three suitcases, one in each hand and one under an arm. Tiffany stood behind him, a garment bag thrown over her shoulder. She was snapping her fingers as she listened to her iPod through earphones.

Tyrone stepped in and placed the luggage on the floor, then gave Charmaine a quick but warm kiss on the lips and hugged Kenny enthusiastically. Tyrone looked genuinely happy to be home, but Tiffany was another matter. She slid in behind her father and brushed past everyone without a word, heading straight to the stairs and her bedroom.

"Tiffany," Tyrone called after her firmly. She stopped and turned to look at her father, clearly surprised to be interrupted.

"The least you could do is say hi to Charm and Kenny," Tyrone said. "And remove the earplugs, please."

Tiffany shifted from one foot to the other with annoyance and removed the iPod earphones with so much reluctance you would have thought her dad had asked her to yank one of her teeth out. She waved halfheartedly.

"Hi, Tiffany," Charmaine said, reaching out to hug her around the shoulders. "It's good to have you back." She nudged her son on the arm. "Isn't it, Kenny?"

"Yeah," Kenny said with an equally weak wave.

Tiffany nodded. "Likewise."

As soon as Charmaine released her, Tiffany replaced the earphones and headed up the stairs. Tyrone rolled his eyes to the ceiling. "Sorry about that," he said to both Charmaine and Kenny. "She'll come around."

Charmaine waved him off. "Don't worry about it. Kenny wasn't much more enthusiastic. Had to force him off his Xbox. Give 'em time."

Tyrone punched Kenny playfully. "Didn't want to see me, huh?" Tyrone teased. Kenny laughed and the two of them pretended to box each other for a few seconds. Charmaine smiled.

"It's good to be back," Tyrone said as he picked up the luggage. Kenny helped him carry the bags upstairs and then went back to his Xbox. Tyrone came down, and he and Charmaine walked into the kitchen and popped and poured the wine. They sat at the table and clicked their glasses together. "To new beginnings," Tyrone said.

"I like that," Charmaine said.

"Again, I want to apologize for Tiffany's attitude just now. I talked to her as we drove over here, but it didn't seem to help much. I'll work on that."

"It's going to take some time for both of them," Charmaine said. "She understandably resents Kenny for being able to live here all year with you, and she doesn't like the idea that I'm sort of replacing her mom."

"But I haven't been married to her mother for several years now. And her mother is fine with me and you."

Charmaine shrugged. "I'm sure Tiffany still wishes the two of you would get back together. It's the dream of any child of divorce to see their parents together. I'm not saying it's an excuse for her behavior. It's not. Just trying to see her side."

"You're probably right, and it's going to be tough to get her to shake those feelings," he said. "I'm going to have to be straight with her from now on and make it clear to her that I won't be getting back together with her mother and that she shouldn't hold that against you or Kenny."

"And I'll explain to Kenny that it's going to take some time for her to get used to sharing her father and that we all have to be patient with her. Kenny should be able to understand that, since he had to get used to you when you moved in."

"I told Tiffany that they won't become best buddies overnight, maybe never, but they have to learn to get along and respect each other."

"We have to work together on this," she said. "They'll come around if we're united."

He nodded in agreement. "Being away from you got me to thinking. There's going to come a time when Tiffany will go off with some dude to start a family of her own, and I don't want to find myself all alone when that happens."

He reached across the table for her hand and squeezed. It was good to hear him talk like this, Charmaine thought.

"I've given some thought about how to handle this," he continued. "I can start by showing more respect for you and Kenny around Tiffany. I have to make it clear to her just how important we are to each other. She'll grow to like you both better if she sees how much you mean to me."

Charmaine smiled broadly. Now *that* was her man talking. "That's a plan I can get with."

He leaned over and kissed her on the lips. Then he gave her a seductive look and delicately ran the tip of his forefinger along the outline of her low-cut top. "The kids are occupied with their Xboxes and iPods," he said. "What do you say we two grown-ups sneak upstairs. We're overdue for some serious making up."

Charmaine nodded eagerly. "That's the best idea you've come up with in a long, long time."

He picked up his wineglass, she grabbed hers, and they held hands as they slipped up the stairs.

Chapter 31

Dinner with Reuben at the Crab Shanty in Ellicott City seemed to fly by for Evelyn. One minute he was knocking on her door and helping her into his black Lexus sedan; the next he was tipping the waitress. In between, they had dined on some of the best seafood in Maryland, all the while talking and laughing nonstop.

It had been decades since Evelyn had dated, and she had not been looking forward to the prospect. Truth was, she had been separated just under a month and hadn't really had time to think about anything as far out as dating again. She suspected that if she'd had much time to think, it would have scared her silly. Yet here she was having the time of her life with a man who was fun and flirtatious and made her feel alive again.

They held hands and walked back toward Reuben's car as the sun was falling, creating a luminescent glow in the evening sky. It was the first moment of silence between them since he had picked her up at six that evening, nearly three hours earlier. She looked up at him and smiled, and he squeezed her hand gently.

He pulled out of the parking lot onto Plum Tree Drive and turned onto Route 40, heading toward his new condo in Columbia. She had agreed to stop by and see it before he drove her the thirty minutes to her home in Silver Spring so she could meet up with Kevin and give him the keys to the house as promised. She honestly didn't want the date to end. Reuben was upbeat and pleasant to be around. And she found him even more attractive now than she had when he was younger. Some people tended to grow better-looking with age, and Reuben was definitely one of them.

She had even toyed with the idea of calling Kevin and telling him to come later that night so she could have more time with Reuben. Going from Reuben to Kevin was going to feel like walking from daylight into darkness. But she decided against doing that. She didn't want to overplay her hand with Reuben and have him get tired of her before they got started.

His condo was right in the midst of downtown Columbia, within walking distance of the shops and restaurants in the area. He pointed out a group of new town houses being built near the mall, where he hoped to buy once he and his wife sold their house in Prince George's County.

"You excited about being a bachelor again?" she asked.

He threw his head back and laughed out loud. "Yes and no. Meaning that I'll probably enjoy it for a while, but I'm really a one-woman kind of guy. I appreciate an evening out with good company like we just shared, but what I really enjoy is having a steady companion. What about you? Are you looking forward to getting back into the dating scene?"

Evelyn shook her head. "Not even a little bit. If anything it makes me nervous. I'm so rusty when it comes to all of this."

"You shouldn't be nervous. You won't have any trouble getting dates and you were fine with me tonight."

"It's sweet of you to say that. But I think I was comfortable with you because we already knew each other. And at my age, most men are taken, gay, or too old to get it on."

He chuckled. "Well, thanks a lot for that vote of confidence."

"No, not you. I didn't mean it like that. See? I'm rusty at this dating thing."

They laughed and continued their discussion of the ups and downs of newfound singlehood in Reuben's kitchen as he removed two wineglasses and a bottle of cabernet sauvignon from the cabinet. He popped the cork, and she picked up both glasses and held them as he poured.

"I do want to say that you've given me more confidence about what it might be like to be single again," she said.

"Have I, now?"

"Definitely."

"Glad to be of help." He finished pouring and placed the bottle on the countertop. But instead of taking one of the glasses from her hands he took them both and set them down. She looked up at him, a puzzled expression on her face.

"You know what I want before we toast, drink, and all of that?"

A chill ran up her thigh, which was odd, she thought. Usually they ran down her spine. "What?" she asked, smiling at what she thought was coming.

"This." He leaned in and pressed his lips to hers as he gently touched her chin with his fingers.

She closed her eyes and held her breath. Even though she was expecting this, she was in a mild state of shock. It had been ages since she had kissed any man besides Kevin, and it had been months since she'd kissed Kevin. But she liked it. She really liked it. She liked it so much that when he released her and moved to pick up the wineglasses, she put a hand out to stop him. She tugged lightly at his shirt until he bent over and kissed her again. This time she didn't freeze up but let herself enjoy the feelings as he wrapped his arms around her and tightened his hold.

Evelyn wasn't sure what came over her, maybe something that had lain dormant for far too long. But she found herself arching her body against his urgently and pressing tightly as she felt him become more aroused. They wriggled and moaned and he backed her up to the countertop.

At that moment, as he kissed her passionately on the neck, a voice in her head told her to put a stop to this. Things were going too far too fast. She pulled her lips away from his and placed her hands on his chest. But before she could push him away, his lips found the crevice of her breast, and the sensation of his hot tongue on her bare flesh sent her into a frenzy. He reached down and hiked up her skirt.

When she felt his hand tugging at her bikini underwear, she knew they were approaching the moment of no return. If she was going to back out, she needed to do it now. Goodness knew she hadn't seen this coming. She'd had no idea how needy her body had become all these many months with no affection from Kevin.

She had no false illusions of love forever after with Reuben. She understood that if she had sex with him now, it could well become a one-night stand of hot passion. Could she live with that?

Hell yeah. She helped him tear off her panties; then they both moved to the zipper of his slacks. She kicked off her heels and he pulled her down to the cold, hard kitchen floor. They flipped around and she lifted her skirt and anxiously straddled him. She could tell that he was as startled by her sudden burst of eagerness as she was.

He pulled her face to his and reached for her lips, kissing her gently at first and then more excitedly. The kiss became wetter and more urgent, until finally at the height of passion she bit him, shuddered, and moaned loudly.

"Ouch!" he muttered, reaching up to touch his bottom lip. "You're a wild one tonight." He laughed softly.

"Sorry if I hurt you," she said as her heartbeat slowed down a bit.

"Don't be." He flipped her beneath him and landed on top of

her. Their hips moved rapidly, and she could feel her passion beginning to inflame anew.

❧ ❧ ❧

Reuben pulled into Evelyn's driveway and leaned over to the passenger seat to kiss her softly on the lips.

"I'll call you tomorrow," he said.

Evelyn smiled, remembering how those words used to leave her so hopeful when she was dating years ago. She could recall many nights waiting near the telephone for him—whoever he was at the moment—to phone her.

Now the words had an entirely different meaning to her—or little meaning at all. She would be flattered if Reuben called. She enjoyed his company, and he had reawakened feelings that hadn't burned through her body in eons. But she also knew that if she never heard from him again, she'd be just fine with that too.

He placed his hand on his door handle, preparing to get out and walk her the short distance to the side door, and at that moment she remembered that she was supposed to meet Kevin there between ten and eleven. She knew without even looking at her watch that it had to be close to midnight. After their hurried lovemaking on the kitchen floor, they moved to Reuben's bedroom with the wine bottle for a second, more leisurely session.

Now she felt bad about forgetting Kevin. Oh, wait. No, she didn't, not really. Anyway, there was a good chance that Kevin hadn't even shown up, knowing him.

She reached out and touched Reuben's arm. "You don't have to get out."

"You sure? I don't mind."

"I'm positive," she said, smiling. God knew that if he walked her to the door they'd probably end up in her bedroom. "I'll be fine." She removed her keys from her bag, they kissed briefly once again, and she climbed out. He waited as she unlocked the door and entered the house, and then he backed out of the driveway and took off.

She removed her heels, and picked them up. She walked across the kitchen floor to the stairs in her bare feet, all the while humming softly. She felt as if she had not a care in the world. It was amazing how much a little loving could do for a woman, she thought as she skipped up the stairs.

Just as she reached the landing a knock came at the side door. Maybe she had left something in Reuben's car or maybe he just wanted more of her. For a moment she tried to think of what she would say to get rid of him. Then she realized that she didn't want to get rid of him. She wanted him to make her feel good again.

She dropped her bag and heels on the floor and ran back down the stairs. When she was close enough to the door to see the figure through the glass panes, she realized that it wasn't Reuben coming back to make more love to her. It was Kevin.

She opened the door slowly. Kevin stood on the threshold, a look of bitter astonishment on his face.

"I don't believe you just stood me up," he said angrily as he brushed by her and into the kitchen.

Evelyn closed the door softly and turned to face him patiently. She was determined that he was *not* going to alter her joyful mood. She was feeling too peaceful, too contented about her time with Reuben to allow Kevin to ruin the moment.

"Sorry to be late getting back," she said. "I, um, got held up."

"I bet you did," he said sarcastically. "Was that him?"

"Was who him?" she asked with studied innocence. She knew it was a stupid question the minute she asked it. He had obviously been parked outside waiting for her to return. But she was enjoying every minute of watching Kevin squirm, and she wanted to string it out for as long as she could.

"The dude who just dropped you off," he said. "Who the fuck else would I be talking about?"

Evelyn had to struggle to keep the smirk off her face. "Oh, you mean Reuben. Yes, that was him."

"Where have you been all night?"

"Out. With Reuben."

"Smart-ass," he hissed.

"Have you been waiting here since ten?"

His lips tightened. "What was I supposed to do? I really need to get some things out of the garage and you *said* you would be here."

"I got held up. What can I say?"

"You must be screwing him. What else would you two be doing until almost midnight?"

She studied her fingernails. "I know you're not talking to me. Not when you just slept with my sister's best friend."

"Oh, so that's what this is. Revenge. Payback time."

"No, Kevin. More like 'I have needs too' time. And since you can't fulfill them, I found someone who can."

Kevin stared at her with disbelief. "So you admit you fucked him?"

She said nothing.

"You know, I really do need my tools from the garage, but another reason I contacted you was to see if we could talk and try to work things out. As long as we've been together, it would be irresponsible for us not to try." He shook his head. "But now I don't know. I can hardly believe you did this. Although I guess in a way we could call it even."

By the time he finished his little speech, Evelyn's eyes were as big and round as pancakes. She walked up to him and got right in his face. "If you're going to stand there and compare what I did to you screwing my sister's best friend and try to call it even, then you've become a bigger fool than I realized. And if you think for one minute, for one second, that I would ever go back to your sorry ass after the shit you pulled, then you're the biggest fool on this goddamn planet."

He stared in silence as she hastily went to a kitchen cabinet, opened it, and retrieved two keys from a hook on the door. She removed one key and held it out to Kevin without looking in his direction. As soon as he took the key, she walked to the door and opened it.

"I'll see you in divorce court."

He opened his mouth and looked like he was about to say something until she turned to him and he saw the look of disdain on her face. He quickly shut his mouth and walked out the door. She slammed it right on his heel and swiped her hands together as if brushing him out of her life.

Damn, that felt good.

Chapter 32

Charmaine reached into the dryer and pulled out an armful of freshly laundered dark clothing. It seemed that the load got larger every time she did the laundry, which was now a few times a week. Tyrone and Kenny were the worst. Although Tiffany had more clothes, guy stuff was bigger, heavier, and dirtier.

This batch was going to take at least two trips from the basement up to her bedroom, where she usually did her sorting and folding. The wedding was the day after tomorrow, and she wanted to make sure the kids had whatever clothing they might need, so she was washing everything. She took the first armload, mostly jeans and slacks, and carried it up the two flights of stairs and dumped it on the bed. Then she went all the way back down to the laundry room for the rest of the items in the dryer. Both times she passed Tiffany, lounging on the couch in the recreation area, watching television and talking on her cell phone.

It dawned on Charmaine that she shouldn't have to do this all by herself. She also needed to get dinner on the stove. Tyrone and Kenny were out getting haircuts for the big day and planned to stop at the grocery store on the way home. Everyone was doing their part of the household chores. Why couldn't Tiffany pitch in and do her share?

Charmaine marched into the recreation room and planted her feet between Tiffany and the television set. "Just a second, Dawn," Tiffany said into her cell phone. She paused in conversation, covered the mouthpiece, and looked up at Charmaine with annoyance. "Yeah?"

Charmaine was tempted to tell Tiffany to address her as "Yes, ma'am," but she knew that what she was about to ask Tiffany to do was going to upset her enough and she didn't want to push it. "I need help with the laundry."

"Oh," Tiffany said, acting surprised that Charmaine would dare mention that word in her presence. "Um, I'll be there in a minute, after I get off the phone."

"I need help now. You can call Dawn back later."

Tiffany frowned. "I don't think so. She's getting ready to go out with her mom, and we need to finish this up."

"I would appreciate your help *now*, Tiffany, not later."

Tiffany blinked and started to say something, no doubt something sassy, but the look on Charmaine's face made her decide against it. Maybe it was the fire pouring from her flared nostrils, Charmaine thought as Tiffany reluctantly told her friend good-bye. Tiffany hung up and dragged her feet as she followed Charmaine into the laundry room. She rolled her eyes with disgust as Charmaine removed the laundry from the dryer and piled it in Tiffany's arms.

"That's enough," Tiffany protested as Charmaine started to drop more jeans into her arms.

"Is that the best you can do?" Charmaine asked.

"Yes, this is a lot."

Charmaine rolled her eyes skyward. "Go on and take it up to my bedroom then." Charmaine grabbed the rest of the clothes from the dryer and followed Tiffany up the two flights of stairs. Tiffany walked into the bedroom, dumped the clothes, and made a beeline for the exit.

"Uh-uh," Charmaine said, as she dropped her own pile on the bed. "Where do you think you're going? I need help folding them."

Tiffany stood in the doorway and placed her hands on her hips with indignation. "Most of that stuff isn't even mine. It's Kenny's."

"Some of it is yours. And what difference does that make? We're family, we help each other out. Kenny and your dad are shopping for food. Do you plan on eating any of it?"

Tiffany smacked her lips and walked back toward the bed.

"What do you want me to do?" she said, staring at the laundry as if it was a new species of animal that she had never seen.

"Haven't you ever folded laundry before?" Charmaine asked.

"Sure. But I've never folded boy's stuff, since it's just me and my mom."

Charmaine nodded with pretended understanding at this newfound excuse. "It's simple, really," she said. She lifted a pair of Kenny's running pants and tossed a pair of Tyrone's jeans into Tiffany's arms. "I'll admit that guys are different in a lot of ways, but since they basically have two legs just like us, you shake them out, fold them over like this, then like this. And presto!" She held the folded pants out for Tiffany to see. "Probably the same way you fold your own. Right?"

Tiffany couldn't help but crack a tiny smile at Charmaine's cleverness. "I guess."

They both folded in silence for a few minutes as Tiffany quickly got the hang of it.

"You do much housework at home?" Charmaine asked.

Tiffany nodded and turned up her nose. "All the time."

"Like what?"

"Let's see," Tiffany said. "Laundry. I do the dishes every other day since we take turns. On weekends, I clean up my room and the bathroom. Vacuum."

Charmaine nodded. She was surprised to hear that Tiffany did so much around the house. So she wasn't treated like a princess at home. The royal treatment was more Tyrone's doing than anything. "So your mom makes you help out. That's good."

"Good?" Tiffany asked with surprise. "What's so good about it?"

"It's good that your mama doesn't spoil you all the time like your dad does. A little work never hurt anyone."

Tiffany smiled knowingly.

"You know you got him wrapped around your little finger, don't you?" Charmaine asked.

"Yeah. But that's what dads are for, right?"

"To a point, maybe."

"But you think he takes it too far, don't you?" Tiffany asked. "I know that. He's got the guilt thing going on big-time."

Charmaine paused. She was startled to learn that Tiffany was so insightful about her father and especially that she was willing to share her insights. "So that's what you think?"

"What else? But don't get the idea that I'm taking advantage of him or anything. It's not like that. I love my dad."

"I know you do."

"And I tease him about the guilt thing all the time. I tell him that it's good training for me in dealing with dudes later on."

Charmaine smiled. "Oh, I know your father is no dummy. He does it willingly. His closeness to you is actually one of the things that attracted me to him."

"So, he tells me you two met at a friend's house?"

Charmaine nodded. "A mutual friend's."

"Was it love at first sight?" Tiffany asked with amusement.

"Oh, I wouldn't say that. But we were definitely attracted to each other."

"What did you like about him so much?"

Charmaine thought back. "Hmm. I liked that he seemed strong and confident on the outside but also had a certain vulnerability. A softness."

"Yeah, he can be a pushover when it comes to girls and women.

My mom even says that. But don't push him too far. He'll bite back."

"I think you're right," Charmaine said. "It's something I'm still learning about him. You and your mom are close, aren't you?"

Tiffany nodded.

"I remember very fondly when it was just me and Kenny, since I was a single mom for a while too. He and I are also very close. You develop a special bond when it's just the two of you."

"You know, I don't think Kenny meant to hurt me when we were playing on the Wii. I mean, I did at first, but I don't anymore. I was upset and hurt and I blew it out of proportion."

Charmaine paused at folding the clothes and stared at Tiffany. It was amazing what you could learn when you talked to someone. "Thank you for telling me that. I wish you'd tell your father."

"I told him last night."

Charmaine nodded. "Good. And how are things between you and Kenny?"

She shrugged. "Okay, I guess. Dad talked to us both last night and made us promise to try and get along better when we go bowling tomorrow."

"Bowling?"

"He's going to drop us off and come back and pick us up tomorrow night after Aunt Beverly's dress rehearsal."

This was the first Charmaine had heard of that. "Cool. Do you bowl?"

She nodded. "A lot at home."

"Kenny doesn't bowl much," Charmaine said. "But it should be fun for the two of you."

"I can show him."

Charmaine smiled. "I hope you understand that I'm not trying to replace your mother or anything like that. Your dad will always be there for you, and nothing between us or between him and Kenny changes that."

"That's what Daddy has been telling me. Last night, he said he was kind of lonely before he met you and Kenny and now he's not. He said that you all make him happy. So that's good."

Charmaine was pleasantly surprised to hear that Tyrone had talked to Tiffany about these things. This was probably a first, and a very nice first. It looked like Tyrone was sincerely trying to mend the relationships. "That's all I want," Charmaine said. "To make him happy, and I think Kenny and I do that. Just like you do."

Tiffany smiled, a genuine smile. That was also a first, Charmaine thought. "You should smile like that more often," Charmaine said. "You're even prettier when you do."

Charmaine realized that Tiffany wasn't totally won over with one conversation and a few smiles between them. There would be many more ups and downs in this crazy blended family. But she felt as if she had made a bit of progress; hopefully she would make even more in the days ahead if she and Tyrone continued to work together.

Chapter 33

Evelyn knelt on the ground, grabbed a handful of weeds, and pulled. She had neglected her flower garden something awful that summer, with all that was happening between her and Kevin. The weeds were getting dreadfully out of hand, and she couldn't put off tending them for one more day. As soon as she had returned home from Beverly's dress rehearsal on Friday evening, she changed into shorts and tennis shoes, went out back, and got busy. It was dusk and she didn't have much time.

Evelyn had noticed that Beverly seemed out of it at the dress rehearsal, so much so that Evelyn couldn't get Beverly's behavior out of her mind. Beverly wasn't at all the happy, upbeat woman one would have expected on the day before her wedding. A couple of times their mother had to call Beverly's name twice before she responded. And she kept stumbling over her vows, even when she was repeating after the minister. It took several attempts before Beverly finally got the vows right. Strangest of all, she and Julian had arrived at the church and left in separate cars.

Evelyn was very worried. With anyone else, a lot of this could be dismissed as simply pre-wedding jitters or confusion or whatever. But this was Beverly they were dealing with. And she was notorious among their family and friends for backing out of weddings at the last minute.

Evelyn stood up. She couldn't let this slide as she had with Beverly's two previous engagements. She needed to get on top of things. She brushed the dirt off her knees and walked into the house. In the kitchen, she picked up the phone and dialed Beverly's numbers but got no answer. She thought a moment and then dialed Charmaine's home phone.

Charmaine arrived home from the dress rehearsal, dropped the dry cleaning she had stopped to pick up for Tyrone onto a kitchen chair, and grabbed the ringing phone.

"Hello?"

"Hi, Charm," Evelyn said.

"Oh, hey."

"I've been calling and calling," Evelyn said.

"I had to make some stops," Charmaine said. "What's up?"

"I've been trying to reach Beverly, but she's not answering her cell or home phone," Evelyn said. "I wanted to talk to her since she was so subdued at the dress rehearsal."

"I noticed that too," Charmaine said.

"What do you think is going on with her?" Evelyn asked.

"If you ask me, she's still got that thing with Valerie on her mind," Charmaine said. "Understandably."

"Yes, but you know how she is," Evelyn said. "And she and Julian arrived in separate cars. I'm more than a little worried."

"I don't think she'll cancel tomorrow, if that's what you're thinking. She told me that she and Julian were getting together for dinner after the rehearsal."

"Oh, good," Evelyn said. "I didn't know that. So I can stop worrying."

"I'm sure she's fine," Charmaine said. "Julian is special and she knows that. But how are *you* holding up? And how did things go with Reuben? I didn't get to ask you at rehearsal." Everyone was so worried about Beverly with the big day approaching, which wasn't surprising, given Beverly's shaky history with weddings, Charmaine thought. But Evelyn was the one going through the roughest time.

"My date couldn't have gone better, actually," Evelyn said. "Until Kevin showed up, that is. He was waiting when Reuben dropped me off."

"You're kidding!"

"Nope."

"What happened?" Charmaine asked.

"It was a mess," Evelyn responded. "But I said what needed to be said to him and kicked his butt to the curb."

"Good for you," Charmaine said. "Are you really over him emotionally? It's been less than a month since he left."

"Honestly, I'm so over him it ain't even funny. Do I still have feelings for him? Of course. But I'm past the point of wanting us to get back together because I know it would never work. Our relationship had been strained for years, and after what he did with Valerie, I would never be able to trust him again. And I can't be married to someone I can't trust. I've definitely moved on."

"You slept with Reuben, didn't you?"

Evelyn gasped and laughed out loud. "Now where on earth did that come from?"

"I hear it in your voice, girl. You sound like a new woman."

"Really?"

"Yes, and it's about damn time too!"

Evelyn laughed again. "I know. Better late than never, I guess."

"Damn straight. I'm so happy for you. When are you seeing him again?"

"He might come to the wedding with me tomorrow. We're discussing it."

"So you're a couple already?" Charmaine asked.

"I wouldn't go that far," Evelyn said. "But you know what? I'm not even anxious about things like that, like I would have been after sleeping with a man years ago. If we become a couple, fine; if not and we decide to move in different directions, that's fine too."

"Yes! I never thought I'd hear you talking like that."

"Neither did I, to tell you the truth," Evelyn said. "How about you and Tyrone? How's that going since he moved back in?"

"So far, so good," Charmaine said. "We're getting along better. So are Tiffany and Kenny. He looks like a keeper. Got my fingers crossed."

"Tyrone seems like good people," Evelyn said. "I'm glad you all are working things out. Sounds like he must have come around."

"We both did. I had to ask myself whether I wanted to win every argument or I wanted to be married. I decided to swallow a little of my pride and offer to meet him halfway, something I would never have done before. I would have insisted on having it my way, ninety-nine percent." Charmaine chuckled. "A sure prescription for divorce."

"So you compromised," Evelyn said. "Good. But don't bend too much. You have to draw the line somewhere."

"Marriage is a trip, isn't it?" Charmaine said. "A constant juggling act. Why is it so hard?"

"Good question."

"You're the therapist. What do you think?" Charmaine asked.

"If I knew the answer, I wouldn't be just a therapist. I'd also be a best-selling author."

Chapter 34

When Tyrone returned from dropping Kenny and Tiffany off at the bowling alley on Route 40, Charmaine was buck naked and posing seductively for him in bed. He stripped on the spot, letting all his clothing fall to the floor, and climbed in beside her. They were both so eager that they actually bumped heads, then fell back laughing. They got so little time alone together that it almost felt like they were vacationing in the Bahamas.

Twelve minutes later she was gripping the brass headboard, gyrating wildly as the pleasure welled hotly through her loins, and calling out his name. Her voice incited him, and he went deeper, sending them both to new peaks of bliss.

No sooner had he rolled off her and onto his back than the telephone on the nightstand next to her side of the bed rang.

"Damn," Tyrone said, pulling the sheet up over his waist. "Perfect timing, whoever that is."

"No kidding." Charmaine looked at the caller ID. The number that showed up was the only one she would have bothered to answer at that moment—Kenny.

"Hi," she said. "You two aren't ready to come home this soon, are you?"

"Ma." Kenny paused, but even with only that one word,

Charmaine could tell from the tone of his voice that something was wrong. She sat up straight, and Tyrone turned toward her, a big question mark on his face.

"What's wrong, baby?" Charmaine asked.

"We got into a fight," Kenny said.

"*Who* got into a fight?"

"Me and Tiffany."

Oh, hell, Charmaine thought. Not again.

"What's going on?" Tyrone asked anxiously.

"They got into a fight," Charmaine whispered as she covered the mouthpiece.

"Oh, boy. Anybody hurt?" he asked.

"Are you both all right?" she asked Kenny.

"Yeah, we're fine, but can you come get us?"

Tyrone was already up. He grabbed his clothes off the floor and went into the adjoining bathroom.

"We'll be right there," Charmaine said.

Within ten minutes of the call, Charmaine and Tyrone were pulling out of the driveway and heading toward the bowling alley.

"Do you think we should call and talk to them while we drive?" Tyrone asked.

"He said they were both fine."

Tyrone shook his head. "They seemed to get along better lately. They were laughing and joking while I drove them to the bowling alley. What do you think happened?"

"I don't know. But I still believe we're making progress. This is just a temporary setback, and whatever happened, we have to be impartial. The goal is to get them back to getting along again."

"I agree," he said, nodding his head.

"They're teenagers. Hormones and tempers flying. Rivalries."

He patted her thigh. "Don't worry. I won't lose my cool this time. You're absolutely right."

Charmaine smiled but prayed to herself that they wouldn't get there and find things were so bad that one of them was unable to stay calm and neutral.

"Wonder what it could have been about," Tyrone said.

"We'll find out soon enough," Charmaine said as he turned into the parking lot in front of the bowling alley. Almost immediately, Charmaine spotted Kenny and Tiffany sitting side by side on the curb in front of the bowling alley. Tiffany was holding what appeared to be wet brown paper towels from the bathroom up against Kenny's eye.

Tyrone and Charmaine looked at each other with confusion as Tyrone pulled into a parking space. It looked like Kenny had gotten injured despite his claims to the contrary, but at least they weren't still trying to punch each other out.

Tyrone shut off the engine, and they both jumped out of the car and ran up to Kenny and Tiffany. The two teens stood up, and Tiffany removed the towels from Kenny's eye. Charmaine winced and examined him closely. She didn't like what she saw. Kenny's eye was starting to swell up. No telling what it would look like tomorrow for the wedding. Why couldn't these two get along?

"Oh, no, Kenny," she said.

"Let me look," Tyrone insisted.

Charmaine stepped aside to give Tyrone a chance to examine Kenny's eye.

"That's a real shiner you got there, but it will heal," he said. He reached for the wet paper towels in Tiffany's hand. They were filled with slowly melting ice. "This is good. Keep that on there until we get home," he said, moving her hand back to Kenny's face. "Now, tell us what happened."

"And why are you-all out here?" Charmaine asked.

They both looked at each other and grinned. Charmaine frowned. This was getting more puzzling by the minute. The two of them seemed strangely chummy for two people who had just fought each other.

"We got kicked out," Kenny said.

"What?" Charmaine and Tyrone cried in unison.

"The manager told us not to come back until we grow up some," Tiffany said.

"Or bring our parents with us," Kenny added.

Tiffany and Kenny both laughed.

"For some reason you two find this funny," Tyrone said. "Go ahead. I'm waiting to hear exactly what happened."

"So am I," Charmaine added.

"Well, this girl in there was picking on me," Tiffany said.

"What girl?" Tyrone asked.

"Danita," Kenny said. "She goes to my school. I don't know her all that well, 'cept I know she's a troublemaker, always starting stuff with people."

"Why was she bothering Tiffany?" Charmaine asked.

Kenny shrugged. "You have to ask Tiffany that. I was inside with some of my boys when all of a sudden I heard shouting where Tiffany was hanging with some girls. I looked over and I saw that it was Tiffany and Danita."

"She said I thought I was all that," Tiffany said. "'Cause I'm from California, I must think I'm cute. She was getting all up in my face. So I told her, 'Back off, bitch.' That's when she shoved me and I hit her back."

"So if you were the one fighting," Tyrone said, "how did Kenny get the black eye?"

"He tried to stop it," Tiffany said.

"Yeah, I stepped in, trying to break them up. Then Danita's older brother started messing with me, telling me to mind my own business. Next thing I know me and him are going at it."

"So you both got thrown out," Charmaine said. "Did the other teens involved in this get thrown out too?"

Kenny and Tiffany both nodded.

"I know we shouldn't have been fighting, but they started it," Tiffany said.

"You always told me not to start fights but to protect myself, Ma," Kenny said. "I couldn't just stand by and watch that girl pick on Tiffany. We're family."

Charmaine sighed deeply.

"Are we in trouble?" Kenny asked.

Charmaine and Tyrone looked at each other, both trying to suppress the smiles about to break out on their faces. She wasn't exactly overjoyed to see Kenny all banged up or to hear that he'd been in a fight. Yet she was thrilled to hear that he was standing up for Tiffany and to see the two of them getting along so well.

"I just got one thing to say," Tyrone said. "I hope the other dude is busted up at least as bad as you are, man."

Chapter 35

Beverly dashed out of the Baltimore Hyatt hotel room and down the corridor, her overnight bag flung across her shoulder. The heated exchange with Julian of only moments ago was fresh and vivid in her mind.

"Bev, please. I love you and I want to get married tomorrow. Don't do this to us."

"I'm sorry, Julian. I can't go through with the wedding. I just can't."

She reached the elevators out of breath and pressed the down button. She couldn't shake the sad and disappointed look of rejection she saw in Julian's eyes when she had removed the diamond ring from her finger and held it out to him.

"C'mon, c'mon," she mumbled as she paced in front of the elevators. She needed to get away from there. She saw something moving out of the corner of her eye and turned to see Julian scrambling down the hallway toward her, dressed only in the slacks he had hastily thrown on.

"Bev, come back to the room so we can talk," he said.

She shook her head firmly and turned away from him. "No, Julian. We've done enough talking."

"You're not making sense, Bev." He reached out and touched her shoulder. "What are we going to do about tomorrow and all the people coming? Our family and friends?"

Beverly knocked his hand away. She couldn't think about tomorrow. If she did, she might go through with something she would live to regret. She had to think about what she was feeling at this very moment. And what she felt was scared. "I'm sorry, Julian, but I can't think about that right now. Please, go away."

"Is this because of Valerie liking me? I told you it was just a silly crush that she had on me for a while. That's all."

Beverly pressed the elevator button again, anxiously willing it to get there. She didn't want to discuss this anymore. They had talked about it constantly ever since Valerie admitted her feelings for Julian a few days ago. As soon as Beverly arrived home after visiting Valerie on Tuesday, she'd called Julian.

"I don't understand why you didn't tell me all this time if you knew Valerie liked you romantically," Beverly had said after Julian admitted that Valerie had expressed her feelings to him once or twice.

"Maybe I should have, but she told me that before you and I met, and nothing ever happened between us. Not even a kiss."

"We're planning to get married, Julian. There should be no secrets between us, especially about something like this."

"You're right," he said. "The two of you were such good friends, and I didn't want to come between that. But I misjudged."

"I think she still has feelings for you."

He nodded. "That's why I changed jobs."

Beverly frowned. "So the reason you changed jobs was to get away from my best friend because you knew she was attracted to you and you never even told me?"

"I didn't think that she was still interested," he said. "She hasn't said anything to me lately, but I was never really comfortable working with her after you and I started seeing each other."

"Jeez!" Beverly said. "Something's really wrong with this picture."

"I screwed up by not telling you," Julian said, standing behind Beverly at the hotel elevator. "I know that now. From now on, I promise to come to you. No secrets."

"Sorry, there won't be a next time. Just go away."

A middle-aged couple, obviously tourists, approached the elevator, and Beverly and Julian quieted down. Good, Beverly thought. Now maybe he'll shut up and leave me the hell alone.

But instead of walking away, Julian moved closer to Beverly and lowered his voice. "Snap out of this, Beverly. You're panicking about nothing."

"It's not about nothing," she said, straining to keep her voice down. "How can you keep saying that? You don't understand what this . . ." He touched her arm, and she slapped his hand away, this time with more force.

"Stop it!" she snapped, turning to glare at him.

The couple standing nearby gasped and stared openly. Julian backed off and held his hands up in defeat. The look of embarrassment on Julian's face made Beverly feel sad. The look of surprise on the couple's faces made her feel humiliated.

Stupid slow elevator. She felt like kicking it. She looked up and down the hallway for the exit sign to the stairs. She spotted one and took off in that direction, never looking back, praying that Julian wouldn't follow her. She had to get out of there that minute. She was torn and confused. She didn't really understand what she was doing now or why. She just knew she couldn't go through with marriage when it felt so wrong.

She opened the door and flew down the stairs two at a time. She would think about all of this when she got back home. After she put some space between herself and Julian, she would be able to see things more clearly. He made her feel so good, both in and out of bed, and that sometimes messed with her head. She couldn't possibly make a rational decision about him when she was right there under his powerful aura.

She exited the stairwell and ran through the hotel lobby, clutching the overnight bag in her arms. Now more than just a single couple was staring at her. Everyone was turning to get a glimpse of the crazy woman flying through the Hyatt. Only when she was outside on Pratt Street did she slow down. But she didn't stop. She kept up a brisk pace all the way to the garage across the street.

She ran up the stairs until she reached the level where her Lexus was parked. She stopped and leaned on the side of her car to catch her breath. What had she just done back there? She shook her head. Maybe she really was crazy. Here she was deserting the man of her dreams, the man she had waited nearly forty years to meet. Tomorrow was their wedding day, and she was running away from him.

A part of her wanted to turn around and flee back into Julian's arms. She always felt so safe and happy with him. What happened?

Her sisters' troubled marriages. Her best friend's betrayal. Her fiancé keeping secrets from her. That's what happened. It was too much.

Chapter 36

"Charm, wake up!" Evelyn yelled into the phone as Charmaine, on the other end of the line, rubbed her sleepy eyes and scrambled to sit up in bed. The shrill voice blasting through the telephone had sent a chill up Charmaine's spine, and her heart thumped fiercely. Tyrone stirred on his side of the bed and switched the light on.

"My God, Evelyn, you're scaring the shit out of me," Charmaine said. "What is it?"

"Ma just called and she's panicking. She hasn't been able to reach Beverly all morning."

Charmaine glanced at the clock radio on Tyrone's nightstand as he leaned on one elbow, facing her. "It's only six-thirty," Charmaine said. "The wedding's not until two. Maybe she's still out with Julian. You know how they are."

"Then why doesn't she answer her cell phone? No one has talked to her since the rehearsal yesterday evening, unless you did last night."

"No, I didn't. That is kind of strange, I admit. But I wouldn't panic just yet."

"I wouldn't either if this was anybody else, but this is Beverly. I'm afraid that she's doing it again. You know. Ducking out at the last minute." Evelyn sighed deeply.

"Lord, I hope not," Charmaine said. "Did you try to reach Julian?"

"I called his house and there was no answer. I don't know his cell number."

"See? There you go. They're out together. I have his number here somewhere. Let me hang up so I can go and find it. I'll call you back."

"I'll be waiting," Evelyn said.

Charmaine hung up the phone, jumped out of bed, got her purse off the chair, and dumped the contents out on her side of the bed.

"What's going on?" Tyrone asked as he sat up.

"It's Beverly. Seems no one can reach her."

"You tried her cell?"

"Evelyn did."

"So what are you looking for now?"

"Julian's cell number. I know I have it here somewhere. I just never used it and I don't know where I put it." Charmaine finally found the sheet of paper she was searching for buried in a stack of papers inside her day planner. Just as she was about to pick up and dial Julian's number, the phone rang.

"Charm," Evelyn said hastily. "Julian called me right after we hung up. He said he hasn't been able to get in touch with Beverly since last night. He said they were staying at a hotel in Baltimore and had a big argument and she ran off."

"Oh, Lord."

"He's in a panic now, too," Evelyn said. "He doesn't know what to do. *I* don't know what to do. What do you think?"

Charmaine threw her arms in the air. "Damn if I know. What did they argue about?"

"He didn't go into it much, but apparently Beverly is still upset about what happened with Valerie. He said they argued about the wedding and that she was getting cold feet."

"Shit! What is the matter with that child? I know she better not be pulling this crap again. She's had months to get used to the idea of getting married. Or to back out. This is nuts!"

"Calm down, Charm. It does no good to get mad now."

"I'm not mad. I'm just saying, it's so childish of her to pull this every time she gets close to the altar."

"I agree one hundred percent," Evelyn said. "I just don't think getting upset with her is going to help. But go ahead and get it out of your system so we can get busy trying to find her."

Charmaine let out a deep breath. "You're right," she said in a softer tone. "Any suggestions for where we should start looking?"

"Meet me at Bev's in half an hour. Can you do that?"

"Yes, but what good will that do?" Charmaine asked. "She's not answering her phone."

"She might be there and just not picking up. And if she's not there, then we can decide where to look next. Maybe that place down the street where she likes to go for coffee on weekends."

"I'm on my way," Charmaine said. "I'll see you in a bit."

Chapter 37

Evelyn pulled up in front of Beverly's town house in her Benz just as Charmaine was climbing out of her Honda. It was obvious that both of them had dressed in a hurry. Charmaine wore cutoff blue jeans and furry house slippers, and Evelyn had tossed on off-white cotton slacks and a pair of worn leather flats.

They met on the sidewalk in front of Beverly's house, nodded their greetings, and walked hastily up to the front door in silence. Evelyn knocked and stepped back; then they waited. And waited. No answer. Charmaine approached the door and pounded with a lot more urgency as Evelyn pulled her cell phone from her shoulder bag and dialed Beverly's house and cell phone numbers, probably for the tenth time that morning. There was still no answer, and Charmaine backed up and yelled at the windows.

"Beverly, if you're in there, you open this door right this minute! You hear me?"

When there was still no response by door or phone, Evelyn put her hand on her hip and frowned deeply. "Where on earth could she be on the morning of her wedding?"

Charmaine threw her hands in the air. "Knowing her, she took off running down I-95. Let's try the coffee shop and then that park near here."

Just as the two of them headed back down the walkway

toward their cars, they heard Beverly's front door squeak open. They turned to see their youngest sister standing in the doorway looking tired and despondent in bare feet and some old pink-and-white pajamas.

They rushed up the walkway to the door.

"What the *hell* is going on with you?" Charmaine snapped. "What took you so long to come to the door?"

"Good to see you too," Beverly said sarcastically as she stepped aside and let them enter. Charmaine brushed past first and then Evelyn stepped in. As Beverly turned her back to them to shut the door, Evelyn nudged Charmaine on the arm and gave her a look imploring her to chill. The three of them walked into the living room and sat, Charmaine and Evelyn on the couch, Beverly on a side chair in front of the window. Beverly curled her feet up into the chair and looked as if she were bracing herself for the criticism that she knew was coming.

"Ma has been calling and calling you," Evelyn said. Evelyn thought she'd try the guilt approach first. If anything would snap Beverly out of this attitude it would be the feelings of their parents.

Beverly sighed. "I know and I'll get in touch with her soon. But I'm not ready to talk to anyone now."

"What happened?" Evelyn asked. "What's wrong?"

"I just don't feel right," Beverly said. "I'm so confused."

"You're being pretty damn selfish, if you ask me," Charmaine said.

"Well, I'm not asking you," Beverly said sharply.

"Look, Beverly," Charmaine said. "This isn't just about you. Julian's worried half out of his mind too. He called and said you were having second thoughts about the wedding. Is that true?"

Beverly's jaw clenched. "Yes."

Evelyn twisted her lips with regret. "I'm sorry to hear that."

Charmaine rolled her eyes to the ceiling.

"I know y'all think I'm being silly or childish or whatever, but I can't help what I feel," Beverly said.

"No, you can't," Evelyn said. "But it's not all that unusual to feel nervous just before your wedding, Beverly. Please try and get some perspective."

"Heck," Charmaine said. "I was scared before all four of mine, but I still went through with them."

"Thanks, Charmaine," Beverly said glumly. "That makes me feel a hell of a lot better, given that you've also been divorced three times."

Charmaine smiled sheepishly. "You know what I meant. It's natural to get cold feet."

"I just ask that you consider this carefully before you do anything rash," Evelyn said.

"What do you think I'm doing?" Beverly asked, clutching a pillow from the chair tightly in her arms. "That's why I haven't answered the phone. I need time to think, and I can't think with everybody bugging me."

"Why now, Bev?" Charmaine asked. "Why are you doing this *now*? That's what gets me. You've had months to think about this—that's partly what long engagements are for—and yet you wait until the day before the wedding to pull this. Why?"

"A lot of stuff has come up recently. You have to admit that."

"This is about Valerie and Kevin, isn't it?" Evelyn asked.

"Partly, yes. And you and Kevin and the problems that Charm and Tyrone are having."

"We made up," Charmaine said. "We're fine."

"For now, yeah," Beverly said. "But what about next month? Or the month after that?"

"Thanks for the vote of confidence in my marriage," Charmaine said.

"I didn't mean it like that," Beverly said. "But I'm scared and I'll admit it."

Charmaine was about to tell Beverly that she needed to snap out of the funk she was in when the telephone rang. Evelyn stood and headed toward the kitchen, where the extension was. "I'm going to answer that. It could be Mama or Julian."

"You can answer if you want," Beverly said. "But I'm not talking to anyone yet."

"I understand," Evelyn said. "But they need to know that you're all right." Evelyn left the room and tossed Charmaine a don't-be-too-hard-on-her look. Charmaine had already decided that being tough on Beverly would probably only frighten her further. She had noticed how tightly Beverly was curled up in her seat and how she seemed to be withering right before their eyes. The girl was frightened out of her mind.

"You really are afraid to go through with this, aren't you?" Charmaine asked in a gentle voice.

"Yes," Beverly said. "Do you think I want to do this? I know that it will hurt a lot of people if I back out now, and it's killing me. But so is the idea of going through with it."

Charmaine nodded with understanding. "If you're that scared, then don't go through with it."

Beverly blinked. "You don't really mean that."

"Damn sure do. A lot of people will be disappointed, me included. And poor Julian. It will crush him. But it will be worse for the both of you if you get married when you have serious doubts."

"I do have doubts," Beverly said. "I don't know how serious they are, but I do have doubts."

"About Julian?"

Beverly nodded.

"Did he do something that brought this on?"

"It's more what he didn't do," Beverly said. She paused when Evelyn entered the room.

"That was Mama," Evelyn said. "I told her you were fine and that I'd call her back."

"Did you tell her that Beverly is having second thoughts?" Charmaine asked.

Evelyn shook her head. "I don't want to worry her yet. I told her something had come up, but that we were working it out and that I'd call her back when I knew more. I don't think we should tell her the whole story until we're certain what's going to happen."

"I agree," Charmaine said. "Beverly was just about to tell me why she suddenly has doubts about Julian."

Evelyn sat back down on the couch. "Go on, please. I need to hear this."

Beverly straightened her legs and planted her feet on the floor. In a way she felt relieved to be talking about this with her sisters. She knew she could count on them to be straightforward and honest with her. She might not agree with what they said, but they would be fair. "I went to Valerie's house a few days ago to talk to her."

"You spoke to her?" Charmaine asked with surprise.

"Why didn't you tell us?" Evelyn asked.

"I just didn't. It wasn't a nice exchange. In fact, it got real nasty and I slapped her."

"No, you didn't," Charmaine said, clearly surprised.

"What did she say that made you hit her?" Evelyn asked.

"She was very defensive about what happened with Kevin. She even had the nerve to tell me that it wasn't all that bad, because he and Evelyn were separated at the time it happened."

Charmaine scoffed and shook her head incredulously.

"She's saying anything to justify it," Evelyn said with a wave of her hand.

"I agree," Beverly said. "But that's not all she said. You're going to be shocked. I know I was."

"What?" Charmaine tapped her foot impatiently on the rug.

"She told me that she's had feelings for Julian since before I met him."

"Get out of here," Charmaine said. "For Julian?"

"Let me get this straight," Evelyn said, sitting up on the edge of her seat. "Valerie likes Julian, *your* fiancé? And that's why she slept with *my* husband?" Evelyn's voice dripped with sarcasm. "I wouldn't take anything that woman says seriously. She's obviously very confused."

"Even if it's true that she likes Julian, that's hardly his fault," Charmaine added. "So what are you mad at him for?"

"Valerie said Julian knew about her feelings all along. Or she hinted that he did, and when I asked him, he admitted that he knew she was attracted to him. Yet he never said anything to me. Never! This wasn't some random girl at the office who was coming on to him, this was my best friend. If we're going to be a married couple, he can't keep secrets like that from me. How can I trust him?"

"Did you ask him why he didn't tell you?" Evelyn asked.

"He claims this all went down before he and I met and that he didn't want to come between our friendship."

"At least he meant well," Evelyn said.

"Look, obviously he didn't handle it the best way possible," Charmaine added. "Or the way you would have wanted him to, but he was trying to be considerate of you."

"I understand that," Beverly said. "But he still should have told me. They were working for the same company all that time, right up until he left a couple of months ago."

"You don't think he cheated on you with her, do you?" Evelyn asked.

Beverly shook her head. "No, he said nothing happened, and I believe him. In fact, he told me that the real reason he left his previous job was to get away from Valerie."

Charmaine's eyes widened. "He left because of Valerie? Interesting."

"Shows how much he cares about you, if you ask me," Evelyn said.

"I agree," Charmaine added. "Not many men would do that. I'm not so sure Tyrone would leave his job if a woman there had the hots for him."

"I know, I know," Beverly said.

"You are definitely blowing this way out of proportion, girl," Charmaine said.

Evelyn nodded in agreement.

"That's not the only reason I'm having second thoughts. I look around at you all and others and . . ." Beverly paused to collect her thoughts. She didn't want it to seem like she was blaming her sisters.

"I admit it doesn't look promising when you do that," Evelyn said.

"I wonder, why go through with this when everyone I know who gets married just seems to end up getting a divorce?" Beverly looked at Evelyn. "I thought you and Kevin were an exception, that you two had it all figured out. I thought you two had the perfect marriage, and that it would last forever."

"So now everyone knows that we didn't have the perfect marriage," Evelyn said drily. "I don't think you can ever be certain that a marriage will last forever, because nothing in love is guaranteed. If you want a guarantee, buy a new television. If you want love, you have to take chances."

"Preach it, sister," Charmaine said, snapping her fingers. "I'm going to give it my best shot with Tyrone. I'm gonna try harder than I ever have before to make this one work. If I fail, guess what? I'll move on. I'm proof that even when it doesn't work out, you can pick yourself up and start over. There's no such thing as a foolproof marriage because every man out there has faults. So does every woman."

"Instead of asking yourself if Julian is perfect or if your relationship is," Evelyn said, "you need to ask yourself whether you can live with Julian's faults."

Beverly paused to let that sink in. Obviously, Julian was not perfect, but could she live with his faults? He didn't tell her about Valerie's feelings for him, but he was trying to spare her friendship with Valerie. And he had left his job to mitigate the situation. Then when she confronted him about it, he admitted the truth. She also suspected that he would handle something like this a lot more to her liking in the future.

"We're not saying you should go through with this if you have strong doubts," Evelyn said. "Just be realistic. This is marriage we're talking about, not a fairy tale. It's going to take a lot of work, and even with that, you might still fail."

"Either way, you'll be fine in the end," Charmaine said.

"Okay, okay, I get it," Beverly said, easing up on the pillow.

Evelyn noticed a small smile appearing around Beverly's lips for the first time that morning. Hopefully they were getting through to her and had averted pending disaster. "So should I call Ma and tell her everything is fine? And that you'll be at her house to get into your dress by ten o'clock as planned?" Evelyn held her breath while waiting for the answer.

"Not so fast," Beverly said.

"You mean all this lecturing from us and you still haven't made up your mind?" Charmaine said teasingly.

"I know, I know," Beverly said. "And what you all said makes a lot of sense. I just need a little time to be sure. I'll call Ma probably within the next hour or . . ."

The doorbell rang and Beverly jumped and looked at Evelyn and Charmaine in a panic. "Is that Mama?" she asked. The last thing she needed now was more pressure to make up her mind.

Evelyn stood up. "No. I don't think it's Mama. Like I said, I told her I would call her back."

"Then who could it be?" Beverly asked.

Evelyn squared her shoulders. "Um, it's probably Julian."

"But he doesn't know I'm here," Beverly said. "I haven't talked to him since last night and I haven't answered his calls."

"I know," Evelyn said. "I called him after I talked to Mama and told him you were here. He was worried about you and needed to know that you were safe."

"Shit!" Beverly said under her breath. "I'm gonna kill you, Evelyn." Beverly hopped up, ran across the room, and flew up the stairs.

Chapter 38

Evelyn opened the door to see a worried-looking Julian standing on the stoop dressed in loosely fitted, knee-length shorts and a T-shirt. She pulled him in, hugged him, and shut the door. He and Charmaine greeted each other warmly.

"So?" he asked. "How is she doing?"

"She ran upstairs when she found out it was you at the door," Charmaine said.

"Not good," he said. "Should I go up after her?"

"I would give it a few minutes," Evelyn said. "I think we were making progress with her."

"Whatever you two decide is best," he said. "I know she thinks the world of you both. Me? I'm in the doghouse." He chuckled sadly.

"It's not entirely your fault, Julian," Evelyn said. "This has always been an issue with her, as you know."

"I'm going to go put some coffee on," Charmaine said. She walked back toward the kitchen.

"Did she say what the problem is?" Julian asked as Evelyn sat on the couch and he sat in the armchair facing her. "'Cause we were fine until last week. And then this thing happened with Valerie and it's like she blames me for everything."

"I honestly don't think it's about you, Julian. Beverly has always had a problem taking this step."

❖ ❖ ❖

Beverly lay across the bed and hugged a pillow in her arms as she relived the past week in her head. They weren't pretty memories. In fact, thinking back was enough to make her want to cut and run. She grasped the pillow tightly, as an anchor to keep her from fleeing.

Fleeing what? She wrinkled her brow and tried to think. The man downstairs, that's what. And those women. All three of them were trying to get her to do something she wasn't sure was the right thing to do.

She thought back through the similar episodes previously. Painful as it was to dredge the memories up, it was something she needed to do if she wanted to make the right decision now. With both earlier engagements, she had thought she was madly in love. And both times she had panicked weeks before the wedding when she realized she was in love only a little if at all.

This time it was different. Although she and Julian had been physically attracted to each other immediately, their feelings developed more slowly. People always expected fireworks when they found their soul mates. But with Julian it was more like a steady and soothing hum that grew in intensity with time. He made her feel loved and secure and always put her feelings first. Even the worst thing he'd ever done to her—hiding the stuff about Valerie—was done to protect her feelings. If that was the worst, she had little to complain about.

❖ ❖ ❖

Charmaine placed three mugs of hot coffee on the table, and then sat down on the couch next to Evelyn and picked up her mug.

Evelyn glanced at her watch and tried to think of the best approach to put an end to this madness. Julian tapped his fingers on the arm of his chair and then suddenly jumped from his seat.

"I'm going to go up. I think I can get her to come around if we talk about this."

"Probably a good idea," Charmaine said.

"What happened when she backed out before?" he asked. "Was there an argument?"

Charmaine and Evelyn looked at each other. Evelyn squinted, trying to remember. "I don't think it was an argument as much as her feeling like she was being boxed in or forced."

Julian sat back down. "Maybe I'll give her a few more minutes."

Suddenly all three of them turned in the direction of the stairway as they heard Beverly skipping down the stairs. Before any of them could react, Beverly had sprinted across the living room floor and flung herself into Julian's lap. She snuggled close and hugged him. "I'm sorry," she said softly.

Julian wrapped his arms around her and murmured gently as Charmaine and Evelyn exchanged glances. Happy ones, this time. Charmaine placed her coffee mug on a side table, and both she and Evelyn stood up.

"Looks like we should step out," Evelyn said.

"I agree," Charmaine said. "I do have a question first. Should we expect you at Ma's at ten, like we planned?"

Beverly sat up and looked into Julian's eyes. "Do you still want to marry me?"

"I have since almost the day we met."

"Aw," Charmaine said.

Beverly smiled and looked at her sisters. "I'll see you at ten, then." She looked back at Julian. "Meanwhile, we got some making up to do."

"Works for me," Julian said.

"Let's get out of here," Charmaine said.

Evelyn smiled as she reached for her cell. "This is wonderful. I'm going to call Ma right now, but you know what she's going to say, Bev."

"What?" Beverly asked.

"She's going to insist that one of us stay here until you're ready to come to the house to make sure you don't change your mind again. And she's going to be real upset to know that Julian is here. Bad luck and all that."

"So don't tell her he's here," Charmaine said.

"Know what?" Beverly said. "The last thing we want to do is start things off with bad luck." Beverly stood and ushered Julian toward the front door. She smiled at him. "If we're going to get married, let's do it right."

Chapter 39

Evelyn held the bouquet in her hand and walked down the aisle of the community church. She reached the front pews and caught a glimpse of Kevin sitting with Andre and Rebecca on the bride's side. At the last minute, Evelyn had asked Reuben not to attend. They were planning to see a movie together later that evening, and she was excited to have something to look forward to. But it was too soon to spring a new man on Andre and Rebecca. It would only confuse them, maybe even anger them. If she and Kevin could agree on anything at this point, it was to make the upcoming divorce as painless as possible for their son and daughter.

She smiled at the minister as she approached the altar. Could she see herself ever getting married again? Maybe, maybe not. She wasn't ready to think that far ahead. She had descended into a dark hole when Kevin left, and for a while she had lost her way. Wife, lover, soul mate. That woman had been coldly tossed aside. She had wandered about dazed, confused, and bitter, trying to get her bearings until the news about Kevin and Valerie snapped her out of her stupor. Now a new woman was emerging, one with no ties to Kevin or any other man, and she would get through this one day at a time.

Charmaine fussed with the veil on Beverly's face just a few seconds longer and then turned and walked down the aisle behind Evelyn. She soon spotted her family near the front of the church. Tiffany and Kenny sat on opposite sides of Tyrone. Russell sat next to Kenny. Both Kenny and Tiffany looked totally miffed. Tiffany was pouting. Kenny had folded his arms tightly across his chest.

Not a good sign, Charmaine thought. The two teens had had a spat that morning about something so trivial that Charmaine couldn't even remember what the heck it was. That Tyrone had felt the need to plant himself between them at the church meant they hadn't made up. And to think they were getting along so well at the bowling alley just last night. Obviously, she and Tyrone still had much work to do when it came to those two.

She looked at Tyrone, and he winked at her when she passed by. Yeah, Charmaine thought as she smiled and winked back at him. This was definitely a man worth working hard to hold on to.

Beverly slipped her hand under her father's arm, and he patted her hand as if to soothe her nerves. She laughed softly and whispered in his ear. "Don't worry, Daddy," she said. "I'm not going anywhere."

They marched down the aisle together behind Charmaine, and Beverly saw her mom in the first pew on the left side smiling proudly. Julian's parents were holding hands and smiling from the opposite side.

Beverly glanced toward Evelyn and Charmaine, standing on the altar, looking gorgeous in their coral-colored gowns. Thank God for those two, Beverly thought. With a lot of loving patience and a little sisterly prodding they had helped her finally get past her silly fears to this point.

Her father handed her off, and she lifted her gown and stepped up to the altar with Julian, the man who would help her navigate from here on out. She and Julian faced each other before the minister and clasped hands together. Beverly looked into Julian's eyes and smiled. She was ready to say, "I do."

Reading Group Guide

Discussion Questions

1. For those who have read *Sisters & Lovers*, how have Beverly, Charmaine, and Evelyn grown or changed over the past ten years?
2. Which of the three sisters has grown the most? Which has grown the least?
3. Did Beverly make the right decision about whether or not to marry Julian? If so, why? If not, why not?
4. Do too many American women have unrealistic expectations of marriage? Do they expect marriage to be a perfect life, or like a fairy tale?
5. What are Beverly's greatest strengths and weaknesses?
6. What are Charmaine's greatest strengths and weaknesses?
7. What are Evelyn's greatest strengths and weaknesses?
8. Which sister is your favorite and why?
9. Which sister is you least favorite and why?
10. Was Charmaine right to go to bat for her son Kenny, even at the risk of destroying her marriage?
11. Do you think that Beverly and Julian will last?
12. Do you think that Charmaine and Tyrone will last?

Essay by Connie Briscoe

When I wrote *Sisters & Lovers*, the prequel to *Sisters & Husbands*, I had recently entered my forties. I was single after a divorce many years earlier, and most of my girlfriends were also single. I remember thinking how different life was for me and many of my girlfriends than it had been for my parents' generation. Back then, most women were married with children in college by age forty. Yet women in my generation was less inclined to even marry before reaching their thirties. Many of us, whether single by choice or by chance, had to learn to accept living much of our lives without a permanent mate. That's how Beverly was born. When *Sisters & Lovers* opens, she's thirty-nine, still single and struggling with her situation.

Flash forward. In *Sisters & Husbands* it's ten years later and Beverly is engaged to be married. After a string of lovers, she's about to take a husband, or so it seems. By this time, though, Beverly has learned to accept life as a single woman and even to embrace it. She questions the necessity of marriage, especially since she's nearly past childbearing age. Plus, over the years she's seen the marriages of her sisters and girlfriends all fall apart, whether they were married two years or twenty. Beverly's fiancé is the man of her dreams, but she's she not convinced they need to marry. When *Sisters & Husbands* opens, she's got cold feet.

I went through a similar phase. I first got married in my twenties. It lasted less than a year. He wasn't the right man for me, and I got out. I couldn't understand how I could have been so mistaken about a man, and the experience soured me on marriage for years. But I've always liked the idea of marriage—companionship for life, a sex partner for life, raising children and growing old together. My parents had that. So fifteen years later I decided to give marriage another try, and my husband and I are married going on ten years now.

With age, wisdom, and experience maybe you can succeed where before you failed.

Questions and Answers

1. *Sisters & Husbands* is the sequel to *Sisters & Lovers,* your first novel. What was it like revisiting the three sisters after fifteen years?

It felt almost like a family reunion, and I honestly get teary-eyed thinking about it at times. Beverly, Charmaine, and Evelyn hold a special place in my heart because it all started with them, and *Sisters & Lovers* was so enormously popular. It succeeded beyond my wildest dreams. I think it took me fifteen years to revisit them only because *Sisters & Lovers* was my first novel, and I wanted to try other topics with new characters. Now that I'd done that, I was more than ready to go back to the women who helped launch my career as a novelist. Also, my life had changed so much over that period, and I was ready to share and explore some of my recent experiences—such as marriage—through the sisters.

2. How has your career changed over the years?

There are two answers to that question. The writing part is basically the same. Writing is hard work. It's also a fairly lonely pursuit. But it has tremendous rewards that make it more than worthwhile, one of the best being the freedom you have to determine your work schedule. No clocks to punch, no boss hanging over your shoulder. Of course, that freedom must come with responsibility and discipline on the writer's part or you won't survive in this business. I sometimes work more hours than I would if I had a nine-to-five gig. This is all just as true now as it was when I wrote *Sisters & Lovers.*

I think what has changed for me most has been the business side of writing, particularly when it comes to promoting my work. I'm a reserved and sort of private person. I don't open up easily or willingly until I get to know you. I'd prefer to just write and leave the selling to others. But you can't in this business, and that's even more true now than it was fifteen years ago for a number of reasons, such as increased competition and changing market preferences. Although I'll never be one hundred percent comfortable with it, I think I'm getting better at promoting myself and my work.

3. What are you working on next?

Another relationship novel but one with a twist. The theme is a basic one: Money doesn't buy happiness or love. It's about a woman who wins a few million dollars in the lottery and thinks the money will solve all her problems. Of course, it doesn't. I firmly believe that happiness comes from within.

I remember traveling to Dakar, Senegal, years ago with my best friend. We visited with people who lived in huts on the outskirts of the city. They weren't starving or anything. They could catch fish in the sea and pluck fruit from trees. They didn't have many of the luxury items that we've come to crave or think we're entitled to here in the U.S., but they were full of joy. My girlfriend and I sat in front of a fire on the beach with a group of Africans, and it was the most peaceful moment watching the sea and sky and engaging in good conversation as the sun went down. I was utterly content.

The poorest or unluckiest person on the planet can still be happy. The richest can be miserable. I've always known that and the point was reinforced for me last year, when I went through the worst summer of my life. I had a few really bad months and I still have bad moments. But when I came out of my fog and realized that I was still a happy person and content with my life, I was amazed. I think I would bounce back from just about anything. Sometimes we have to experience tragedy or life on the other side to realize or remember what's really important.

Winning a multimillion lottery
may be the best—or the
unluckiest—thing in her life.

Please turn this page
for a preview of

Money Can't Buy Love

Available in June 2011

Prologue

Lenora stood above the polished chrome faucet in her master bathroom, razor blade held firmly in one hand, and thought of slashing her wrist. She had just stumbled through the most turbulent year of her life, filled with highs and lows, ups and downs. And now she was at the bottom of the pit. Her fiancé had dumped her, her girlfriends had deserted her, and her brand new BMW had been repossessed. Last month, she had to give up her prized photography studio because she could no longer pay the mortgage.

And just now, she got the news she dreaded most of all. The bank was going to foreclose on her beautiful five-thousand-square-foot, million-dollar dream house. After months of default notices and frantic calls back and forth to the lender begging for time and patience, she was served with the papers that morning. Every time she thought her rotten life couldn't possibly get any nastier, it did.

Lenora shifted her eyes back and forth between the sharp edge of the blade and her bare brown wrist. *Go on, you pitiful bitch. Go on and end the misery right now. You're beyond feeling pain anyway at this point.*

She squinted and touched the blade to her skin. The hard, sharp prick jolted her eyes open. She grimaced. Maybe this wasn't the answer to her troubles after all, she thought. As bad as things had become, taking her life was something she could not bring herself to do. She was afraid to go on living, but she was terrified of death.

She lowered her arm and placed the razor blade on the countertop just as the front doorbell rang. "Shit!" she muttered as she pushed her dark, unkempt, shoulder-length hair back off her face and stared at her puffy eyes in the mirror. Who else would disturb her at 9:30 a.m. on a weekday morning? She had no job, no friends, no man. They had taken her car and her house. So now what the fuck?

The bell chimed again, and Lenora dragged her bare feet across the ceramic tile floor to the carpeted master bedroom suite. Paws, her white-haired Lhasa apso, scurried from her doggy cot near the fireplace and bounded down the stairs as Lenora grabbed a dingy terry cloth robe from the foot of her unmade bed.

Downstairs in the foyer, she peered through the glass on the double front doors to see a petite blonde woman standing on the threshold. The woman's hair and jacket were damp from a steady, unrelenting rain that had been falling all morning, and she had an anxious expression on her thin face. Lenora knew instantly that this was another one of those pesky reporters, and she was tempted to turn around and flee back up the stairs. But the woman had already seen Lenora, and her face pleaded to be allowed inside.

Lenora cracked the door open slowly.

"Hi, are you Lenora Stone?" came the woman's voice beneath the clatter of rain on the pavement.

"Who's asking?"

"My name is Donna Blackburn. I'm a reporter with the *Baltimore View*. We're doing a roundup of people who won a million dollars or more in the Maryland Lottery over the past few years. A feature with the theme of, where are they now?" Donna held a business card in her outstretched hand.

"So, I figured," Lenora said with impatience, pushing the card away. "You're like the tenth reporter wanting to talk to me since I won last year. Most of them had the decency to call first."

"Sorry, but I couldn't get through to you. I don't have your landline number and your cell is, um, discontinued."

That's when Lenora remembered that her cell phone service was disconnected a few days earlier since she hadn't paid that bill either. Still, she didn't feel like talking to any damn reporters. She was a photographer herself and had worked around a ton of them. She knew how persistent they could be. How they would dig into your personal stuff if you let your guard down for even a minute. Then they would go out and blab about your business to the entire world.

"I've said all I have to say," Lenora said. "Go away."

"I won't take up much of your time," Donna pleaded. "You won five million dollars in the Maryland Lottery almost a year ago, and I've heard about some of your recent misfortunes."

"You and everyone else," Lenora said sarcastically.

"It would give you a chance to air things out if we talk."

"Sorry, I'm all fucking aired out." Lenora stepped back and reached for the doorknob.

"Sure you don't have just a few minutes?" Donna asked as her eyes darted around the room behind Lenora. Lenora could tell that the reporter had noticed that the large foyer and living room were practically bare, with no furniture, no lamps, no memorabilia. Lenora had sold all of that in a futile attempt to stay afloat. The reporter's expression had changed from mild curiosity to one of eagerness, as she suddenly sensed a much bigger story than the one she imagined when she knocked on the door.

"Yes, I'm sure," Lenora responded and hastily began to shut the door.

Donna stuck a damp shoe in the crack, and Lenora glared at her, ready to punch this interloper smack in the mouth. How dare she intrude so brazenly. Lenora knew that she might be about to lose the house but right now it was still hers. "Bitch, who the hell to you think you are coming in . . ."

"I'll treat you to dinner," Donna blurted out. "Steak, seafood, pasta. The restaurant of your choice."

Lenora paused at the mention of free food at a real restaurant, not a quickie meal at McDonald's or a bag of stale chips in her bed. Lenora considered herself a bit of a foodie, so this was like promising drugs to a junkie. Lenora had a sneaking suspicion that the reporter somehow knew this, that she had discovered this tidbit in her research. She pulled her robe tighter around her bulging waistline and cracked the door wider.

"Legal Seafood in Baltimore," Lenora said, thinking of one of her favorite seafood restaurants. She could already taste the steamed littleneck clams.

"You got it," Donna said. "But you have to be open with me. Answer all my questions. We do the interview here first then go to dinner later this evening."

Lenora glanced down at her bare feet on the cold slate floor of the foyer, the place where an antique Oriental carpet once lay, until she sold it on eBay last month. She was still tempted to turn the reporter down. Even a nice dinner in Baltimore for a seafood lover might not be enough to compensate for having to relive the most traumatic months of her thirty-eight-year life. She wanted to forget everything that had happened, not rehash it. She wanted to banish the lottery, Gerald, Ray, Alise, the house, and the studio from her mind forever. But the thought of staying alone inside these half-empty walls just after getting a foreclosure notice was even more depressing.

Lenora opened the door. "Come on in. Find a chair and give me a minute to get decent." She needed to shower, something she had not done for a few days. There was no need since she hadn't left the house or had face contact with anyone.

"No problem," Donna said as she stepped eagerly through the doorway.

Fifteen minutes later, Lenora and Donna were seated across from each other in the kitchen, the dream kitchen Lenora knew she was going to lose soon. It had everything—Travertine flooring and granite countertops, a Viking range, and two sinks. They sat at the kitchen table, the only piece of furniture Lenora had left besides her bed, and nursed two mugs of hot instant coffee. A couple of months ago, Lenora had sold her nine-hundred-dollar coffee and espresso machine on eBay for a fraction of what she'd paid for it, and she had learned to tolerate the microwave variety of coffee.

Lenora now saw the extravagant coffee maker as one of the more rash in a long line of greedy, foolish decisions that she had made over the past year after winning the lottery. Her ex-fiancé Gerald had warned her to slow down. "Five million dollars won't last forever with you spending like this," he said repeatedly. Lenora now wished she had listened to him about the money and a whole lot more.

"So, tell me what's happened with you since you won five million dollars in the lottery." Donna asked.

Lenora sighed. "Long story short, I fucked everything up, that's what happened." She twisted her lips. "But you don't want the short version. You want the whole, sad story."

Chapter 1

One Year Earlier

Lenora's eyes opened and shot toward the clock. "Oh, no!" she yelled, springing up from the bed. She had done it again, slept straight through the alarm going off at 7:00 a.m. on a workday. What was wrong with her?

Paws, the one-year-old Lhasa apso she had rescued from the dog pound a few months earlier, ran to the bed and wagged her tail in anticipation as Lenora tossed the covers aside. She gave Paws a quick pat, stuck her feet into slippers, and raced across the floor of her one-room condominium. Her boss was going to kill her for being late to work again, she thought as she entered the bathroom and sat on the toilet. Why, oh why was she having so much trouble getting out of bed these days? Late-night drinks with her boyfriend Gerald were no excuse.

She grabbed her toothbrush from the holder and quickly applied toothpaste. There was a time when she would never have stayed out until 2:00 a.m. on a weeknight. Her job had been too important to her to allow that. But she was starting to get supremely frustrated with work, especially with Dawna Delaney, the new managing editor at the *Baltimore Scene* magazine, and a woman whose middle name should be "Evil."

So she found herself needing more time to wind down in the evening, more time to chill with her boyfriend or hang out with her girlfriends. Still, she had a mortgage on the condo and a gazillion other bills to pay. She definitely could not afford to do idiotic things like make her boss angry by being tardy for work repeatedly.

She slipped in and out of the shower in two minutes. She had no time for makeup other than a dash of lipstick. That was just as well. She hated putting the stuff on anyway. It was only because she was thirty-seven years old and starting to see a few lines around her mouth that she bothered at all. Some women craved jewelry, others makeup, shoes, or clothes. Her thing was freedom from all of that nonsense.

And food, she thought as she quickly grabbed a pair of loose-fitting cargo pants from the closet, one of only a few pairs that still fit. She muttered obscenities as she squeezed them over her hips. One of these days she was going to admit to herself that her five-foot, four-inch frame was no longer a size six or even an eight and buy clothes that fit properly, she thought as she tugged at the zipper and squeezed the snap. This was why she avoided shopping as much as possible. She hated looking at her short, roundish figure in the mirror. People often told her she had a cute face but rarely commented on anything below the neck, unless it was to suggest that she needed to lose a few pounds.

Slacks or jeans were customary for her, and not just because of her weight. As a photographer for a city magazine, she needed the freedom to bend over, climb, kneel, or whatever a photo shoot demanded without having to worry about anyone trying to sneak a peek up a skirt or that she would snag some nice designer fabric on a nail.

Today she added a loose-fitting berry-colored top to disguise her bulging waistline. Then she glanced at her watch and muttered more obscenities at the late hour as she grabbed her black camera bag off the chair near the small desk in the living area. Her morning commute into Baltimore was at least a forty-minute drive during rush hour. She didn't have time for breakfast, not even a glass of juice, which was just as well, she thought, given that her fat butt should be on a diet anyway.

She ran to the door and was about to open it when she looked down and saw Paws staring up at her with those big brown, puppy-dog eyes. "Dammit!" she said aloud. She had to walk the dog or she'd pee all over the condo. Lenora dropped her camera bag on the couch and quickly put the leash on Paws. "C'mon, sweetie," she said as she opened the door. Paws followed happily as Lenora ran down the back stairs of the two-story building and across the parking lot to a grassy field.

"Hurry and do your thing, girl. You want me to be able to buy your dog food, don't you? That means I gotta get to work." Paws seemed to understand and quickly carried out her business. Then they both ran back up the stairs. Lenora dashed into the kitchen and scooped some dry dog food and water into Paws's dish, patted the pooch on her furry little head, and ran back out. In the parking lot, she jumped in behind the wheel of her ten-year-old Honda just as her cell phone rang. She dug into the side pocket of her camera bag, grabbed the phone, and saw that it was Dawna.

She agonized over whether to answer for a second, then tossed the phone onto the passenger seat next to the bag. She knew what Dawna wanted—to know why the hell she was already more than an hour late for work. Again. And frankly, Lenora didn't want to hear all the snapping and cussing, which for Dawna went with having her morning cup of coffee.

Lenora would take her licks when she got to the office. Dawna wouldn't fire her, at least Lenora didn't think so. Good photographers were hard to come by, and Dawna, who started at the

Baltimore Scene only six months ago, was eager to make her mark at the magazine. Lenora had been there for seven years now and Dawna needed her. Yet Lenora realized that she couldn't continue to press her luck.

She turned the key in the ignition and the worst thing possible happened. The crappy car didn't start. It made some strange noises, sputtered pitifully, and then died. Lenora held her breath and tried again. Same thing. She smacked the steering wheel. She couldn't believe this was happening to her. One of these days, she was going to win the lottery. Or get that boyfriend of hers to marry her. With two incomes, she wouldn't have to freak out about possibly losing her job and her only source of income.

The cell phone rang, and Lenora could see that it was the boss calling again. It took every ounce of will power not to grab the blasted phone and heave it out the window. Instead, Lenora closed her eyes, took a deep breath, and turned the key again.

Chapter 2

"Yes!" Lenora yelled when the engine purred. One day real soon she wasn't going to be so lucky. Her commute between Columbia, Maryland, and Baltimore was over twenty miles each way. The clunker was more than ten years old, and she had already cranked out 100,000 miles on it. But there wasn't a whole lot she could afford to do about that right now. The payment on the adjustable rate mortgage for her condo had recently increased, and the last thing Lenora wanted was to lose her very first home after living in it for barely four years.

The condo wasn't all that much, just one large living area with a separate kitchen and bathroom. But it was hers. The minute she saw the units going up near the mall, Lenora knew she had to have one. She barely qualified, but with a little creativity, the loan officer had managed to set her up with an adjustable rate mortgage that she could afford.

Then the monthly payments shot up, the economy crashed, and reality came knocking at the door. The magazine was struggling to hold on, and Lenora didn't get the raises she expected over the past couple of years. It was a struggle to make her monthly payments. The worst was that she couldn't sell. Because of the recent crash in the housing market, she now owed more on the condo than its current value.

As she pulled onto the highway and headed for the office in downtown Baltimore, her mind tried to get her story ready for Dawna. By the time she pulled up in front of her office building, she still hadn't come up with a decent reason for being so late. She had already used every excuse known to womankind and some she had invented. Like Paws vomiting all over her clothes just as she was about to walk out the door, or waking up to discover that her boyfriend had accidentally taken her car keys home with him the night before.

She grabbed her camera bag and phone and ran into the building. She tapped her foot impatiently while waiting for the slowpoke elevator. "C'mon, c'mon," she muttered. The thing finally appeared, and she hopped on and pressed the button for the fourth floor, praying that it would not stop beforehand. No such luck. It stopped at the second floor, and a silver-haired woman using a walker smiled and stepped in slowly. Naturally, Lenora thought, gritting her teeth. It never failed. Whenever she was rushing about, a slower driver got in front of her on the road or an elderly person dragged his or her feet onto the elevator.

Lenora slowly shook her head. She wanted to slap herself for acting like such a bitch. Her tardiness certainly wasn't this woman's fault. Lenora put her hand out to hold the doors open as the woman settled in. "What floor?" Lenora asked.

"Third," the woman said, smiling in appreciation.

Lenora smiled back and pressed number three. When the elevator stopped, Lenora patiently held the doors open as the woman got off. Then Lenora took a deep breath as the doors shut and the elevator climbed to the fourth floor. As soon as it stopped again, she darted across the hallway and through the double glass doors of the entry to the *Baltimore Scene*. She was about to turn down the hallway toward her office when Jenna, the orange-haired, multi-tattooed receptionist sitting in the foyer, looked up from her paperback horror novel and beckoned with a black polished fingernail.

"Dawna is looking for you," Jenna said. "She wants to see you, like, yesterday."

Lenora nodded and backtracked in the opposite direction. She licked her forefinger and held it in the air, a signal that much of the staff used to get a reading of the boss's mood from Jenna.

"Hot," was all Jenna said before she jumped back into her novel. Lenora squared her shoulders, turned, and walked down the hallway toward Dawna's office. She had a good idea what was coming and it was going to be ugly.

Lenora approached the office, and Dawna looked up from her big glass desk, a scowl on her face. Lenora froze in the doorway. She was always amazed at how such a gorgeous woman—with a flawless tan complexion, beautiful hazel eyes, long dark hair, and a tall, slender size-six figure—could make herself look so mean. Dawna reminded Lenora of Wilhelmina Slater and Cruella de Vil wrapped into one terrifying being.

"Sorry to be late," Lenora said as she slowly inched toward the desk.

"Don't be fucking sorry," Dawna snapped, her long lashes blinking rapidly. "Just be on time. We've got a magazine to get out here. I can't have my key staff late all the damn time. Where the hell have you been?"

Lenora stood stiffly in front of the desk and swallowed hard. All the lies she had prepared were stuck in her throat. "Uh, my alarm never went off. Last night I had to go . . ."

Lenora paused as Dawna held up a hand adorned with thick gold rings and bracelets. "Save the drama for your mama," Dawna said. "I'm running a business here. Do you think I care about your fucking alarm and what you did last night?"

Lenora swallowed harder.

"Whatever is going on in your personal life, I don't give a damn," Dawna continued. "Just come in here on time. That's all I ask. Do you think you can manage that?"

"Yes," Lenora said. "I can manage that." Sometimes she thought her single, overworked boss just needed to get laid. Or have some other kind of fun. All the woman did was work and yell at everybody all day long.

"I damn sure hope so, Lenora," Dawna said firmly. "This lateness has gone on too long. Don't make me have to fire your ass. I will, you know. If you weren't so damn good at what you do, I would have fired you a long time ago."

Lenora bit her bottom lip and broke out into a sweat. That was the first time Dawna had used the word "fire," and it made Lenora nervous. "It . . . it won't happen again. I'll make . . ."

"Here, take this," Dawna snapped before Lenora could finish. Lenora blinked, eased her camera bag onto the floor, reached across the desk, and took the slips of paper from Dawna.

"The address is for a park-like setting in front of a new luxury condo on the waterfront. You're going to see Raymond Shearer, a young hot landscaper in the area. We're planning to run a feature on his work in the August issue. The other slip is the shot list. We want him and his crew getting in and out of their pickup trucks, digging holes, trimming trees. All that good stuff. Now hurry. He was expecting you at the site an hour ago, and I need those shots tomorrow morning for the layout. We go to print next week."

Lenora knew this meant she would likely be working late tonight reviewing and organizing the photographs on her computer. And that meant she'd have to cancel her dinner date with Gerald. She had planned to shop and cook a big meal for him, one that she saw prepared on her favorite cooking show, *Down Home with the Neelys*, on the Food Network. Spicy crab cakes, gazpacho salad, and ice cream with an orange liqueur flambé. It was a diet buster, but the way Gerald smacked his lips in anticipation when she cited the menu had convinced her to skip the diet for one night. Now he was going to have to wait and her diet was back on. Frustrating, but what could she do?

She placed the paper in a side pocket of her camera bag. "Should I focus on the landscaper and his crew or the grounds around the project he's working on? I ask because if it's a new building . . ."

"Didn't I just say he was a hot young landscaper? Of course it's about him. But get photos of the grounds, too. And the crew! All of it! Now, scram! Go do your job and get the hell out of my office. I have a million things to do." Dawna waved her arm to shoo Lenora out the door. Lenora bent down and quickly grabbed her camera bag, all too happy to oblige.

She went to her office to retrieve a couple of extra lenses and filters that were good for close-ups of flowers and plants, then headed back down to the parking lot. She hated rushing about and preferred taking the time to talk to the writer of the piece and to plan her shots before going on location. But that wasn't how it worked with this new managing editor, although she was partly to blame for being late.

Lenora just hoped her lousy car would be kind to her. Her job likely depended on the thing starting up now. She hopped in and hugged the steering wheel for a second, crossed herself and said a silent prayer, and turned the key in the ignition. The engine started right up. "Yes!" she said aloud, pumping her fist in the air. She pulled away from the building and headed toward the waterfront.